THE VILE NARROWS

A gripping murder mystery full of twists

JACKIE ELLIOTT

Coffin Cove Mysteries Book 4

JOFFE BOOKS

Joffe Books, London
www.joffebooks.com

First published in Great Britain in 2023

Cover art by Nick Castle

ISBN: 978-1-83526-057-9

"Each life creates endless ripples." — Frank Herbert

PROLOGUE

April 5, 1958

Gerald Duffy crouched behind a sprawling clump of blackberry bushes at the end of the backyard. He pulled his thin jacket around his shoulders and shivered. He hoped the white steam of his breath in the chill of the April morning wouldn't give his hiding place away.

Gerald knew his mother would only walk halfway down the yard looking for him, because the uneven stone path gave way to an expanse of sparse grass and mud and was riddled with poop from her boyfriend's smelly dog, Carter.

His mother would think he'd already left for school. He'd wait for fifteen minutes until he heard the front gate creak and slam shut behind his mother when she left for her shift on Maud Island, and then he would be free.

Most days, he went to the beach. Plumper Bay was nearby, and Gerald would spend all day foraging for fossilized sea urchins and arrowheads in the rock outcrops until the tide came in and hunger forced him home.

It had been so long since he'd shown up at school, Gerald was sure they'd forgotten he even existed. His mother

1

was so wrapped up in her new boyfriend and his son, she rarely paid him any attention.

Except for today.

Gerald heard the slap of his mother's shoes on the pathway, then they stopped. He waited to hear her retreating footsteps, but they didn't come.

"Gerry?" his mother called out.

He didn't answer.

"Damn it." He heard her sigh, and then he heard the snap of her purse, and seconds later, a waft of cigarette smoke hung in the morning air.

"Gerald," his mother said quietly after inhaling deeply and then exhaling smoke, "I know you're there. You've gotta come inside."

He still didn't move.

She tried again.

"There's no school today, remember? And no work for me."

Doris Duffy stood in the yard and finished her cigarette, while Gerald stayed hidden, not daring to move a muscle.

"Fine," she said at last. "Stay there, then. Don't blame me if you get hurt." And then Gerald listened to her walk up the path and bang the back door to the cottage.

Why would he get hurt? he wondered. And then he remembered. Reluctantly, he left his hiding place.

* * *

Doris Duffy was waiting for him, standing in the cramped kitchen, her arms crossed and eyes narrowed.

Gerald tensed, waiting for the sting of her palm across his head.

It didn't come.

"Shut the door behind you," was all she said. "Then go upstairs and make sure the windows are shut and the drapes drawn. That's what they told us to do."

Gerald pulled off his boots and rubbed the mud off his knees before running up the narrow staircase before his mother changed her mind and came at him. When she started wailing on him, sometimes she couldn't stop.

Gerald poked his head into William's bedroom. His mother had tried without success to get Gerald to accept William as his brother. Gerald hated him. William was a year younger than him, but he was taller, skinny, mean and lazy. And he enjoyed tormenting Gerald.

Gerald usually wasn't allowed in William's bedroom, and he hesitated as the wooden floor creaked. William was still in bed, snoring. He didn't stir as Gerald edged around the bed and checked the window. It was closed.

Gerald backed out of the room and closed the door behind him quietly.

William's father, John, was also still sleeping. Gerald despised him even more than William. Gerald didn't understand why his mother doted on this unpleasant bully and his son. As Gerald pushed open the door, the smell of stale alcohol hit him. Piles of laundry were scattered over the floor, and an empty whiskey bottle was on the nightstand.

Gerald crept around the bed. John groaned and turned over as Gerald checked the window. It was also closed. Gerald wondered for a second what would happen if he opened all the windows. Would shards of glass blow in through them? Maybe one would stick in John's heart, and maybe William's throat would be cut. He stood, imagining how much blood there would be, when his stepfather let out a noisy fart, startling Gerald out of his gory fantasy.

Gerald escaped to his attic room. It wasn't really a bedroom, just a dusty storage space, but it was his sanctuary.

A tiny window looked out over Maud Island, a small rocky outcrop linked to Quadra Island by a man-made track. The mining camp was there. Today, Maud Island would host the show. Gerald sat on his metal-framed cot and thumbed through a tattered book about fossils, waiting for the show to begin.

Today was Blast Day.

Today, Ripple Rock would be blown up, and the dangerous marine hazard which had claimed more than one hundred fishermen's lives would be blasted into a million tiny pieces.

Ripple Rock was an underwater mountain with two peaks which caused dangerous eddies from the strong tidal currents than ran through Seymour Narrows, part of the ocean waterway known as Discovery Passage. John was rarely sober, but he'd told William about his job as foreman at the Maud Island mining camp over dinner one night.

Today, the government was going to literally blow Ripple Rock out of the water.

After that, they would dismantle the mining camp and the kitchens where Doris Duffy worked, and her job would be gone. They would have to leave the tiny cottage which had been Gerald's home for two and half years. Gerald had no idea where they would go.

Doris didn't know either. Gerald had heard the loud arguments for weeks now. Sometimes John would leave the house, banging the door behind him and cursing, to come back hours later, drunk and in a violent temper.

Some mornings, Gerald found his mother sitting at the kitchen table, white-faced, except for bruises and swollen red eyes, and she'd let him silently hug her.

Blast Day. Today, when Ripple Rock blew, Gerald knew his life on Quadra Island would be shattered too.

* * *

It hadn't always been like this.

When Gerald had arrived on Quadra Island two and a half years ago, it was just him and Doris. Gerald had no memory of his father, and the stories about him had always been vague. Sometimes Doris told him his father had died in the war, but she wasn't specific about which war, and Gerald had figured out that he had been born a long time after the last war had ended. When he'd questioned Doris, she'd snapped at him, "There's been more than one bloody war, you know," and then refused to answer any more questions.

"You're well rid of that bastard," his grandmother had told him once. "He was a lazy, stupid, no-good bastard." So now Gerald did not know if his father was alive or dead. But he knew he was a bastard. His grandmother wouldn't let him forget that.

He'd spent the first eight years of his life living in the basement of his grandmother's home in East Vancouver. Doris was an unpredictable mother. Some days she'd cuddle him nonstop, calling him "her little man", until he felt smothered. Other times, she'd barely look at him, or cuff him for no reason.

Gerald's grandmother was far more consistent — consistently mean. She would make him clean her stovetop and scrub the outside toilet and run errands all day long.

"Shouldn't he go to school?" Doris had once asked her mother.

"He's too stupid," Gerald's grandmother had said. "Waste of time." That much was true. He was too stupid. One of Doris's many boyfriends had tried to teach Gerald to read.

"The boy's a retard," he'd told Doris. "Most bastards are retards." Gerald had looked hopelessly at the black squiggles on the page and as he did so, they seemed to lift up and move around, rearranging themselves in unfamiliar patterns.

One day, Gerald's grandmother died.

He'd heard Doris scream and found his mother standing over the prone body of his grandmother on the kitchen floor. Her eyes were open, he noticed, but it was as if a light had been extinguished, and they looked beyond him into nothing.

Gerald was curious about death. What did a dead body feel like?

He reached out to touch his grandmother's white fingers, but Doris hissed at him, "Get away!"

For hours and days after his grandmother's demise, people came and went to the house. Doris sat in a chair, dabbing at her eyes, as different men comforted her. Some people brought food, which was good, because Doris often forgot to feed Gerald.

When people had stopped coming one night, Doris shook Gerald awake.

"Get up," she said. "Pack your stuff. We have to leave."

As Gerald shoved his few clothes into an old duffel bag, Doris told him they couldn't stay at his grandmother's house. "She paid the rent," Doris explained as she moved around the house, stuffing anything that looked valuable into a battered suitcase.

"Don't worry," she said, in a rare attempt at kindness, "we're going somewhere nice. It will be an adventure." And then, clearly reading the doubt on Gerald's face, she added, "I have a job."

* * *

It was miraculous to Gerald, but Doris had been telling the truth.

After travelling all night in a van driven by one of Doris's boyfriends, including two ferry rides, Gerald woke, stiff and sore from sitting on the floor of the truck, to the sound of waves crashing on a beach.

He'd recognized the sound and salty smell of the ocean from an afternoon he'd spent at English Bay, with one of Doris's kinder male escorts.

He climbed out of the truck and shivered in the wind.

Doris pulled out their luggage.

"This way," she said, and they walked for nearly an hour down a rutted track until they arrived at a dilapidated clapboard cottage.

"Home," Doris said, and for once, Gerald thought, his mother smiled a genuinely happy smile.

* * *

Home was on Quadra Island, two miles from the man-made causeway which linked Quadra and Maud Island. Doris did indeed have a job as a cook at the mining camp on Maud Island.

The cottage was run down, but Doris worked hard at fixing it up. Gerald had never seen his mother this happy. Early every morning she left for the two-mile walk to the camp, worked for twelve hours, and returned, exhausted.

Gerald was supposed to go to school. It was nearly two hours' walk to April Point and the one-room schoolhouse. When he arrived the first morning, everyone stared at him, including the schoolmistress.

She was a severe-looking woman with a tight grey bun and thin lips.

"Sit there and read this aloud," she commanded.

Gerald sat and stared at the book she gave him. The words swam and danced in front of him, and he stuttered. He felt his face heat with humiliation as he heard titters of laughter from the other pupils.

"You can't read?" the teacher had asked incredulously and pointed to the front of the room, where the smaller children sat.

"How was school?" Doris had asked when she arrived home, slumping into a chair. She brought food home with her in a covered basket, and Gerald pulled out buns and ham.

"Fine," he'd lied and averted his eyes. He was glad Doris was too tired to pursue the subject.

* * *

After that, he'd stopped going to school. But he was intrigued about the mining camp on Maud Island.

Doris had been vague about her workplace.

"What are they mining?" Gerald asked her. "Gold?" One of Doris's old boyfriends had worked at a gold mine.

She had shrugged. "They're not mining anything," she said. "They're drilling holes into a big rock."

"What?" Gerald had looked at her, confused. "Why?"

"They're going to blow it up," she said and then waved her hand. "I'm tired of all these questions. What does it matter anyway?"

The next morning, Gerald had followed Doris to work. The trail was narrow and there weren't many places to duck down and hide if his mother turned around, so Gerald hung back. When he finally arrived at the mining camp, Doris had disappeared.

Gerald stared at the collection of wooden buildings separated by muddy pathways. The place seemed deserted except for a plume of smoke from the chimney of the largest hut. Gerald could smell food and guessed it was the cookhouse. Doris was probably inside.

A hill cast a shadow over the camp and at the top there was an enormous structure which looked like a tower.

Gerald did not know what it was.

He was crouched behind a clump of blackberry bushes and wondered what to do next. There wasn't much to see.

Just then, a deafening wail emitted from the camp. Gerald leaped from his hiding place, preparing to run, when he realized it was a siren.

A large grinding sound came from the tower, and men materialized from every direction. All at once, the camp was noisy with men's chatter.

Gerald realized they could see him.

He swung round, but a hand clamped on his shoulder.

"What are you doing here, son?" a not unkind voice boomed above him.

"Nuthin'," Gerald answered sullenly. And then, remembering his mother could appear at any moment, he added, "Nuthin', sir. Just looking."

"Well, it's dangerous here for a young boy like you."

Gerald looked up to see a tall man with broad shoulders and an unsmiling face looking down at him. The man looked different from the other workers. His clothes were newer and his hands were big, but smooth and clean.

"Where are you from?" the man asked, not loosening his grip.

Gerald jerked his head towards the trail.

"A boy like you should be in school. Getting some learning in. Otherwise, you'll end up in a camp like this one. You don't want that, do you?" The man had a strange way of speaking.

"What's that for?" Gerald's curiosity overcame his fear. He nodded at the tower at the top of the hill.

"That's a mineshaft," the man said. "Those men you see there?"

His hand came off Gerald's shoulder and pointed. Gerald could have run, but he wanted to know.

"I see 'em."

"They will go down to work and change shift with the men who are already down there."

"Down where?"

The man sighed but answered. "In the rock below the ocean. They are drilling tunnels and planting explosives. One day, we will explode the rock."

"Why?"

"Because that rock causes boats to sink."

He looked down at Gerald and must have seen the confusion on his face. "The ocean between here and the mainland, it's called 'the Narrows'." He gestured with his hand. "The rock is in the Narrows, under the ocean, and the way the water swirls round that rock — it sucks in whole boats. Kills people. So, the rock has to blow."

Gerald thought he understood, but he was having trouble picturing men drilling into a rock underwater.

"Those men? They're underwater? In the rock?"

The man nodded. "Drilling tunnels into the rock. It's dangerous work. They carry explosives. There are explosives stored all over the camp. This is not the place for a young boy."

He bent down so their faces were close. Gerald tried to pull back, but the man had clamped his hand back on his shoulder.

"Listen to me, young man. Run back down that trail, and don't let me catch you here again, you hear me?"

Gerald nodded. He wanted to ask more questions, but knew his time was up.

"All right, then." The man straightened up. Gerald thought there was a glimmer of a smile on his face, but just then he heard a familiar laugh. He looked up to see his mother standing outside one building, smoking a cigarette and smiling at a man who was bent forward, saying something in her ear.

As she flung back her head to laugh again, Gerald twisted away from the man's grasp on his shoulder and took off running towards the trail.

* * *

That evening, Gerald waited for Doris to get home. He hovered nervously around her, expecting her to grab him and demand an explanation. He was sure she hadn't seen him, but what if that man had said something?

But Doris was preoccupied. She hummed to herself as she prepared a half-decent dinner for them both, but seemed lost in her thoughts, a smile playing on her lips as she lit a cigarette once they had finished eating.

"I'll do those," she said as Gerald cleared the table. "You go up to your room."

Gerald stared at her and then realized what was going on. That man he'd seen with her earlier in the day. The one who'd made her laugh.

Doris was always like this when she met a new man.

She brought John home a week later.

He was a small man with a thin face and slick black hair. He ruffled Gerald's hair.

"Well, then, little man," John said, cocking his head to one side and fixing him with his ice-blue eyes. He reminded Gerald of a bird. "Well, then," he repeated, looking Gerald up and down. "A fine lad," he said to Doris, as if Gerald wasn't there. "I can see he gets his good looks from his mother."

Doris giggled, and John grinned at her, showing a row of sharp teeth. The grin didn't reach his eyes.

Not a bird, Gerald thought. *A rat.*

"John has a son," Doris said, pulling Gerald towards her and giving him a hug.

Gerald pulled away, annoyed.

"His name is William, and he's just a year younger than you. I bet you'll be the best of friends."

Gerald shrugged and stayed silent.

"John and William are coming to tea on Sunday. You boys can get to know each other."

Doris winked at John, and they laughed, as if they were sharing a huge joke.

* * *

William was a smaller version of John. He eyed Gerald in the same way his father had done.

Doris had prepared a spread, the way she always did when she had a new man-friend to impress.

She poured tea for all of them, and John laughed.

"What's this? Tea? Got a beer, darlin'?"

"Of course," Doris said with a smile and got up from the table.

"That's my girl," John said, and slapped Doris on the behind as she passed him. He winked at the two boys, but only William laughed.

Later, Doris sat on John's knee and shared his beer. Gerald left the table and went outside, wishing the end of the afternoon would come soon.

William followed him into the small backyard.

Gerald had intended to bolt through the backyard and head to the beach, but he didn't want William to follow him, so he hesitated.

William punched him in the shoulder.

"Dad says you can't read. You some kind of retard?"

Gerald didn't answer, but glared back at William's sneering face.

They both heard a peel of laughter, followed by a shriek in the kitchen.

William's face broke into a grin.

"My dad's gonna fuck your mom," he said.

Rage boiled up from the pit of Gerald's stomach, and he launched his small body at the taller boy. Roaring, he jammed his thumb into William's eye.

William's howl of pain competed with the laughter from the kitchen, and Doris burst through the back door.

"What the bloody hell is going on?"

"It was him," William whined. "I just wanted to be friends and then he attacked me for no reason."

Gerald stood stock-still, his expression blank, as Doris and John took turns beating his body until his legs buckled. When they were done, Gerald turned to face William, who had a smirk on his face. Gerald felt the burning rage within him die, and a steely coldness take its place.

John and William moved in a week later.

Gerald vacated his tiny room for William and moved his few belongings into the attic.

He didn't care.

He could see the ocean through the dirty windowpane, and there were dark cubbyholes where he could hide his rocks and seashells.

Gerald spent most days at the beach now. He hid behind the blackberry bushes until Doris left for work with John, before slipping away to his sanctuary. Nobody asked about his day or checked if he was in school.

I am a ghost, Gerald thought. *Nobody can see me anymore.* Some days it made him sad, others he was grateful to be invisible — especially to William.

William lay in bed until noon most days and then disappeared with a gang of hoodlums who spent their days pilfering anything that wasn't nailed down from the island residents. At home, he'd turn on the charm, smiling at Doris and offering to help with the dishes or chop firewood.

Gerald hoped his mother's relationship with John would end as quickly as all the rest, but he knew he'd have to endure through this honeymoon period while Doris was blind to all John's faults.

Already, John had displayed his temper and had struck Doris across the face when she was too slow to bring him a beer.

William smirked and carried on eating. Gerald started out of his chair, but Doris shushed him, and John said sharply, "Sit down, boy, or you'll get the same."

Now, alone as usual, Gerald sat on his narrow cot in his attic room and hoped that wherever they were going after Ripple Rock blew, John and William would not go with them. But nothing he ever hoped for came true.

He lay back on the thin blankets and waited for his world to explode.

CHAPTER ONE

Present day
New Year's Eve

The man counted out two thousand dollars exactly into Ron's outstretched hand. The full price was three thousand.

Ron was impatient to get going. He needed to catch the tide, but he allowed the man to take his time. Ron had been shorted cash before, and in his line of work, there was no official complaints process.

The man shifted from foot to foot nervously and looked at Ron. He looked up and down the dock as if he expected someone to be watching.

Ron sighed. It was six in the morning of the last day of the year. It was cold and wet, as it usually was in Campbell River, and nobody was around. The man had insisted on meeting Ron this early.

"How do I know this is going to work?" the man said at last. "This better not come back on me."

Ron was expecting this. All new clients were worried at first.

He gave his most reassuring smile.

"You've asked around about my service, right?" he said. "Have you heard any complaints?"

The man shook his head slowly, but still didn't finish counting out the cash.

"And you'll do all the paperwork?" he asked.

They had been through this before.

Ron spoke slowly. "You've signed the boat over to me. Once I've been *paid*—" he emphasized the word — "I'll register the boat in my name, and then I'll tow it away. What happens after that is down to me."

The man nodded. "OK, OK . . ."

Ron frowned at the man.

"Look, if you don't want to do this, I'm OK with that. You can call someone else and pay the full *official* price. No skin off my nose." He gestured, as if to give back the cash in his hand.

That worked.

"No, no, I'm good with this," the man said hastily and finished counting.

Ron smiled inwardly. Of course he was OK with it. A salvage company — a legit one — would charge twenty thousand dollars to dispose of this tug. Oil, diesel, asbestos — all that had to be dealt with in accordance with environmental regulations. Then there was the plastic, metal, glass; the list went on. Some parts could be reconditioned and sold on. But it was a long, expensive process, and a small company with limited space in the yard could only work on one or two boats at a time. This way was far more lucrative. And worked out well for all parties, as long as everyone kept their mouth shut.

Once Ron had safely tucked the cash in his pocket, the two men walked down the dock. The ancient tugboat was tied up at the outer finger of the dock. It sagged in the water, resigned to its fate. Ron noted the gaping holes of rust along the bow and peeling paint on the wheelhouse. He had stepped on the deck before the negotiations began, and had hastily stepped off again, as the rotten boards sunk and creaked under his weight.

The small tugboat was definitely at the end of its life.

"When will you take it?"

"It'll be gone in a couple of days. I can't register the tug until the office is open on the second."

The man looked at Ron suspiciously, but the deal was done now.

Ron nodded at his anxious customer reassuringly. The man turned without shaking Ron's hand and hurried back along the dock.

Probably going home to plan tonight's big New Year's Eve celebration, Ron thought. He imagined what that would be like. Everyone dressed up, eating and drinking and waiting for the big countdown. Then there would be hugs and kisses and good wishes for the year ahead.

He couldn't remember the last time anyone kissed him on New Year's Eve. *Maybe next year*, he told himself. He whistled softly to ward off the heavy weight of loneliness and walked along the length of the old tugboat. It was listing a little in the water. It wouldn't take long to get rid of this one.

Then he hopped in his boat, started the engine and chugged slowly away from the dock. An hour and he'd be in Campbell River. At this time of the year, he could slip in and out of the marina easily without paying moorage.

Ron patted his pocket and smiled. He settled back in his seat and pushed the throttle forward a little, satisfied with the morning's work. Business had ended on a high note at the end of this year. Maybe he'd head into town, grab a bottle of Crown Royal and have his own New Year's party.

Captain Ron's Environmental Salvage Company had taken a while to catch on, but he was proud of his venture. The idea had just come to him one afternoon. He'd been laid off as a labourer when the property developer he was working for had been caught paying cash and avoiding taxes. To make ends meet, Ron picked up pop cans and turned them in to the recycling depot for a few cents a can. One afternoon, he was in a ditch outside a fancy home in Steveston, emptying stagnant water and cigarette butts from beer cans, when the house owner shouted and gestured at him.

First, Ron thought the man was telling him to clear off, and he waved the dirty cans to show what he was up to. But when the house owner got nearer, to Ron's surprise, he was gesturing for Ron to follow him to his garage.

"Can you get rid of these for me?" the man asked. "There's two hundred dollars in it for you."

Ron was suspicious. Four bulging garbage bags were piled in the garage.

"What's in 'em?" Ron asked. How did he know this guy wasn't a serial killer, and the bags were full of body parts?

"Asbestos," the man admitted. The contractor who'd just finished his bathroom reno had left them there and now wasn't answering calls. Ron knew why. It cost a fortune to dispose of this shit properly.

"Five hundred," he said.

Ron thought the man would object, but he disappeared into the house and came out with five brown notes and pressed them into Ron's hand.

Later that night, Ron crept onto the building site he'd been working on a few days before and tossed the four garbage bags into the dumpster. Now he and his previous employer were even, he figured.

The next day, he knocked on the man's door.

"What do you want? I'm not giving you more money . . ."

Ron explained that he'd be delighted to help again when needed. He told the man he'd be in the neighbourhood the following Tuesday.

From those lowly beginnings, Captain Ron's Environmental Salvage Company was born. Ron bought a tired old troller boat, moored just outside Steveston on the Fraser River. Instead of paying moorage, Ron cleared the dock of rusty metal and fiberglass remnants and old paint pots. Nobody asked Ron how he got rid of all their crap.

Ron figured that nobody much gave a shit about the environment anyway. Oh sure, there were the groups of weirdos who would turn up waving banners and trying to stop pipelines and such, but if they really wanted to save the world, why didn't they give up their big houses and fancy cars? These were the same people who made a big fuss about recycling. Didn't they know all their shit went straight into the landfills? They spent all that time washing out tins and smugly piling up their cardboard from all their online purchases, and it was a total con. A big fucking lie.

Well, if the government could get away with it, so could Captain Ron. He was no more a captain than he was an environmentalist. In fact, he'd never been on a boat until he bought this little blue troller.

He was helping people. Much better he did this than return to breaking and entering, which was his main occupation when he aged out of the children's home.

He wasn't breaking the law; he was bending the rules. What had his mentor told him?

"It's a regulatory infraction, not a crime. You can't plead ignorance if you break the law, but if you break a rule, well, they change so often. How were you to know?"

Ron wasn't so stupid that he didn't know it was against all the rules to dump garbage on empty lots or out to sea, but nobody seemed to care. Just like the tugboat owner. He just wanted the rusty vessel gone. And Captain Ron was happy to oblige.

One day next week, when it was dark, this tugboat would meet its fate on a nicely hidden rocky outcrop on the north side of an uninhabited island in the Georgia Strait. The only observers of the sinking tugboat would be a few scrawny sheep.

The tugboat would become a new home for crabs and whatnot. Captain Ron grinned to himself.

He felt the top pocket of his shirt vibrate, and he pulled out his cell phone. He frowned. Ron recognized the number, even though it had been months since he had talked to the caller. The conversation had been terse. The older man seemed to think Ron owed him a cut of the profit.

"A royalty," he called it. "Payment for all the tuition over the years."

It had incensed Ron. "I've paid all my dues," he said. It took some courage. The caller was cunning. He knew people, bad people. People you don't want to cross, as he kept reminding Ron. But this time, Captain Ron held fast.

He should have known he wouldn't give up.

The phone kept ringing and before it went to voicemail, Ron tapped the green button and accepted the call.

"Hello?" Ron shouted above the engine noise. He listened for a minute. He was relieved. The man's tone was friendly.

"You're where? When? OK. I can do that." Ron was cautious, but this was a small favour.

He ended the call, and immediately the phone rang again. This time, he didn't know the number on the call display. Ron was instantly suspicious. But it might be business, so he throttled back the engine and took the call.

"Hello there, Captain Ron speaking." Ron kept his tone light. He listened for a few seconds.

"A job for me? What kind of job?" Ron listened again.

"And how did you hear about me?" He couldn't keep the excitement out of his voice.

"You'll pay me how much?"

To hell with it. This was a big job. Ron was certain it wasn't a setup. He'd heard about the Fish Plant development in Coffin Cove.

"When do you need it gone? I have something else to do . . . OK, that works fine. See you then."

* * *

Ron started his tuneless whistle again as he tapped his phone to end the call. He had plenty of time for the favour he'd promised and then it would take him the rest of the day to get to Coffin Cove, which was a lot of fuel. But if his luck held, he could tie up at the dock without being seen. Captain Ron had been there before. He remembered the old guy in the office spent more time at the pub than collecting moorage fees. Hopefully, the job would take two or three days, and then he could come back for the tugboat. It was a good plan.

Humming, he pushed the throttle, and his little boat picked up speed. He stared out of the window as the fog cleared. Watery sunlight filtered through, and Captain Ron smiled. "Happy New Year," he murmured to himself.

CHAPTER TWO

Present day
New Year's Eve, Quadra Island

The old man eased out of his chair and leaned heavily on his cane until he was confident his trembling legs wouldn't fail him. Then he shuffled slowly, pushing one foot and then the other forward until he reached the small pile of wood beside the hearth.

Groaning with the effort, he bent forward, and with one hand clutching the cane to prevent himself from toppling forward, he picked up a small log and dropped it into the fire. Sparks flew up the chimney. Still holding his cane, he picked up the brass tongs, poked at the fire and rearranged the logs.

Exhausted from the effort, he stood there, resting on his cane before he returned to his chair.

New Year's Eve. His twentieth since his wife had died.

The first years after her death, his son had attempted to be home for the holiday season, until the old man had persuaded him not to make the journey.

"One day is like any other," he'd said simply. "Christmas, New Year, birthdays . . . they're all the same."

And they were.

He kept his mind as sharp as possible by reading. His eyes still worked, thanks to the miracle of cataract surgery, and his brain was in better shape than his body. He forgot things, but only inconsequential things like butter on his grocery list, and what day of the week it was.

But the young fella came once a week to mow the lawn and keep the property tidy in the summer, and to chop wood in the winter. He'd employed the young fella when his wife got sick. He didn't like to leave her side. When she was awake, he read to her.

The young fella looked after the house and ran errands. When his wife finally died, the young fella made sure they had groceries and remembered to eat.

These days, the "young fella" was thicker around the middle and had grey hair. Just before Christmas, when he'd finished piling up kindling, he'd shown the old man pictures of his first grandchild.

"You must show them to . . ." he'd said, and then remembered. His wife was gone. The young fella seemed to understand and squeezed his shoulder.

He'd seen his wife just the other day, he wanted to say. She was standing right there in the garden. She loved her flowers. Sometimes Maeve, the little girl from next door, would help her weed the flowerbeds. They would work together, his wife pointing out the different flowers and their Latin names until the sun sank behind the trees and Maeve's mother would call for her. When he saw his wife this time, she was alone. She was wearing a big floppy hat to keep the sun off her face and was holding a trowel in one hand. Her knees were dirty from kneeling on the grass. She was wearing a sundress, one of his favourites. It was blue with yellow flowers, and it clung to her breasts and her thighs. She was laughing, her head back exposing her white throat. He didn't know why she was so happy, but it didn't matter. He felt the warmth of the sun on his face, and when he looked at her, he felt a stirring, a surge of energy as she smiled at him. She pushed a stray strand of her dark hair under her hat and beckoned to him. She was trying to say something to him, he was sure. She kept gesturing, so he knew it was important, but all he wanted to do was hold her in his arms again. As he moved forward, desperately wanting to kiss her, her smile faded along with the warmth. He could see her lips moving, but then she was gone, and he was looking at a hard brown patch of mud where the flowerbeds used to be.

She must be fed up with waiting for him. He was one hundred years old, and it was all he could do to put a log of wood on the fire. How she would laugh when she saw the wispy hair on his head, and the liver spots on his wrinkled skin.

He wasn't feeling sorry for himself; he was just tired of living. Every day he woke up exhausted and amazed he was still breathing. He wished it would end soon, preferably before he was whisked away to a nursing home where they'd pump him full of medication and speak to him in sing-song voices as if he'd regressed into childhood.

He doubted he would last another year. He doubted he would last another month. Maybe seeing his beloved wife was a sign.

This would be his last New Year's Eve, he was certain. *He was hopeful.*

He wondered why he didn't have a picture of his wife wearing that dress. They had been so young. Just the two of them, before life had become complicated. Before the tragedy had blighted his marriage. He'd tried so hard to make her happy, turn her back into the laughing woman in the blue-and-yellow sundress. But it had never been possible. Even that one act, the one sacrifice he'd thought would bring her happiness. It had just hung over them like a black cloud.

The black cloud had bothered him recently. It was a weight he'd carried for so long, he barely noticed it. One impulsive act. But it had been for the greater good. He was a logical man, a scientist, accustomed to weighing theories and calculating outcomes, and he was certain he'd done the right thing. So why was the past visiting him in his dreams and sometimes when he was awake?

He wasn't a man who liked to talk, but recently he'd felt the need to tell someone. He'd even called Maeve. She'd always loved his wife, even nursed her, and maybe she would listen and reassure him he'd done the right thing. Then he could rest easy.

The room became chilly, as if there was a window or door open. It was light outside. Morning? Time was confusing to him now. He'd eaten a sandwich earlier. He was never hungry, but it was an instinctive survival mechanism, even at his advanced age.

The young fella had left food in the fridge for a week. He'd cut lots more wood than usual and had collected the old man's mail. He'd left the envelopes on the table and had sat and chatted for a while. He couldn't come for two weeks, he said, and the lady from the Health Authority wouldn't be there for a few days either.

The old man didn't mind. That lady wasn't much company, and she kept telling him he would be so much happier in a facility.

He felt a breeze on the back of his neck. Maybe he'd left the back door unlatched.

He readied himself to rise out of the chair again. Then he heard a sound. And then another, he was sure. Maybe it was the young fella. Perhaps he forgot something. But usually, he shouted a cheery greeting. "It's only me. How ya doing?"

The old man struggled to his feet. He made slow progress to the kitchen and then stopped at the foot of the stairs. Grey light filtered into the kitchen. It was still morning, he was sure. Another waft of damp salty air billowed around him.

"Is someone there?" he called, his voice thin and reedy. "Young fella?" And then, with hope, he added, "Maeve? Is that you?"

He heard another noise. This time, he recognized the click of the back door closing. "Who's there?" he demanded, his voice a little stronger.

A figure moved into the kitchen. The light was so dim, and it was hard to see who it was. The old man fumbled for the light switch, but he staggered a little, so grabbed his cane again to regain his balance.

"Who are you?" The old man wasn't afraid, just curious. "What do you want?"

The figure moved forward but didn't speak. The old man could see the outline. Did he know this person? Maybe. He was so confused.

"Have you come for me?" the old man asked. "Is it time to go? Have you seen my wife?"

He sensed rather than saw the figure rush towards him. But for a second, he thought he saw his wife standing in front of the kitchen window. He reached out for her and lost his balance as he felt a rush of air. Both hands were so close to her, but before he could touch her, a face loomed in front of him. He felt severe pain in the side of his head and then warmth and wetness on his face and neck. As he fell, the last thought he had was that he had always known it would end this way.

* * *

"I wish you'd stay with us for a few more days," Monica Drummond said, as she opened the car door for her mother. "I don't like to think about you alone."

Maeve Drummond swung her legs out of the car and stood up straight, unaided. She was nearly eighty years old, but she kept herself active. She wasn't one to sit and knit, as she liked to tell her daughter.

"I'll be fine, honey. I need a few quiet days. You go to your party tonight and have fun."

"If you're sure." Monica pulled her mother's bag from the back seat and linked arms with her. They both walked to the door of the small house, Monica's childhood home, and until two months ago, her parents' house. It was her mother's house now. Her funny, larger-than-life father had collapsed and succumbed to a massive heart attack.

The house was dark and quiet, as if in mourning. Monica realized it was the sounds she was missing. Her father's booming voice and belly laughs, the whining of a chainsaw, or the radio turned up loud because he was going deaf and refused to get hearing aids.

"I sure do miss him," Monica said as her mother fiddled with the door keys. She turned her head so Maeve wouldn't see the tears forming in her eyes.

"I know, honey. Me too."

They stood for a moment, and then Monica bent and kissed her mother's cheek. "You know, I think I'll just walk down to the beach for a few minutes while you go inside. Why don't you put the kettle on? I'll stay for tea."

"All right, then. Don't be long, it's getting cold. Forecast says we're in for some snow this week."

Monica Drummond followed the pathway around the side of the house, passing the small workshop full of her father's tools. Would they get rid of his stuff, she wondered. Maeve, ever practical, had already started sorting out her father's clothes.

"They have a lot of wear in them yet. Someone will need them. It's what your father would have wanted."

It wasn't what Monica wanted.

They had survived the first Christmas without her dad carving the turkey and wearing his ugliest Santa sweater. Without him toasting the Queen of England, even though he'd left the country of his birth seventy years ago, and without him insisting they all pull crackers and wear the silly paper hats for the entire day.

Christmas had been at Monica's house. She thought the void which her father had left would be less noticeable in the new holiday surroundings. They had all made an effort, her mother especially. They'd sung carols and told all the jokes from the pulled crackers. Monica's husband Derek had carved the turkey, and she'd lit the brandy around one of her mother's famous Christmas puddings. It had felt like they were all acting a part in a play, but Maeve had smiled and laughed and refused to shed a tear.

"Christmas was very important to your father," she'd said. "He'd have wanted us to celebrate, not mope around."

She was being so brave. It broke Monica's heart for the second time.

Monica took the narrow trail from the edge of the property through a group of spindly shore pine trees. Then she followed the distant thump and whooshing sound of the ocean waves on Plumper Beach. This was her favourite place on Quadra Island. Her father would always take his morning walk along the beach, and she remembered running in front of him when she was little, stopping to examine shells and tiny crabs in rock pools.

It was late morning, and the beach was shrouded in marina mist. Clouds had lowered and obscured the clifftops and had darkened into an ominous charcoal. The breeze whipped off the ocean and lifted Monica's hair. She could taste the salt on her lips and feel the sting on her cheeks. Her mother was right. Snow was coming.

In the distance, she heard the growl of an engine. She looked out to sea and could make out the shadow of a boat in the morning fog. The running lights came on and it roared away. She sighed. Her dad had loved to pull a few prawn traps for a feast on New Year's Eve. She stood for a few minutes, reliving those early mornings on the boat.

When she got back to the house, she found her mother standing in the kitchen with the telephone to her ear. Her parents had refused to switch to cell phones, and still had a landline and an old-fashioned telephone with a cord. When Maeve saw Monica, she put the phone back in its cradle.

"I was calling Randolph," she said. "I promised I'd call him when I got home. But there's no answer."

CHAPTER THREE

"Happy New Year!" A man wearing a black suit with a gold bow tie was welcoming Mayor Jade Thompson's hand-picked guests as they arrived at the entrance of the Cove Bistro and handed over their official invitation. The smiling man took a moment to scan his clipboard before they could join the revelry inside.

It was a nice touch, Andi had thought when she arrived arm in arm with Harry Brown. It emphasized the exclusivity of the gathering, and therefore the status of each guest. Maybe they'd remember on election day.

The Cove Bistro was the first restaurant to open in Coffin Cove since the Fat Chicken, over thirty years ago. And even then, the pub was new in name only. They rebuilt it in the same style as the Timberman's pub, which had stood in the exact spot until it burned down after a fight broke out between fishermen and loggers in the late eighties.

Andi Silvers couldn't see any plaid shirts or overalls in this New Year's Eve gathering, which doubled as the Bistro's grand opening. Instead, she could only pick out a few familiar faces in the elegantly dressed crowd.

"You look handsome," she whispered to Harry. She'd never seen him in black tie before, but he looked at ease as he shook hands with city officials and local business owners.

The Cove Bistro was the jewel in the crown of the rejuvenated Fish Plant site on the Coffin Cove shore front. The dilapidated warehouse had been transformed into boutique retail spaces and trendy apartments with spectacular ocean views, and it also housed the new Coffin Cove Museum. The crumbling pier was now a covered walkway to the Bistro. Decades before, fishermen had tied their boats up here and offloaded their catch to be processed at the Fish Plant. It had been Coffin Cove's economic heyday. Nobody had expected it to end. The town was awash with cash from fishing and logging, and coal barons pivoted to exporting lumber and seafood.

A few purse seiners and gill-netters still tied up at the Coffin Cove Government dock. One sawmill was still operating, but the pulp mill, which converted wood to paper, had cut back shifts to the bare minimum.

When Jade Thompson became the first woman ever to be elected mayor of Coffin Cove just over three years ago, she promised to restore economic prosperity to the town. The Fish Plant development was her triumph, the first delivery of that election promise. At least, that was the angle she expected Andi Silvers to take in the first edition of the New Year. It was an election year. The *Coffin Cove Gazette* had endorsed her last time round, and the invitation to the fancy New Year's Eve celebration came with an unspoken expectation of the same support.

Andi had accepted the invitation. She was acting editor of the *Gazette* and represented a local business, but she didn't feel any obligation to endorse Mayor Jade Thompson. The endorsement, as well as Andi's vote, would have to be earned. The *Gazette* would take a neutral stance until other candidates had thrown their hat into the ring.

Jade's tenure hadn't been plain sailing. Her predecessor, Dennis Havers, had been a self-serving, corrupt individual who rewarded himself and his cronies with shady deals and lucrative contracts. Coffin Cove had narrowly avoided bankruptcy and the resulting loss of independence. Jade Thompson had battled to stop the community from becoming another sub-urb of Nanaimo, the second-largest sprawling metropolis on Vancouver Island, but had made enemies. She had purged city staff. Business and residential taxes had increased, and she'd offered contractors "take it or leave it" deals. When Dennis Havers and his family were the victims of brutal murders, the outpouring of shock and sympathy in the community had recently transitioned to nostalgia for Dennis's leadership style.

"We need someone to look after local people," was the sentiment Andi was hearing. "All the money is going to attract newcomers. Nobody cares about us."

Mayor Jade Thompson had done little to quell that complaint this evening, Andi thought. The Bistro was owned by Paul Brecon, an already successful restaurateur who'd revitalized the mediocre dining scene in other struggling communities and had supposedly provided a boost to failing economies by hiring and buying locally.

Andi didn't recognize any of the serving staff, who were mostly young women. They were all dressed head to toe in black and expertly kept champagne glasses filled in between fading into the background.

What financial incentives had Jade offered Paul Brecon? It was a risky venture, opening a fine dining establishment in Coffin Cove. The town was accessible by only one road and was regarded by other Vancouver Islanders as a crime-in-fested, smelly mill town. The "smelly" part was unfair. In days gone by, the pulp mill belched steam and sulphur into the atmosphere, so on warm cloudy days the stench of rotten eggs choked the residents, until pressure from environmental groups forced new regulations and — if mill owners were to be believed — the decline of the forestry industry.

Jade Thompson blamed the *Coffin Cove Gazette* for the town's reputation for high crime rates.

"We don't make up the numbers, we just report them," Jim Peters, the owner of the *Gazette* and Andi's boss, had reminded the mayor before he left for his sabbatical.

Several high-profile homicides had fuelled the spike in crime statistics and Coffin Cove's reputation. Andi's investigative journalism had drawn attention to the community — unwanted attention, according to Jade Thompson and some business owners who had complained to Andi about a fall in the already dwindling tourism trade.

"We're changing Coffin Cove's story," Jade Thompson had declared earlier, just before she cut the gold ribbon at the door of the Cove Bistro. "This is just the start of exciting and prosperous times ahead for us all."

Andi watched the diminutive figure dressed in a shimmering black dress and high heels, her dark hair swept back from her face. Jade's black-rimmed glasses and sensible suits usually made her look like a librarian, and fooled opponents into thinking she was a pushover. Her appearance tonight brought admiring glances, but, Andi thought, also sent a message: *underestimate me at your peril.*

Harry was talking animatedly to a red-faced, balding man, who was forced to look up as Harry towered over him. Andi recognized the man as a fisheries manager from the Department of Fisheries and Oceans. Andi smiled to herself.

Harry would have preferred to cook a meal on the *Pipe Dream*, his boat, which they both called home, and then for the two of them to share a bottle of wine, sitting under blankets on the deck, watching the stars.

At least this evening would be productive for him. Beads of sweat were forming on the man's bald head, and his eyes were darting around the room, looking for an escape. Harry must be sharing his thoughts on the DFO's proposals for this year's upcoming herring season.

Andi let the man suffer. Instead, she wandered around the edge of the room, admiring the black-and-white vintage photographs of the Fish Plant and other historical landmarks in the town.

"That's my father."

Andi turned to see Peggy Wilson standing behind her. Peggy Wilson owned the only motel in Coffin Cove and

31

was a gossip with a mean streak. Her voice was the loudest, protesting against the mayor's economic policies.

It did not surprise Andi to see her at the reception, despite Peggy's vigorous objections to the Bistro's existence. Peggy wouldn't have been able to resist the opportunity for a first-hand dining experience, not least because she'd be able to bad-mouth literally everything about the new establishment. Jade Thompson invited Peggy, Andi was sure, because her political instincts were to keep her enemies exactly where she could see them.

This evening, Peggy looked almost regal. Her hair was piled up high, and she wore a black dress covered in sparkles. Peggy was wearing more make-up than usual, and Andi remembered there had been some gossip about Peggy being on the lookout for a new husband. Her first husband had died about fifteen years ago.

"To get away from her," Harry had said. He had little time for Peggy and her gossip.

Peggy was gesturing at the photograph on the wall. "My father opened the first gas station in Coffin Cove."

Andi looked again at the black-and-white print. A man wearing overalls and a cap in front of old-fashioned gas pumps was smiling directly at the camera.

"Is that you, Peggy?" Andi pointed to a small girl wearing similar overalls, with curly hair and a dimpled smile.

"Yes. My mother was horrified when she saw that picture. She always tried to make me wear a dress, but I was a tomboy back then, I suppose. Like that one, there."

Peggy was nodding towards Hephzibah Brown, Harry's sister, who was standing with her partner, Ruth Cloutier. As Andi looked at the couple, she saw Hephzibah throw back her head, laughing at something Ruth had said, and then slip her arm around the other woman's waist. They made a striking couple. Hephzibah's long silver hair was hanging loose down her back, and she was wearing a midnight-blue gown which brought out the Nordic ice blue of her eyes. Ruth Cloutier wore a red dress with a plunging neckline. The beaded necklace at her throat was a nod to her indigenous heritage.

"I've never seen that one dressed up to the nines. She was always *very* boyish."

Peggy Wilson's tone was soft, and she smiled, but Andi wasn't buying it.

Her remark was deliberately calculated to hit a nerve.

Hephzibah was one of the most beloved members of the community. Despite Harry's repeated efforts to help Hephzibah's Café turn a profit, Hephzibah refused to stop waving away payment for coffee and sandwiches from people she knew were struggling financially. Or allowing seniors to enjoy the warmth of the wood stove in winter to save on their own heating bills. Hephzibah was always ready with a hug or a willing ear.

The long sleeves and skirt of her gown hid the burn scars from a fire, still red and vivid many weeks later. Ruth Cloutier had also been a victim that tragic day, and the trauma had drawn the two women close together.

Their relationship had raised eyebrows in Coffin Cove, with some of the most disappointing reactions from the very people who'd accepted Hephzibah's kindnesses over the years.

Peggy's remark did not surprise Andi. She had already experienced Peggy's bigotry. The self-righteous woman had formed a coalition of business owners which she'd named the Concerned Citizens Committee, purporting to be advocates for Coffin Cove's economic future, the reduction of crime rates and reversing the decline in morality of the community. The inaugural meeting was scheduled for later in the week. Andi suspected it would be a forum for small-minded bigots like Peggy.

Peggy's seemingly innocent remark had a vicious under-current, and Andi opened her mouth to deliver a sharp rebuke.

Before she could, Paul Brecon chinked a wine glass and announced dinner was about to be served.

Andi took a moment to look around the restaurant as everyone took their seat. Peggy Wilson and the other business owners were seated with the mayor. There was an empty chair next to Peggy, and as Andi watched, Peggy turned in her seat to glance at the entrance.

"What are you looking at?"

Harry was looking at her.

"Oh, nothing, just wondering if Peggy Wilson has a date. There's an empty seat beside her."

"I feel sorry for him, whoever he is." Harry pulled out Andi's chair, and she sat down.

They were seated at a round table, herself and Harry, Hephzibah and Ruth, her father, Bob Hinton and the newest addition to the *Gazette* team, Charlene Davis.

"Are you having the chicken or seafood?" Hephzibah asked her brother.

Harry was an excellent cook, and rarely liked to eat out, unless it was a burger at the Fat Chicken.

"The chicken, I bet," Andi said with a smile. "Harry only eats seafood he prepares himself."

"Not true," Harry said. "I'm having the halibut."

Hephzibah loved to tease her brother. "Are you going to check the freshness of the fish first? And help the chef?"

"I know the fish is as fresh as it can be, because I've already asked about their supplier. And no, I'm an invited guest. I have no intention of spending any time in the kitchen," Harry answered coolly, and ignored his sister and Andi as they collapsed in giggles.

Paul Brecon approached their table, smiling.

"You all look as if you're having fun." He gestured to a young woman hovering behind him. "This is Juanita. She'll be taking your orders and looking after you this evening."

"Can I take your orders for the main course, please?" Juanita smiled.

Bob looked up from his menu. "Is that a Mexican accent I hear?"

The server dropped her smile for a second. "No, I am from Argentina."

"Really? I've travelled a little through Argentina. Which part are you from?"

Juanita smiled again. "Buenos Aires. I moved here to be with family. You like the chicken or seafood?"

"Chicken, please." Bob smiled back at Juanita. "I know Buenos Aires well. Which part of the city?"

"I live all over," Juanita said. "Why you go to Argentina?"

"I was working as a freelance journalist. What brings you to Canada? And Coffin Cove?"

"Dad, leave the poor girl alone," Andi said.

"Is OK. I move here to be with my brother."

Juanita moved on to take orders from Ruth and Hephzibah, but not before she gave Bob another flash of her smile.

Andi rolled her eyes. "Dad, stop flirting with the server." Her father grinned in reply.

Harry filled their glasses with wine, pausing when he came to Charlene. "You old enough for this?"

"Of course." Charlene grinned. "But I'm driving later, so I'll stick to water."

"Very wise," Harry said. "So, how are you enjoying working at the *Gazette*?"

Charlene, or Charlie as she preferred, had joined the *Gazette* three months ago and had just finished her probation period. Andi would officially confirm Charlie's permanent position as a junior reporter when they got back to work. Charlie was a serious young woman, but when she smiled, it lit up her entire face and made her deep brown eyes sparkle. She was quiet but possessed a dry sense of humour. She was also a talented writer.

She had very little work experience, but at her interview she had showed Andi an article she'd written about her mother's treatment in the Emergency department of Nanaimo's hospital. Charlie and her family were First Nation and members of the Three Cedar Band. Charlie's mother had twisted her ankle badly, and they both waited for six hours in the waiting room before a nurse examined her injury. The young woman was furious when the nurse asked if her mother had been drinking. The nurse wasn't satisfied with the answer — which was no — and then Charlie had asked why the hell that would be relevant.

The exchange became heated, and Charlie was asked to leave the waiting room. After that encounter, Charlie had taken it upon herself to interview other native people about their experiences in the health system. She'd submitted her article to the Nanaimo newspaper, but they'd ignored it.

Andi was impressed, not just with the writing, but with the systematic way Charlene had gathered evidence to support her argument that native people were not getting the health care they needed because of racist attitudes and stereotyping in the local hospital.

Andi hired Charlie on the spot.

It was working out well. Charlie was bringing a new perspective to the *Gazette*, and already print circulation had increased.

It was fun having new people in the office. Andi had felt overwhelmed when Jim Peters had left for his sabbatical. Until then, Andi had been the sole journalist for the *Gazette*, while Jim focused on the editorial duties and the business side — selling advertising space, dealing with the printers and distribution, everything Andi had ignored. Luckily, her father also joined the team when Jim left.

Juanita, their server, arrived back at the table. She was holding a bottle of red wine.

"The mayor would like you to have this with her compliments," Juanita said in her charming accent.

"Let's try it." Bob beamed. "Looks like a good one."

They all turned and raised their glasses to thank the mayor.

Andi was intrigued to see Peggy Wilson stand and wave vigorously at a man who was standing at the door of the Bistro.

"Over here," she called, and Paul Brecon led the man over to the empty chair.

"Ah, Peggy's mysterious date," Harry said, following Andi's gaze. "He must have been tending his flock."

"What do you mean?"

"Look what he's wearing."

Andi looked and saw what Harry had spotted. "A dog collar. Peggy's dating a pastor?"

Peggy Wilson was all smiles as the pastor sat down beside her. He was a thin man, with grey curly hair and glasses. As he'd walked over to Peggy's table, he'd reminded Andi of a strutting pigeon. He was dressed in a shabby corduroy jacket over a denim shirt and his white dog collar.

"She'll be worse," Harry commented. "She'll think everything she says and does is sanctioned by the Almighty."

"We don't know for certain she's dating the pastor," Andi said. "He looks quite a bit older than her."

"Oh, come on, she's all over him. And what about all the make-up and the wig?"

"You are terrible," Andi laughed. "Don't be mean." But she remembered Peggy's sly comment about Hephzibah and Ruth and didn't feel guilty about laughing.

"Damn it!" Ruth's annoyed voice brought Andi's attention back to her own table. When she looked, a dark stain was spreading down the front of Ruth's gown, and red wine dripped off the table.

Juanita was dabbing at the pool of liquid and Hephzibah grabbed a handful of napkins off the table and pushed them into Ruth's lap.

"Oh no, your lovely gown!" Hephzibah was upset.

"*Lo siento, señora*," Juanita said, lapsing into Spanish.

Paul Brecon rushed over. "What happened here?" he snapped at Juanita, whose face turned sullen.

"It's nothing," Ruth said. "Accidents happen."

"I am so sorry," the manager said. "Juanita, get this lady another plate immediately and a fresh glass."

Hephzibah finished wiping off the excess red wine and handed the stained napkins to the dour server, who disappeared.

"I am so sorry," Paul Brecon repeated. "Please give me your dry-cleaning bill, or if it can't be cleaned, we'll replace your dress."

"Thank you," Ruth said. "Please don't worry."

Juanita appeared again and placed a fresh plate of food in front of Ruth. She banged it a little, Andi thought, and then said something unintelligible under her breath. Ruth's head jerked around, but the server was already moving away.

"What did she say?" Andi asked.

"I'm not sure," Ruth said. "I'm sure she's just embarrassed." She waved off Hephzibah's fussing. "Please stop, Hep. Everyone's looking."

Hephzibah left the table, carrying more stained napkins, leaving a tense silence behind her.

Andi leaned forward and pointed to a bracelet on Ruth's wrist.

"That's unusual. Where did you get it?"

Ruth smiled and broke the tension. "Hephzibah gave it to me. It belonged to her mother."

Harry looked up. "Is that the copper bracelet she used to wear?"

"Yes, is it OK that I have it?" Ruth looked anxious.

"Sure it is. I just remember it, that's all. It has an engraving on it, doesn't it?"

Ruth slid off the copper bracelet and held it out for Harry to see. "It's quite worn, but I think it's a native design, probably a raven."

Harry nodded. "I'm sure my mother would be happy for you to have it."

Ruth nodded and smiled and put the bracelet back on her wrist just as Hephzibah arrived back. She looked relieved to see Ruth was all smiles, and the conversation had moved on.

After dinner and when the tables had been cleared, Charlie excused herself to go to a house party to see in the New Year.

"Ah, to be young again." Harry smiled as they left. "I'll be struggling to stay up to midnight."

Andi was about to agree when her phone buzzed in her purse. "Who'd be calling at this time?"

She smiled when she heard the voice on the other end of the call.

"Jim! Happy New Year! Guess where we are at the moment? . . . Yep, the Cove Bistro, it's pretty fancy. Yes, all the usual players are here. We're all guests of the mayor . . . OK, we'll stay to the end. Keep in touch. We miss you."

Andi grinned at Harry as she ended the call. "He says Happy New Year and we have to stay to the end. We'll get the best stories when the crowd gets drunk and rowdy."

CHAPTER FOUR

January 2

Andi woke up when she felt the bed creak. Through the gloom, she could see Harry's outline as he pulled on the clothes he'd left neatly piled the night before. Briefly, Harry blotted out the charcoal-grey morning light as he moved through the stateroom doorway and out to the galley.

Andi said nothing, just lay cocooned in warmth. She delayed getting out of bed as long as possible on these dark mornings. Harry was always up early. He liked his routine. Andi heard the coffee grinder shatter the silence, and then the hiss of the gas stove as Harry got the pot percolating before heading out to the deck. His movements made the large aluminium boat sway gently as he checked the tie lines and disturbed the seagulls while he waited for the coffee to brew.

Andi stayed still until she heard the chink of mugs and the splutter from the percolator. She swung her legs out of bed and took a sharp intake of breath as her bare skin met the chilled January air.

She pulled on sweatpants and a fleece jacket and then went out to the galley to pour herself a coffee. Harry had left her mug full of hot water to keep it warm.

Andi liked Harry's small, considerate gestures. Hot coffee every morning. Sometimes he'd have bacon sizzling, other mornings they'd have breakfast at Hephzibah's Café on the boardwalk if she wasn't rushing to the office.

She took a sip from her mug and stepped out on the deck to join Harry. Andi sat on a canvas chair on the deck and shivered a little in the morning breeze. The clouds parted briefly in the grey morning sky and allowed a glimmer of weak winter sun to appear on the horizon.

Harry got up and went back into the galley. He returned with a refilled mug and a blanket for Andi.

"Thanks. At least it's not raining," she said.

"It might snow this week," Harry said. "There's a cold front coming down the island. It should hit the north end today and then come for us."

It had rained a lot this winter. It was hard to keep anything dry on the boat, and most evenings, they'd sat in the galley with steamed-up windows and the oil stove burning at full capacity to reduce the dampness.

Harry had warned Andi that living on a boat wasn't as romantic as she might imagine.

She watched the January sun attempt an appearance on the horizon before a heavy cloud blotted out the faint orange glow. Andi's cheeks were cold, but her body was cosy in the blanket and she didn't want to move again.

"Slow news week, you think?" Harry commented.

"Not at all." Andi reached an arm out from under the blanket to pick up her coffee. "The mayor will expect a congratulatory article about her New Year's Eve triumph for starters."

"Wasn't it the Bistro's triumph?"

Andi gave a short laugh. "Not according to Jade. She made the Fish Plant happen, therefore any triumphs which occur in or around it are hers alone."

Harry smiled at her sarcastic tone. "Let me guess, she's taking credit for the triumphs but not the disasters — is that right?"

"Correct. They've sold none of the apartments. There are still two commercial vacancies, and then there's the mess the contractors left." Andi gestured towards the Fish Plant, where several dumpsters still stood, three months after construction had finished.

"No doubt the *Gazette* will hold our mayor's feet to the fire." Harry stood and stretched. "Got time for breakfast with Hephzibah? It's her first day back at work. Then Ike wants me to collect moorage fees from a boat which snuck in and tied up when nobody was watching."

Andi shook her head. "No, I'd better get to the office. Tell her I'll be in for a coffee later."

"Going to take a shower first?" Harry grinned at her.

It had become a running joke. Ike, the grumpy manager of the Coffin Cove Government Dock, had walked in on Andi when she was taking a shower in the washroom at the end of the dock. It was one of the less cosy aspects of living on a boat. The *Pipe Dream* had a washroom, but it was tiny and it took ages to heat enough water for a two-minute shower.

Ike had the other key to the shower block, and he'd just about fainted on the spot when he emptied the coins from the washing machine and found Andi barely covered by a towel.

"I'll wait until this evening. Ike goes home around three. It'll be safe after that."

* * *

Andi waved at Ike as she passed the office and smiled as he met her eyes and briefly raised his hand before turning away. The poor man was still embarrassed. It wasn't his fault, either. It was against the dock regulations to have live-aboards tied up at Coffin Cove, and he'd always turned a blind eye to Harry living on the *Pipe Dream*. Harry, in turn, did his best to help Ike out by collecting moorage fees and acting as a deterrent to would-be petty thieves.

Andi had moved onto the *Pipe Dream* because she had nowhere else to go. She'd been unable to continue living in her apartment over the local pub after she'd made the traumatic discovery of a murder victim one morning at the foot of the stairs leading to her apartment. Andi still saw the pool of dark blood, the grey pallor and the unseeing eyes of the corpse in her dreams.

Andi had initially moved into Hephzibah Brown's cottage. She'd found peace for a while, living with Harry's gentle sister. But now Hephzibah and Ruth Cloutier, her new partner, needed space and privacy as their new relationship blossomed.

Andi passed the boardwalk and the line of wooden shacks which faced the ocean. They used to house fishing tackle stores, net sheds and mechanic shops, back in the days when commercial fishing was booming in the tiny town. Hephzibah's Café was at the far end, and a kayak rental store had opened last year, but the rest of the shacks were boarded up or used for storage.

Andi glanced back at the new Fish Plant development before she turned onto Main Street.

The morning light reflected off the glass wall, and for a moment, Andi found the image jarring, as if the Fish Plant was an alien spacecraft landed in the middle of the town.

"A rising tide lifts all ships," the mayor had said in her grand opening speech last year. But despite Jade's plans for more projects and grants for existing businesses, she had achieved little apart from the Fish Plant. The tired buildings on Main Street and the boardwalk seemed to sag resentfully in the shadow of the gleaming new building.

It would be an interesting year, Andi thought as she climbed the stairs to the *Coffin Cove Gazette* office, which occupied the second floor over a vacant store.

Andi heard laughter coming from the office and realized she wasn't the first to arrive. She pushed the door open and saw her father, Bob, sitting at her old desk. He was talking on the phone, but looked up when Andi walked in.

"New business!" he said with a smile as he ended the call.

"Great," Andi replied. "We need cash." Jim Peters, the owner of the *Gazette*, had taken every opportunity to impress on Andi the importance of cash flow for the *Gazette*'s survival.

Her boss had departed for a year's sabbatical, travelling and writing a book about his life as a war correspondent for international media outlets in the years before he came back to Coffin Cove. He'd returned to take over the local newspaper when his father, the *Gazette*'s founder, became ill.

"I've already made some calls, and I think we have three new clients, plus the religious fella on the phone," Bob explained.

"Religious fella?"

"The pastor, the one who turned up at the New Year's Eve party with Peggy Wilson. He's starting a new church, or religious group, or something. He'll be in to talk about it later today."

Andi shrugged. "All business is welcome, religious or otherwise. What else have we got?"

Bob rummaged through a pile of papers on his desk, and Andi pulled up a chair as her father went through his notes from his early-morning calls.

This was the first time in Andi's life she and her father had worked together. In fact, it was the first time since Andi was a small child that she had spent any time with him. Bob Hinton had made his name in Ottawa as an astute journalist working on Parliament Hill, unafraid to ask politicians the tough questions and persisting until he got an answer.

He'd sold out, according to his peers, switching to the more lucrative and sensational celebrity stories, before dropping off the radar altogether. Rumours swirled about drinking and drugs, and it was about the same time that Bob had left his wife and young daughter, and had sunk into obscurity and out of Andi's life for decades.

Andi's eyes wandered to the long windowless wall in the office, used as a visual story wall. Documents, pictures and scrawled notes from the *Gazette*'s most recent investigation were still pinned and taped to the wall.

This unfinished investigation, Bob's obsession and the reason for his absence in Andi's life, had brought him and Ruth Cloutier to Coffin Cove.

Ruth was searching for her sister, who had disappeared on a camping trip in the 1970s. Bob was on the trail of a killer, a powerful figure who'd evaded justice for a string of unsolved murders. Their paths merged and unexpectedly ended in Coffin Cove.

Ruth had eventually found the remains of her long-dead sister, another victim of Bob's elusive killer. Andi and her father had joined forces for the investigation and uncovered the truth. But, yet again, the killer was one step ahead and protected by friends in very high places. The only piece of physical evidence underpinning their investigation had been suspiciously "misplaced" by the prosecuting authorities.

The story remained unpublished, but Andi had refused to clear the story wall. "It stays until we publish," she'd said.

Bob followed her eyes and then rummaged on his desk.

"I received this today," he said, handing a document to Andi. She saw from the elaborate letterhead it was from a lawyer.

Andi was silent for a moment while she scanned the letter. "A civil case against Elizabeth Halwell? Ruth is going through with it?"

Ruth had decided to pursue justice for Essie George, her sister, through the civil courts. The threshold for conviction was lower, and if successful, it could prompt a re-opening of the criminal prosecution. It was a long shot.

"Looks like it. Good for her. Politically, it's the best possible timing for the case."

Andi sighed. She had watched the tragic images of heartbroken parents and relatives of First Nations children who'd been torn from their families and placed in so-called "schools" run by the government and Christian churches. It had been the abhorrent policy of successive Canadian governments until the 1990s. First Nations people had long told horrific stories of abuse and worse at these schools. Now, discoveries of mass graves containing the remains of their children were the proof of these tragic stories.

Ruth had said simply, "This is not news to our people. They took children from their families and they never came back. What else could have happened? White people refused to believe us. Now we have the evidence."

Bob leaned towards Andi. "Don't be naïve, Andi. Everything is political. If native communities want justice for their children, and if Ruth wants any kind of justice for Essie, these cases have to be brought while the country is still in shock. Otherwise, politicians will delay and obfuscate, until the media moves on. Ruth has to do this now, while powerful people are on the back foot."

"You think Elizabeth Halwell is on the back foot?" Andi asked. She wasn't convinced that Halwell, the ruthless psychopath who'd viciously taken Essie George's life, would be alarmed by Ruth's legal action. Halwell was the daughter of a diplomat and now the wife of a wealthy politician. She seemed beyond the reach of the law and the influence of a small west coast newspaper.

Bob sighed and sat back in his chair. He seemed deflated.

"I don't know," he said finally. "She's evaded any accountability for her actions, however abominable, for her entire life."

"So you'll help Ruth?" Andi asked, although she knew the answer to that already.

"I will," he said. "I'll do everything I can."

Andi heard the thump of feet on the stairs, and a moment later, Charlie Davis pushed through the door.

"What's going on?" Charlie asked cheerfully.

"You tell us," Andi teased. "I hired you to get all the local news, remember?"

Charlie smiled. "I was just in the café. I heard Peggy Wilson talking about the meeting this week. Are we going?"

"The inaugural meeting of the Concerned Citizens Committee? It's Friday night, same time as the museum lecture," Bob said. "I know where I'd rather be."

"I'll go to the meeting," Andi decided. "I know Jim thought they were just a bunch of crackpots, but they're gaining support."

The Concerned Citizens Committee was going to be a thorn in Mayor Jade Thompson's side and her bid for re-election later in the year. The "Concerned Citizens" were mainly local business owners who hadn't felt lifted by the rising tide of economic prosperity the mayor had promised.

"They have legitimate concerns," Bob pointed out. "The Fish Plant isn't full, the apartments will probably be too expensive for local people and the Bistro is in direct competition with the Fat Chicken. It might attract diners from out of town, but how will that benefit any other business?"

Charlie said, "They're all upset about the new band office. And now Mayor Thompson's started the project on Hope Island, they're complaining that too much money is going to the natives." She rolled her eyes. "I should cover the meeting."

Andi shook her head. "No. I'd like you to cover the lecture at the museum. I think your first solo outing for the *Gazette* should be something less controversial."

"Dinosaurs? Really?" Charlie slumped back in her chair.

"Yes. It's a big deal for Katie Dagg. She's worked hard to get the museum up and running, and this is the first of a series of lectures. Apparently, the professor is highly sought after on the lecture circuit. Get some background, go to the lecture and make sure I have something for next week's deadline, OK?"

Charlie nodded, still not displaying much enthusiasm.

Andi stood up and stretched. She walked over to Jim Peters' worn oak desk and opened her laptop to start work.

"Trust me, Charlie," she said to her unsmiling junior reporter, "there's plenty of politics for us all to cover in this town. I've got a feeling it's going to be an interesting year."

CHAPTER FIVE

January 4

Juliette Parsons wished she'd taken another day off. The office was quiet and most people wouldn't be back until the kids were back at school. She had traded the week in between Christmas and New Year with a colleague for this week. She'd thought she'd been the one with the best end of the deal. Now she was looking at the schedule and saw the meeting her colleague had wanted to ditch.

She must have been doing a happy dance, Juliette thought sourly. Missing the meeting with Sylvie Hamm was worth trading a month's holiday.

Maybe Sylvie wouldn't show. Maybe it was snowing too much for the ferry to run from Quadra Island? Juliette knew she was clutching at straws. She had given Sylvie her last warning for missing mandatory meetings, and the weather forecast was snow for a short while and then the storm would continue south.

Sylvie would arrive, and Juliette had no choice but to take the meeting with the least popular Community Health worker on the north end of Vancouver Island.

With a sigh, Juliette pulled out Sylvie Hamm's thick file and slapped it on her desk. Then she went to pour herself a large strong coffee.

At 10.15 a.m., the receptionist called Juliette.

"She's here."

Juliette thanked her. Only fifteen minutes late. It still irritated her. She'd only met Sylvie Hamm twice before, and both times Sylvie had made it clear she resented any "interference" from her supervisors.

To hell with her. She'd have to follow the rules like everyone else. Juliette took a breath and swallowed. She'd be kind but would stand her ground.

Juliette jumped as the door swung open and Sylvie Hamm walked in.

"Sylvie, please knock next time. I could have been on the phone." She was already rattled.

Sylvie Hamm stood towering over Juliette's desk. This wasn't the way Juliette had planned this meeting. She gestured for Sylvie to take the chair in front of the desk. Without saying a word, Sylvie sat down and dropped a large cloth bag on the floor beside her.

Juliette wrinkled her nose. There was a funky smell emanating from the sullen-faced woman sitting opposite her. It was a combination of mildew and body odour. Juliette contemplated opening the only window in her office, but it was high above the filing cabinets and would have involved standing on a chair.

She glanced at the electronic diary displayed on her computer screen. She had allowed an hour for this interview. Perhaps she could shorten it.

"It's nice to meet you at last, Sylvie," Juliette said. "So unfortunate you've had to miss our last two scheduled meetings."

The woman didn't say a word, just glowered at her. Juliette knew from the file that Sylvie Hamm was fifty-seven years old. She had a round moon face, a pink complexion and baby-blue eyes which wandered around the room and had failed to look directly at Juliette until the last reference to the missed meetings. Now the blue eyes were staring at Juliette with a peculiar expression. Vacant or disconnected, Juliette couldn't decide. She could only tell the woman was annoyed by the way she pursed her lips and the small dots of red on both cheeks. It was the woman's hair which fascinated Juliette. It was long and frizzy, almost down to the woman's waist. The hair was swept back from the woman's forehead and then seemed to take on a life of its own. It was grey, almost white in places, and looked as wiry as steel wool. Juliette wondered if it was even possible to brush it.

Sylvie Hamm was the only Community Health worker for Quadra Island, a small island off the east coast of Campbell River. Quadra Island was only accessible by a ferry. Sylvie had enjoyed almost full autonomy, it seemed, from the main Community Health office in Campbell River under Juliette's predecessor, who had recently taken early retirement.

"Good luck with that one," the departing manager had told Juliette, as she dumped Sylvie's thick file on the desk. "You'll need it."

Juliette tried again.

"So why exactly were you not able to attend the last meetings? They are mandatory. And—" she tried a gentler tone, recalling her predecessor's written evaluations of Sylvie Hamm — "these meeting are to help you, Sylvie. I'd like you to consider me as a resource. You know, someone to call on when you need to chat about clients . . . or difficult situations . . ." Her voice trailed off. Sylvie's face was set in the same expression, which Juliette now interpreted as angry.

Difficult. Aggressive. Inconsistent. Juliette glanced down at Sylvie's file. She wished she'd read it all before this meeting. Why was this uncommunicative woman still employed?

"Sick. I was sick." Sylvie spoke in a gruff voice but refused to meet Juliette's eyes.

"I see. For both meetings?"

"Yes." Sylvie looked at Juliette, and now her expression was different. *Is she challenging me?* Juliette wondered.

"It's office policy to send in a doctor's note if you are off sick, so please bear that in mind in the future." Juliette kept her tone pleasant but brisk. "Let's address another issue." Juliette turned the pages of Sylvie's file until she found the relevant information. "On a number of occasions, clients have complained to this office that you are not answering your cell phone during office hours and—"

"Which clients?"

"I beg your pardon?" Juliette looked up, startled at Sylvie's angry tone.

"Which clients complained about me? I have a right to know."

"It doesn't matter, Sylvie. The point is, you are not answering your cell phone. Is there something wrong with it? Do you have it with you?"

"No."

"No, there's nothing wrong with it, or no, you don't have it with you?" Juliette was losing her patience.

"I lost it."

"I see."

The red spots on Sylvie's cheeks were burning brighter. Juliette could clearly smell wafts of stale sweat coming from the folds of Sylvie's clothes.

It was an odd ensemble. Sylvie wore a long black skirt that had dragged on the floor when she entered the office. Over the top, she wore a knitted brown tunic, a black scarf and a long wool cardigan which once may have been white or cream, but now was a grubby shade of grey. Sylvie Hamm was a large woman. She had broad shoulders and big hands. Juliette noticed that Sylvie didn't wear a ring, although her file mentioned she had a son. She sat in front of Juliette's desk with her legs slightly apart, leaning forward. It was a masculine pose, Juliette thought. Intimidating, even. Her skirt was hitched up at the front, and Juliette could see her mottled skin bulging over brown socks, and her feet stuffed into worn running shoes.

Juliette decided not to fight this battle today.

"Well, I'll make sure to arrange a new one for you as soon as I can." Juliette reached for her keyboard. "Now, I'd like to schedule a day with you to visit clients. I'd like to get a feel for your workload and see for myself where I can help. So, how does January eighteenth sound? It's a Thursday."

Sylvie made a strange sound, like a growl in the back of her throat. Juliette looked up in surprise.

"Sylvie?"

The woman's entire face was flushed red.

"I don't like to be spied on!" Sylvie rose to her feet and towered over the desk. She had balled her hands into fists, and she held her arms rigid by her sides. Her hair stuck out at the sides, so it looked like she was wearing a grey shroud.

The force of Sylvie's words made Juliette sit back in her chair. Her mouth had fallen open in shock. She'd done many hours of conflict resolution and de-escalation, but she was totally unprepared for Sylvie's hostile reaction to a simple request.

Juliette fought to keep her voice calm but authoritative.

"Sit down at once, Sylvie."

To her surprise and relief, the large woman did what she was told. Her face remained red, and she pushed her fists into her lap.

"I have no intention of spying, Sylvie. Why would you even think that? I am new in this district, and it's my responsibility to get to know our clientele so I can advocate for the best resources. I am spending a day with all the Community Health workers in the field. Now, if the eighteenth doesn't work, please suggest an alternative date."

Sylvie seemed to struggle to compose herself. At last she said gruffly, "January eighteenth is fine."

Juliette decided it was time to bring this meeting to a close. A few minutes later, she was watching Sylvie's back disappear out the office, and in a last act of — defiance? anger? — Sylvie banged the door shut.

Juliette sat back in her chair, exhausted by the encounter. She looked at Sylvie Hamm's file on her desk but couldn't bring herself to open it again.

"I've had enough crazy for one day," she muttered to herself.

* * *

Two hours later, Sylvie Hamm eased herself behind the steering wheel of a red, nearly new GMC Sierra truck. She sat for a long moment, and then gently ran her hands over the leather-clad steering wheel. She breathed deeply and savoured the "new truck" smell. Everything was different and better. The dashboard was free of dust, there were no stains in the cup holder and, in place of the radio and CD player in her old junker, a touch of the computer screen would find her favourite radio station and magically operate her cell phone. She hoped her supervisor would get her a new one soon.

The salesman rapped on the window and waved some documents in the air. He was young and thin, with dark hair that hung limply over his forehead. He reminded Sylvie of Cody.

"Miss Hamm? You still have to sign this paperwork. For the loan, remember?"

Sylvie eyed him with suspicion. "Loan?"

"Yes ma'am, er, miss. You've paid the cash deposit, but you have to fill in paperwork for the monthly payments. So we can take them out of your bank account."

Sylvie detected an impatient tone in his voice, but the salesman was still smiling and nodding at her.

Probably he'll get a big fat commission for this sale.

Sylvie smoothed her hands over her skirt and pulled on the handle to open the driver's door. She swung her legs around and slid to the ground, exposing her feet and ankles. The smile left the salesman's face. Sylvie saw another expression. Was it disgust? She balled her hands into a fist and then forced down the flare of anger that had formed in the pit of her stomach. Why should she care what this boy thinks? She took a deep breath. She wanted this truck. She was going to get it.

"I'm so confused, dear," she said, smiling as sweetly as she could, and raising her voice an octave above her usual gravelly pitch. "Can't I just come in every month with cash?"

The salesman's mouth dropped open.

"Well, no," the young man said after a moment of silence, during which he hopped awkwardly from foot to foot. "I'm afraid we don't do that . . . Oh no. Please, Miss Hamm, don't . . . don't cry . . ."

In a short while, Sylvie Hamm drove off the dealer's lot and headed her new truck towards the ferry terminal. The salesman had agreed to accept monthly cash payments as long as Sylvie Hamm lived close by and *promised* not to be late. *Ever.*

"Otherwise, it'll be my job gone," he'd said with a nervous grin. "And my wife would kill me, what with the baby on its way . . ."

Sylvie heard his words, but she didn't bother to acknowledge him. She was too busy admiring her new purchase and enjoying that lovely feeling she always experienced when she had just acquired a new possession.

The tears had worked, she thought, as she lined up for the next ferry to Quadra Island. She'd given the salesman the address of a colleague in Campbell River. He wouldn't check it, she was sure. That lie, plus the tears, had sealed the deal for this nearly new red truck. Tears always worked on Cody too.

"OK, Mom, please don't cry. I'll buy it for you." He always gave in — nearly always. He'd been firm about not buying her a truck, even though she'd pleaded. No matter now. She'd figured it out on her own.

She would have to pay the monthly instalments. It would be OK. Right after her monthly meeting with her supervisor, she would take an envelope of cash to the dealership for the next twenty-four months. She was certain it would be fine.

All organized, she thought, satisfied with her plan. The ferry line-up moved. Sylvie turned the key in the ignition, and the truck immediately responded with a reliable purring sound. She smiled. It had been a good day, after all.

Except . . . her thoughts returned to her supervisor and the meeting she'd had before she set off to the dealership. Sylvie shook her head as if to dislodge the thoughts. If it hadn't been for that woman, she would have never bought the truck. The truth was, she'd been thinking about this truck for weeks. The need to own it had been building and building until she couldn't think of anything else. It was like a slow, smouldering fire within her, which had erupted into flames when that bitch had picked and poked at her, pretending to be her friend. Sylvie had practically run from the office down the road to the dealership.

But now, just as quickly as the impulse to buy this truck had taken hold and propelled her to wave excitedly at the salesman this afternoon, the fear set in. She wrote a cheque. She'd promised Cody she would never do that without talking to him first. How would she explain it? Even if she transferred the money from her secret account, he would see the cashed cheque. Maybe she could say it was a mistake?

The thoughts jarred her.

What was it Cody kept telling her?

"You can't buy happiness, Ma."

It wasn't true. Buying things, anything, made Sylvie happy. But she had to admit that recently, the warm afterglow of her purchases dissipated quickly, leaving nothing but an empty anger and gnawing impulse to do it all over again.

Sometimes in Sylvie's life she'd been able to control herself. She had even cleaned out the towers of cardboard boxes that filled most of the rooms in her small cottage. She'd donated many of the items — some which she hadn't seen for years or had forgotten about completely — to charity shops up and down Vancouver Island. It had been hard to let them go, but she had to admit she felt lighter without all the stuff to worry about. It was becoming more of an effort to find places to store her purchases from each spending spree.

It wasn't the possessions she craved. It was the thrill of the transaction, the moment when she had a new thing in her hand. The *thing* could be anything — clothes, ornaments, kitchenware, furniture . . . new or second-hand, Sylvie didn't care.

Dwindling finances had slowed her down. Cody, her son — her rich son, as she kept reminding him — had spent many hours admonishing her and trying to agree budget plans with her, so he didn't have to constantly top up her meagre monthly salary.

At least she owned her cottage. Well, technically, Cody owned the cottage. He had paid off the tax liens and the loans which Sylvie had secured against the property when he found the final demand notices from the city and the bank. Since then, the cottage had belonged to him, and there was no way Sylvie could borrow any more against the asset to fund her spending. Cody also paid for the utilities, Sylvie's cell phone, her second-hand car, the insurance and all the maintenance bills. He had drawn the line at a new truck.

"No way!"

The ferocity of his response to Sylvie's request angered her. She figured he had a new girlfriend. These little bitches he picked up at the hospital always tried to come between her and her son.

She'd tried her usual approach.

"If it hadn't been for me, you'd never have been a doctor."

Sylvie truly believed that. She had always wanted Cody to be a doctor or a lawyer. She imagined him living in a big house on the ocean somewhere. She'd have her own private wing, and she'd retire and take up painting.

When Sylvie's parents died, they'd left their cottage to their daughter, but had wisely tied up the rest of their estate in an unbreakable trust for their only grandson. They, too, wanted him to go to college. Sylvie's ex-husband had been the executor of the will. When he refused to challenge the trust, or give up the executorship to Sylvie, she threatened to divorce him. He didn't need a second prompt. For a few years he paid Sylvie some alimony and child support, but when Cody received his trust money and went to university and then medical school, Sylvie never received another penny.

Cody had become a doctor — an emergency doctor in Calgary. He worked long hours, was highly paid and was still single.

He was saving to buy a house, he said. That meant he couldn't keep paying all Sylvie's bills.

What was it he'd said?

She'd have to tighten her belt. Live within her means.

Sylvie jammed on the brakes, coming to a stop inches away from the car in front of her. Just thinking about that phone call made her hands tremble.

She had slammed the phone down. If Cody wouldn't help her get the truck, she would find another way. And she had.

Sylvie came to a stop at the ticket booth. She fumbled in her bag and found enough cash to pay for her ferry ride back to Quadra Island.

As the ferry neared the Quathiaski Cove ferry terminal, Sylvie's chest tightened. The January sky was darkening, and she wanted to drive straight back to her cottage. But she couldn't do that yet.

As she drove off the ramp, Sylvie kept her eyes forward. But she couldn't help sneak a glance at the figure in bright yellow rain gear directing the ferry traffic.

She saw a woman's face streaked with rain, her dark hair sticking to her forehead. The woman glanced once at the truck and then stared directly at Sylvie, who deliberately slowed down.

The woman's face gave nothing away. It was a mask of stone.

Sylvie didn't care. Monica Drummond had said terrible things about her. Now she could see that Sylvie was successful enough to own a nearly new truck. Monica could never do that. She'd never earn enough money to buy anything more than second-hand junkers.

Thinking about money made Sylvie remember her task. She put her foot on the gas, glancing once more to see if the figure in yellow was watching. She wasn't.

Sylvie drove across Quadra Island, the soft swoosh of the wipers keeping the windscreen clear of the January drizzle. In half an hour, Sylvie made the turn onto a gravel road near Plumper Beach on the west side of the island.

She'd made this visit at least once a week for the last ten years.

Sylvie was the only Community Health worker based on Quadra Island, serving the increasing number of elderly residents. As a young woman, she'd wanted to be a nurse. Her grades had been poor at school, and her many applications had been turned down.

As a community worker, she assessed the needs of seniors on the island, recommending the allocation of resources and services. Much of her day was spent chatting with her clients over cups of tea. Sylvie was popular with them. She had lived on the island her entire life and she paid attention to gossip. She wasn't afraid to repeat and sometimes embellish the juiciest of rumours.

But Sylvie wasn't popular with her supervisors. It wasn't her fault. She tried to complete the paperwork on time. She worked as hard as possible and still they always hated her. And then there was that trumped-up complaint last year. That Monica Drummond hated her too. She'd been mean in high school and nothing had changed.

Sylvie stopped her truck in front of a mailbox. Leaving the truck running, she slid out of the seat. She rummaged in her pocket and pulled out a small key.

There were several envelopes in the box. Sylvie immediately saw the brown one. Her heart skipped a beat. She pulled out all the mail, locked the mailbox and stuffed the brown envelope in her pocket with the key.

She should leave now, she knew that. She had what she needed. Just one more day and then she'd call the police. But what if someone else had been to the cabin?

Cold fingers of fear clutched her heart. For a moment, she contemplated putting the brown envelope back in the mailbox. But what about the others? What if someone started digging? No, she had to stick with her plan. She'd check the cabin, although she didn't want to, and then she'd go home and have a nice cup of tea. She'd call Cody and tell him she'd got a big raise and had celebrated by buying a new truck all on her own. He'd be happy and proud of her. That thought put a smile on her face.

Sylvie scrambled back in the truck.

The next turn-off after the mailbox was a rutted track under a canopy of trees. Sylvie marvelled at the comfort of her new ride, as she barely felt the truck drive over the potholes. After a minute or two, she stopped the truck and turned off the ignition. She sat for a moment, listening to the ticking sound of the warm engine.

The cabin stood in a clearing. Once upon a time, it had been well maintained. Now the cedar shakes on the roof were covered in moss and some were cracked and peeling. Paint flaked off the windowpanes and the front door. Drapes were open, but there were no lights at the windows. It would be pitch black in an hour. Sylvie knew she had to be quick.

Not wanting to stumble, Sylvie turned the key in the ignition and turned on the headlights. Immediately, the cabin was illuminated with a stark white light.

Sylvie got out of the truck and walked to the front door, her heart pounding against her ribcage. The front door wasn't locked. Last time she was here, she had just pulled it shut. Now, she turned the handle and pushed the door open wide, allowing the light from the headlights to flood into the cabin.

Sylvie half expected the old man to call out as he usually did. "Is that you, Sylvie?"

Instead, a stench filled Sylvie's nostrils, and she clamped her hand over her mouth before she gagged.

The body lay at the foot of the stairs, just as she had left it two days ago. The beam from the headlights turned the old man's face and unseeing eyes into a silvery death mask. The blood, which had been oozing and red in Sylvie's memory, was black as an oil slick under the man's head. It had seeped into the rug in the living room. The garish light had turned the entire scene into shades of black and white, as if Sylvie were viewing an old movie. If it wasn't for the smell, and the faint buzz of flies, even in the January chill, Sylvie could have believed someone had created and then abandoned an elaborate display for Halloween.

Sylvie turned to leave. Nobody had been here. But then, a small box on a coffee table caught her eye. She'd seen it many times before. She had sneaked a look when she'd been left alone in the room. She knew what was inside that box, and suddenly she knew she had to have it.

Carefully, she hoisted her skirt above her knees.

Then she shuffled into the room, coming perilously near the man's head when she reached the table. She stretched out one hand, not wanting to take another step, in case she left a footprint in the blood. Her fingers just touched the box, and she held her breath as she eased it towards her. Finally, she got hold of the box securely in her palm. Still holding up her skirt, she edged backwards until she was at the door.

Sylvie couldn't wait. She snapped open the box and smiled when she saw the contents. Two gold rings. One was wider than the other, just a plain gold band. The other was delicate and inlaid with tiny diamonds.

Sylvie closed the box and backed out of the front door.

She scurried back to the truck, started the engine and swung the truck in a wide circle, before heading back along the narrow track to the road.

It wasn't until she arrived at her cottage that she remembered the mail. Her hand flew to her pocket. It was OK. She still had the brown envelope.

Humming quietly to herself, she opened her front door and squeezed past the boxes in the hallway, then headed to her kitchen to make a cup of tea.

CHAPTER SIX

January 5, morning

Peggy Wilson eased off her office chair and walked over to the coffee machine, which was strategically placed on a small table by the window.

Peggy didn't want more coffee. She'd already drunk three large cups and was fighting an urge to pee. For the moment, she ignored the pressure in her bladder. She emptied the old grounds into a garbage bin, spooned more coffee into the machine and checked there was enough water before pressing the button once again. Peggy stood by the window as the coffee machine gurgled into life, and the aroma of freshly brewed coffee filled the small office. The window faced onto the motel parking lot, and Peggy, the owner, was looking for someone.

He had promised to help her this morning. She hoped he hadn't forgotten.

She was keeping her eye on cabin 410. There were only twelve cabins, but when Peggy's husband was alive, he'd thought it made the motel complex seem bigger and therefore more desirable if they started the numbering at 400.

There was only one vehicle in the parking lot and it belonged to her guest in cabin 410. They had arranged to meet this morning.

She danced from foot to foot and then gave in to the urgent call of nature, abandoning her lookout station.

After relieving herself, Peggy washed her hands thoroughly and stared at her reflection in the small mirror above the sink.

"Not bad," she murmured to herself. She'd tried to keep herself trim. She ate healthy food and didn't drink.

Peggy ran her hand over her tight curls and pursed her lips. The wig itched a little. Her hair had never grown back properly after the chemotherapy. The pallor and dark circles under her eyes showed her insomnia. She hadn't let it slow her down, though. She didn't want pitying looks from anyone.

Keeping busy was the key, and that meant staying involved in the community.

At one time, she had single-handedly run the Women's Institute, and after that she'd started the Welcome Wagon for newcomers to Coffin Cove. More recently, she and other tradespeople had started a business association, and because there were so many people in the town who were worried about its future, Peggy had proposed opening up membership to any like-minded town resident.

"The Concerned Citizens Committee," she said to her reflection in the mirror. She liked how it sounded.

A muffled sound of a door slamming grabbed Peggy's attention, and she remembered her mission.

She hurried back into the office and over to the coffeepot. She didn't want to appear to be looking out for her guest, so she made a show of checking the pot and then arranging brochures and notices on a cork board which hung next to the window.

She need not have bothered. When she casually looked out at the parking lot, she could see the truck still in its parking space. Darn, had he left on foot?

Peggy went back to her desk and eyed her ledgers. When Dennis Havers was mayor of Coffin Cove, before that young woman had taken over, the Coffin Cove Motel was full all year round. Dennis had many associates who needed accommodation regularly, plus the contractors working on his projects, and then there was the usual tourist season. There weren't many tourist attractions in Coffin Cove, but the fishing was good. Peggy had always made a decent living in the summer from sports fishermen who tied up their boats in Coffin Cove and preferred a comfortable bed and ensuite bathroom rather than the austere shower block at the dock.

Business had slowed since Jade Thompson became mayor. Peggy knew Dennis Havers lined his own pockets when he was in office, but at least he kept the cash flowing through the town, even if he benefited the most.

Mayor Thompson used local contractors for her Fish Plant project, and they didn't need accommodation.

Then one morning last summer, Peggy woke up and didn't have the energy to get out of bed. It took her a month to summon the courage to go to the doctor, who solemnly confirmed Peggy's worst fears. After that, she relinquished control to doctors and specialists, nurses and counsellors and spent hours in waiting rooms and treatment clinics, the weight of terror in her stomach every time her name was called.

Just before Christmas, Peggy's doctor delivered some tentative good news. The surgery and chemotherapy treatment had been successful; the tumour had receded.

"You'll need to take these," the doctor had said, handing Peggy a list of drugs, "but other than that, Peggy, try to live your life and put this behind you."

"But what if the cancer comes back?" Peggy blurted out. She hadn't succumbed to tears throughout the whole ordeal, but the thought of being abandoned by the team of people who'd taken over her entire existence and left only with a few pills to keep the monster at bay, that terrified her more than the original diagnosis. Tears poured down her cheeks.

The doctor looked at her with sympathy and took Peggy's hand.

"You've received excellent treatment, my dear. The likelihood of your cancer returning is very low. You must have *faith*," he said.

Until then, Peggy had only attended church for weddings and funerals, but still considered herself a practising Christian. After her last appointment with her doctor, she attended the four advent Sunday services, a carol service, the children's nativity and the Christmas morning service. But the small Methodist church in Coffin Cove was sparsely attended, even on significant religious occasions, mainly because of the uninspired sermons from the ancient Pastor Jones.

Peggy needed to be inspired. She needed to *believe.*

Out in the Valley, old Fred Harding used to preach in an old wooden church he built himself, and that was all fire, brimstone and the Devil. Peggy shuddered as she remembered the one Sunday she'd been persuaded to attend, and how embarrassed she'd been when several of Fred's congregation writhed on the floor spouting all kinds of gibberish. "Talking in tongues," they'd called it. Utter nonsense is what Peggy called it, snorting to herself. Maybe faith would find her.

She continued to examine herself daily in the shower and then kneel beside the bathtub in her housecoat and pray to be delivered from the fears which kept her awake at night.

It wasn't just the return of the cancer which kept Peggy tossing and turning.

The motel had been all but closed since fall. Peggy's savings were dwindling. She'd applied for a city grant to renovate the motel rooms, but she hadn't had the energy to interview contractors. Besides, with little or no revenue, she might need to borrow from those funds to keep the motel afloat.

Peggy glared at the ledgers. She'd need divine intervention to keep the damn business going. Or a new mayor. That Fish Plant was supposed to attract new people to the town. But what use was a new museum and shops for her? Now Mayor Thompson was planning on some kind of resort on Hope Island — a partnership with the Indians of all things. How was that supposed to bring more guests to the motel?

Peggy took a deep breath. Stress was bad for her. She needed to be grateful for her blessings, and one of those was her guest in room 410.

Pastor Michael Nelson had called to make the booking before New Year's Eve. Peggy had been dozing beside the fire and hadn't wanted to go to the office. Even when the motel had been busy, she rarely had visitors between Christmas and New Year.

The man was short, with greying curly hair which touched his shoulders. He was wearing a dark trench coat, black jeans splattered with mud and scuffed running shoes. If it hadn't been for the white dog collar at his neck, Peggy would have thought twice about letting him stay.

He had an odd way of looking at her. He wore glasses with thick lenses which magnified his eyes, and he put his head slightly to one side when he spoke. He reminded her of a bantam hen, as he held himself with his shoulders back and a barrel chest protruding slightly from the trench coat.

Peggy had glanced over his shoulder into the parking lot. He was driving an old, battered pickup truck.

"Good morning," she'd said, and had introduced herself, even though she was already thinking of reasons she could turn him away. Her curiosity got the better of her.

"A pastor? Which church?" she'd asked.

He'd shrugged. "I'm not sure yet, Mrs Wilson. All I know is that I've been called to this small town to do God's work. They must need here me to save lost souls. All will be revealed in time, I'm sure." His tone had been sincere.

"I see," Peggy had said, although she didn't. "So you'll be staying for a while?"

"I believe so." Pastor Michael had smiled and then handed over enough cash to pay for a week.

"Oh, cash . . ." Peggy usually took a credit card number to secure bookings and cover deposits, especially useful if a guest broke the rules and smoked or allowed their dog to soil the carpets.

"Is that a problem, Mrs Wilson?"

"No, not at all, Pastor," Peggy had found herself saying. There was something about this man. A man of God, a saver of lost souls — of course it wouldn't be a problem.

Pastor Michael had flashed his warm smile again and gathered his keys.

Peggy had wanted to ask more questions, but decided there would be time enough for that. Later that evening, she'd been distracted from her TV soap operas with thoughts of the enigmatic Pastor Michael Nelson. It all seemed cryptic, a pastor turning up with no church, no congregation and no idea why he had been "called" to Coffin Cove.

She was unsure how Pastor Michael Nelson would have received his instructions to save lost souls. Wouldn't he have a supervisor who decided all that? On the other hand, it was no secret Coffin Cove was overrun with "lost souls". Violent crime had risen, what with all the terrible murders — something else which had started when Jade Thompson became mayor — and wasn't that why she'd formed the Concerned Citizens Committee? Because of the lack of morality and Christian values?

There was something interesting about this new pastor. The way he held her attention. Peggy wasn't sure what it was, but he made her smile. Made her feel better about herself somehow . . .

You're getting old and silly, she'd scolded herself. But then her eye caught the gold-edged invitation on her table. She'd decided not to attend the New Year's Eve party at the Cove Bistro. Why should she support the new restaurant and the mayor? The mayor was to blame for her current financial state.

But wasn't it important to know what was going on in the community? And wouldn't it be a wonderful opportunity for the new pastor to meet everyone? In a moment of impulse, Peggy grabbed the invitation and in a few minutes was knocking on the door to room 410.

Peggy had to admit she'd enjoyed the party. It had distracted her from her worries, but as she sat looking at her ledgers, afraid to open them, reality overwhelmed her.

The cash for the one room had helped a little. Peggy had paid her bills, which came due on 1 January, and had tried not to worry about her dwindling bank balance. But she needed cash fast, or she'd have no option but to borrow against the grant money and hope she could replace it before the city accountants started asking for receipts.

The inaugural meeting of the Concerned Citizens Committee was that night. It was imperative that business picked up in this town, and the only way to do that was to make that mayor understand the plight of hard-working local people.

Peggy checked her reflection in the washroom mirror once again and pulled on her coat. The forecast on the radio had called for snow. She picked up the posters she'd printed and stepped outside, locking her office door behind her.

"Mrs Wilson!"

Pastor Michael Nelson stood in the doorway of room 410, beaming.

"How are you this morning? Are you ready?"

Peggy's mood lifted. She held up the posters and explained what she was about to do.

"Well then, how about I buy you a cup of coffee and then I'll help you with those? I have a few ideas about your committee I'd like to share with you."

Peggy thought about the pots of coffee she'd already consumed that morning, and then she looked into Pastor Michael's over-large blue eyes, which seemed to bore into her soul from behind his glasses, and nodded her head in agreement.

CHAPTER SEVEN

Fred Harding sat hunched over the steering wheel of his old pickup. The truck was parked by the boardwalk, facing the ocean. He'd arrived in town far too early for the hardware store to be open, but some days he liked to watch the sun come up and turn the ocean from a metallic grey to shimmering gold. He felt near to God and His infinite power, granting humanity another morning.

The hardware store opened at eight, and Fred had found what he needed. He would just have a little coffee before he went to the grocery store. Then he would drive back to the Valley.

Fred's arthritic hands fumbled with his thermos and shook a little as he poured black coffee into a tin cup. He cursed under his breath as he spilled some, then bent his head in apologetic prayer.

The Lord didn't need to be listening to his potty mouth.

Fred wished sometimes the Lord would see fit to ease his physical suffering. His arthritis, fading eyesight and virtually non-existent hearing were making each day a trial to be endured. *Why am I still here?* Fred wondered every day as he wheezed and spluttered, heaving himself from his bed at five a.m., just as he had done for nearly all of his ninety years.

That's why he made these trips to town to watch the dawn break. It gave him a reason to still be alive. Yet, what was left for him now? Ruth, his wife, had been gone for years. Sue, his daughter, visited regularly, although not as frequently as Fred would have liked. It was his fault she kept away, he sometimes admitted to himself on long dark evenings with just the distant roar of the river to break the silence.

Sue had begged him to move into town. "Assisted living, Dad," she'd said. "It's not so bad. You'd have company, you could play cards and have coffee with other seniors."

Fred had gazed at her in fury and astonishment. Did she not know him at all?

"Play cards!" he'd spat back at her. "Gambling? With those heathens?"

Sue had stood her ground. "You could go to church," she'd insisted, not shrinking away from her father's anger. "Join a Bible reading group." Her tone had softened. "Dad, it's OK. You can leave her now."

"Leave me be, girl." He'd turned away, not wanting his daughter to see the tears that threatened in his eyes.

Leave her? He couldn't do that. As he'd watched Sue's truck back out of the dirt driveway, his eyes turned to the old tire hanging by a frayed rope from a maple tree. In his mind he saw and heard Sarah, his granddaughter squealing with laughter and shouting, "Higher, higher!" as he pushed the little girl, her blonde hair trailing in the wind.

God had blessed him with one grandchild and then taken her away in her teenage years.

Not God, he corrected himself. *No, sir, not the Almighty. Satan himself.*

Sarah had been murdered decades ago. For years, he and the rest of Coffin Cove had blamed a charismatic environmentalist who had charmed Sarah and much of the Coffin Cove youth. Sarah had snuck away to a protest and had never returned. Sue, her mother, had never fully recovered. It was only when the terrible truth of Sarah's killing had been uncovered that Sue found the strength to move on.

But Fred's bitterness had continued to fester. He turned in on himself in anger. Had it been his fault? Had he driven his granddaughter away? Was it his devotion to the Lord which had blinded him to the needs of his family?

Fred Harding had been a pastor of an evangelical Christian church. The old rotting building, which had once echoed with his fiery sermons and rousing hymns, was on his land, a few acres beside the Coffin Cove River, which locals called simply "the Valley".

In the early days, the church had been crowded with the devoted, the repentant and the sinners. But the Devil had strode within their midst and tempted his flock away. And now, Fred thundered his sermons to empty pews covered with mildew, as the chilled wind lifted the damp pages of the hymn sheets scattered on the floor.

Fred's house and the church stood on low ground. Over the years, the river had often burst its banks and flooded the Harding place. Mildew clung to the drapes and black mould edged up the walls of his home. Fred kept a wood fire burning year-round, but still the damp persisted, clutching and squeezing Fred's lungs, keeping him permanently short of breath. Some days, he could hardly shuffle to the kitchen.

In the dawn hours, as he lay in bed, gasping for air, he begged God to take him. He longed to see Sarah again, her blue eyes and cherubic smile, and chubby hands reaching up for her Gramps.

But every morning he was still alive.

God must still have more for me to do, he thought. And Fred was certain God did not want him to live among the heathens in town.

Fred avoided Coffin Cove as much as possible, relying on Sue to bring him supplies. But Sue hadn't been around much, not since the last time Fred sent his daughter packing. So this morning he'd hauled himself out of bed, said his prayers kneeling as he'd done since his childhood, and then driven his old truck along the rutted trucks, wincing as every jolt sent fiery pains through his joints.

A tap on the truck window made him jump, sending more coffee splashing over his hands. Fred gazed irritably at the face pressed at the glass.

"Morning, Fred. How are you?"

"All right," he muttered and nodded, hoping that Peggy Wilson would move on, but knowing it would be hard to get rid of her.

Peggy made a gesture for Fred to wind down the window. He tried to ignore her, gazing straight ahead and sipping his coffee.

Damn woman, he thought, and mentally apologized for cursing again. He loathed Peggy Wilson and her meddling ways. She'd only want to pass on gossip or dig for information.

Peggy rapped on the truck window again.

He sighed.

Maybe if he got out of the truck, Peggy would say her piece and he could be on his way.

Fred climbed slowly out of the truck and steadied himself as his stiff legs adjusted to his upright body.

Peggy was speaking.

". . . terrible what's going on in town, Fred. What with that Hephzibah and her Indian 'friend' living together, and all the tax money being spent on a stupid dinosaur exhibit at this museum, and all the horrible murders and crime we've had to endure . . ."

Fred stared at her, not comprehending. Dinosaurs? What was this stupid woman blathering about?

". . . Concerned Citizens Committee, and I know a God-fearing man like yourself would want to be involved, what with the awful things your poor family has suffered . . ."

Fred felt a chill, yet there was no wind, not even a breeze from the ocean. A truck passed by, drowning out Peggy's words. Fred turned towards the grocery store, hoping that she would get the message and leave him alone.

The morning sun illuminated a figure standing across the street. Fred's eyes couldn't make out if it was a man or woman. He hoped it was someone Peggy would want to speak to. He turned back to Peggy, who was oblivious to Fred's discomfort.

When Fred turned again, the figure was in focus and coming nearer. Fred stared at him as the man smiled, showing his teeth. Fred felt his chest tighten, not because of his lungs, but another unpleasant sensation. It was the same feeling he'd had all those years ago when a police officer stood at his door, waiting to deliver the news of his beloved Sarah's death.

It was fear clutching at his heart as Satan himself strode over to greet him.

CHAPTER EIGHT

"Welcome back! How are you feeling?"

Hephzibah smiled at Katie Dagg, the manager and curator of the Coffin Cove Museum.

"I'm feeling fine, thanks, Katie. Just glad to be back at work. How's things at the museum?"

"Really busy, but great, thank you."

Katie Dagg smiled back at her, and Hephzibah thought how wonderful it was when someone found their true calling in life. Katie Dagg was passionate about local history. Mayor Jade Thompson had hired the young woman to be curator for the new Coffin Cove Museum, and Katie had overseen the design of the new premises and the transfer of all the artifacts from the cluttered old wooden building which had served as the local museum as long as Hephzibah could remember.

"I'll be at the lecture tonight," Hephzibah said as she poured two mugs of coffee for Katie. "Ruth will be there too, if she's not working late. Did you sell all the tickets?"

"We did. And people are coming from as far as Victoria to hear Professor Weber's lecture."

"That's wonderful. Is that the man himself?" Hephzibah said, lowering her voice and nodding at a man who was settling himself in one of the chairs at the far end of the café. The man looked like a professor. He was tall and slim, with grey, thinning hair. He had horn-rimmed glasses perched on his nose, and he was wearing a fraying jacket with leather patches on the elbows. *Traditional dress for academic types*, Hephzibah thought.

Katie nodded. "Yes, he's so interesting. I could talk to him all day about his research. We're so lucky to get him."

"Here," Hephzibah said, sliding two morning glory muffins to her on a plate. "Take these with your coffee. Everything on the house."

"Oh lovely—"

"Business must be good if you can afford to give your products away."

Peggy Wilson had appeared behind Katie, who smiled her thanks and went to join the professor, leaving Peggy standing at the counter.

"Would you like coffee?"

"No, we won't be staying."

Hephzibah looked over Peggy's shoulder and saw a man standing in the doorway. The morning light was behind him, but Hephzibah was sure it was the pastor who had accompanied Peggy to the New Year's Eve party.

"What can I do for you, then?"

Peggy was holding a handful of paper documents. She handed some to Hephzibah, who glanced at them.

"I'd like you to put these flyers on your tables today. The Concerned Citizens Committee is meeting tonight, and we'd like to make sure everyone knows about it. You're welcome to come, of course."

Hephzibah handed the flyers back to Peggy. "I won't be there, Peggy. I'm going to the lecture at the museum. And I don't think I'll be joining your committee. I'm mostly happy with the way Mayor Thompson is running the town. I'll be voting for her again in the fall."

Peggy took the flyers back. "I suppose now you're living with a native *person*, you support the Indian resort on Hope Island?"

Hephzibah heard the sneer in Peggy's voice and kept her voice calm, not wanting to let the woman know she'd got under her skin.

"It's not a resort, Peggy, it's a cultural and language centre, and yes, I support it. I have strong ties to Hope Island, as you know, and Ruth has too. The centre will be dedicated to her sister's memory."

The scruffy man hovering by the door cleared his throat and stepped forward. He held out his hand. "Pleased to meet you, Miss, er . . ."

"Hephzibah. Hephzibah Brown." She took his hand. "And you are?"

"Pastor Michael Nelson," he said, peering at her through thick-lensed glasses. "I'm helping Peggy organize tonight's meeting, and I'm honoured to say she's invited me to lead the committee in prayer and speak to the attendees."

"I hope the meeting goes well," Hephzibah said politely but withdrawing her hand. "But, as I told Peggy, I'm going to the lecture at our local museum. Professor Weber there—" she nodded to the easy chairs where Katie Dagg and the professor were deep in conversation — "is delivering the lecture tonight, and I'm looking forward to it."

The pastor's head snapped round, and he looked at Katie and Professor Weber with interest.

As if they felt his gaze, they stopped talking and looked up.

Pastor Michael Nelson stared for a moment longer, and then spun round and left the café.

"What's wrong with him? And please take those flyers with you, Peggy. I'm not interested and I'm not pushing your negativity on my customers!"

Hephzibah had had enough.

Peggy's face flushed red. "I'm leaving these flyers on the table," she said. "And you should watch yourself, Hephzibah Brown. You'll go the same way as your mother, if you're not careful."

She slammed a pile of flyers on the nearest table and stalked out of the café.

Hephzibah knew it was silly, but she fought to contain tears for a few moments as she watched Peggy leave.

"Are you OK?"

Katie stood at the counter, her face full of concern.

Hephzibah took a deep breath. "Just Peggy's nonsense. She's upset because I won't join her crazies club."

"Let me guess, the Concerned Citizens Committee? I got a flyer at the museum this morning. I guess one thing they're mad about is the money spent on the museum."

"Yes. And the Hope Island Project. And she was quite rude about Ruth," Hephzibah said quietly.

Katie sighed. "I'm so sorry, Hephzibah. Some people in this town are still living in the Dark Ages."

"What's that about Dark Ages?" Professor Weber had joined Katie. "That sounds like my territory."

Hephzibah found a smile. "Some people find it hard to accept change, Professor, that's all."

CHAPTER NINE

January 5, later

"The lecture starts soon, Dad. Are you still going?"

Bob Hinton yawned and stretched his arms above his head. "I don't think so, Andi. Is that all right? I think Charlie can handle it. I think I want to go home and read a book by the fire."

"Of course it's all right. Are you feeling OK?" She propped herself on the edge of her father's desk.

"I'm feeling old," Bob admitted. "But that's all. Don't worry." He patted her hand.

"I can spend the evening with you. Cook you dinner?" Andi was concerned.

"If it was Harry offering to cook me dinner, I'd accept, but you've got that meeting tonight, haven't you?"

Andi ignored his teasing.

"Dad, it's just Peggy riling up the locals. It doesn't matter if I don't go. They'll probably have one meeting and disband, and that will be the end."

Bob looked at Andi, and his voice was serious.

"Andi, that's the wrong attitude. Don't dismiss this meeting. There are people in this town who have real resentment against the mayor and her policies. When their concerns aren't taken seriously, well, that's when tempers flare and problems start."

"You really think so?"

"I do. I've seen it before. There are plenty of people in this town, men mostly, who have little or no future now the forestry and fishing industries are all but finished. You think they're happy with a young female mayor who's spending their money — as they see it — on fancy restaurants they'll never visit and projects with the natives?"

"The shift closures and the lack of fishing aren't Jade's fault. She's just trying to find an alternative way to get tax dollars."

"They don't see it that way. They're looking for someone to blame. Go to the meeting, you'll see."

Andi sighed. "All right, I'm going."

She leaned forward and kissed her father on the forehead. "You go home and read your book."

* * *

Hephzibah had tried to forget Peggy Wilson's outburst all day. *Most people were happy for her and Ruth*, she told herself, or they just didn't care. Why should she let a silly woman's prejudices get under her skin?

It was nearly time to close the café, so Hephzibah busied herself wiping tabletops and loading the dishwasher. At six o'clock, she locked the door and turned off the *open* sign.

She'd have to hurry if she was going to get to the museum lecture on time.

Her eyes dropped to the table nearest the door. Peggy's flyers were still there. Hephzibah grabbed them. The stupid committee meeting was tonight, so she might as well throw these away.

As she moved them, she saw a white envelope which had been tucked out of sight under the flyers. It had her name on it, written in block capitals.

Why would someone leave a note for her here? Why not hand it to her?

Hephzibah tore the envelope and found a single sheet of folded paper inside. She shook it out and read the words, printed in block capitals, the same as on the envelope.

It took a minute for Hephzibah to process the words and their meaning. When she had, she found it difficult to breathe. She looked down at the hand that held the paper, and found that it was shaking.

* * *

Andi had never been in the Coffin Cove Community Hall, she realized, when she arrived for the meeting. It was a small wooden-framed building, next to the Methodist church. It was rarely used and city funding had been reduced since Mayor Thompson's election. If it were not for frequent volunteer efforts to raise funds, the AA meetings, Women's Institute bake sales and weekly Bible lessons would have had to move long ago.

Andi remembered the conversation she'd had with Charlie earlier. She hadn't told the young woman of her own reluctance to cover bake sales and community gatherings when she first arrived in Coffin Cove. She hadn't wanted to waste her journalist credentials on the minutiae of small-town life. Jim Peters had never missed a single local event and had often made room for free advertisements in the *Gazette*.

"We are a community newspaper," he'd often said. "We exist because of the people of Coffin Cove. It's up to us to report on the issues and events which are important to them."

Instead, Andi had been embroiled in criminal investigations and digging up buried secrets. She'd helped to solve cold cases and traumatic murders, and her stories had won her national acclaim, but few friends in Coffin Cove.

Had Andi missed the real story? The one playing out before her eyes, every single day?

She'd dismissed the Concerned Citizens as a coalition of disaffected rednecks who viewed outsiders with suspicion and prejudice. Maybe, as her father had said, they were just figuring out how to keep up and survive in these rapidly changing times.

There were rows of metal chairs set out facing a raised platform at the end of the hall. On one side was a large table, and Peggy Wilson appeared out of a side door carrying a large urn, which Andi assumed was full of coffee.

"Hi Peggy, can I give you a hand?"

Peggy seemed surprised to see her. "We have the media attending, do we?" Her tone wasn't unfriendly, but she ignored Andi's offer of help and marched past her to the table and set down the urn. She disappeared back through the same door and re-emerged moments later with a stack of polystyrene cups. Andi checked her phone for the time. It was still ten minutes before the meeting was due to start.

"Peggy, do you have a minute or two? Would you like to tell me about the Concerned Citizens Committee? A kind of pre-interview?"

Peggy looked at Andi suspiciously, but Andi had calculated correctly. There was nothing that Peggy Wilson loved more than being the centre of attention.

Andi sat down on one of the metal seats and patted the one beside her.

"All right, then. But none of those 'gotcha' questions, OK?" Peggy sat down.

Andi mentally rolled her eyes, but smiled and said, "Of course not, Peggy. I'm just here to cover the meeting, and I'd just like some background about the organization."

"Organization?" Peggy seemed confused.

"Yes. The Concerned Citizens Committee. Is it a business association or political association? Or a non-profit?"

"I don't know anything about that. It's just a group of people who are tired of the way things are being run in this town." Her tone was defensive.

"I see. What things?" Andi had pressed the voice record app on her phone. Peggy looked at the phone and said, "Am I being recorded?"

"It's just easier than taking notes," Andi said. "What things would you like to see changed, Peggy?"

"Well, how the money is spent, for one thing. All that taxpayer's money on the Fish Plant and they're not even finished yet. And then there's Hope Island. The Indians got a bunch of cash, I bet, to do all that building over there. And they just got a new band office. And there's people out of work, and the mill saying they're cutting back another shift. How are all the local people supposed to live?"

Peggy's voice had become shrill. "All the money goes to newcomers, nothing to the people who have lived and worked here all their lives."

Andi knew this wasn't true. She also knew it wasn't worth arguing with Peggy, who had become red-faced, her lips pursed together so hard, her mouth had disappeared.

Andi couldn't help herself.

"Didn't the motel get a grant recently?"

Peggy's red face darkened into purple, but before she could answer, two men wearing plaid shirts and carrying travel mugs walked in.

"Is this where the meeting is?" one asked.

"Yes, it is. Pastor Michael Nelson will open the meeting soon." Peggy stood up, and Andi assumed she would not get an answer to her last question. It didn't matter. She would get a list of the grant recipients from City Hall tomorrow.

By six o'clock, the hall was full and most of the chairs were taken. Andi was surprised how many people had turned out on a Friday evening. She scanned the crowd, looking for familiar faces. She saw a lot of the local business people, including Cheryl and Walter from the Fat Chicken pub. Cheryl waved at Andi with an embarrassed shrug. Walter stared straight ahead, his face impassive.

Andi used to be their tenant. She knew the couple had struggled financially for a long time. She and Walter had clashed when he accused the *Gazette* of profiting from Andi's reporting on the tragic murders in Coffin Cove over a year ago. But hadn't they also received a grant? They had recently converted her old apartment into a smart conference room.

Andi noted down the people she knew. Peggy Wilson, of course, motel owner, and Cheryl and Walter from the Fat Chicken; then there was Bill Richards from the hardware store, several mill workers still in their work clothes, fishermen and loggers Andi recognized from the regular crowd at the Fat Chicken and teachers from the elementary school. Most of the community was represented, although there was an absence of anyone from City Hall. Andi guessed anyone employed by the city would rather be seen supporting the lecture at the museum. She also wondered whether the meeting attendees were all "concerned", or if they were here out of curiosity.

Peggy stood up and walked to the platform at the front of the hall. She cleared her throat and the hum of conversation in the hall died.

"Welcome to the very first meeting of the Concerned Citizens Committee," she began.

"I'm concerned there's no beer," someone catcalled from the back, prompting a ripple of laughter.

Peggy ignored the interruption. "We are all here because we are very concerned about the direction our precious community is taking. And by that, I mean the increase in crime, the lack of investment by our mayor and the city council, the way all our money is being spent on her pet projects, while the hard-working people of this town are left behind."

"Hear, hear!" someone called out, and this time Peggy paused to allow a smattering of applause.

"Not to mention the lack of *morality* and rejection of our values and culture."

Andi thought back to Peggy's snide remarks at the New Year's Eve party and knew what she meant, but as if anyone needed it spelling out, someone shouted, "Yeah, like those two dykes in the café. One of 'em's an Indian too."

"You shut your mouth!"

Andi recognized a fisherman she'd often seen in Hephzibah's Café. He was standing up and addressing his words to a young man with a shaved head and unkempt red beard who must have shouted the slur against Hephzibah and Ruth.

"That's Harry's sister you're talking about, and she's run that café as long as I can remember. And she's always given out food and coffee to hard-up families around here, and that's more than your lazy ass has ever done, you piece of shit."

The young man stood up. He was pale-faced under his beard and his eyes were red-rimmed, as if he'd just woken from a long sleep.

Andi was a few rows back, but she caught the unmistakable waft of weed and body odour as the young man shoved his way past the row of seated onlookers and advanced towards the fisherman.

"Sit down, you little turd," the fisherman said calmly, "or I'll spank your behind."

The hall erupted in laughter now, and the young man flushed red before turning and angrily marching to the door, flinging it open and barging past an elderly man who was coming in.

"Please, everyone, there's no need for any of that," Peggy called. "We are all friends here, and united in our mission."

So far Peggy had outlined no mission, and despite the woman's pleas for peace, Andi knew she'd be in the café tomorrow wildly exaggerating the drama.

Andi turned around in her seat to look at the elderly man who had shuffled to a seat at the very back of the hall with the aid of a hooked stick, like a shepherd's staff. He had a shock of white hair, and a bushy white beard, which might have made him look like a stooped Santa Claus, had it not been for his fierce, piercing eyes. He looked directly at Andi, and she immediately knew who it was.

Fred Harding.

Andi had only glimpsed Fred once or twice in the last two years. He was a virtual hermit these days, and lived just outside of Coffin Cove, in an area the locals referred to as "the Valley". Decades before, the Valley had been a thriving community, with smallholdings along the Coffin Cove River. Then, the logging companies had clear-cut the mountainsides, causing periodic flooding. All the inhabitants had left the Valley except for Fred Harding.

Andi had met Fred and his daughter Sue when she first came to Coffin Cove. Fred's granddaughter had died in suspicious circumstances, and it was Andi's investigation which had revealed the truth.

Sue lived in town now, and she and Andi were on nodding terms, but Fred was a fiercely stubborn man who refused to leave his dilapidated house, despite being flooded out every winter. He had once been a pastor, a roaring "hellfire and brimstone" preacher who did not hide his disgust with the "heathens" who lived in Sodom and Gomorrah, which is how he viewed Coffin Cove.

Fred was the last person Andi expected to see at this strange gathering. Why on earth was he here?

Before she could wonder any further, Peggy clapped her hands.

"Let's continue," she said loudly. "I am delighted to welcome Pastor Michael Nelson. He has travelled around Canada and helped many communities like ours who are being trampled on and forgotten. He has some interesting things to say, and I'm glad he has the time to talk to us."

Peggy clapped, and a few people in the front rows politely clapped with her.

The first thing Andi noticed about Pastor Michael Nelson was the way he strutted onto the stage. He didn't display any nervousness, but spread his arms wide.

For a small man, he had a commanding voice.

"Hello friends. How many of you are tired of being told what to do by people who know nothing of your life or your values?"

He paused as if he expected an answer. A couple of people shifted in their chairs, and someone coughed.

The pastor continued, "The federal government, the provincial politicians and, yes, even mayors and city officials, seek to oppress our liberties and impose their own woke agendas. They even spend our hard-earned tax dollars on their own follies, rather than on supporting their own constituents . . ."

This sounded like a political rally rather than a gathering of local businesspeople, Andi thought.

Pastor Michael continued, his voice louder now.

"What happened to family values? Or support for hard-working Christian men and women? Our beliefs and traditions are being undermined by those who worship false gods and who protest against Christian family life as decreed in the Bible . . ."

A dog whistle.

The pastor was pulling some of his audience in with his quasi-evangelical rhetoric. Some were sitting up in their chairs, paying attention. Andi's father had been right all along.

But what was Pastor Michael's angle? Why was he here? Time to do some digging into his résumé.

He ended his speech with references to Jesus being a simple fisherman and pledging to help the downtrodden folk of Coffin Cove rise against their oppressors. He held his hand up in salute and then gave a theatrical bow in response to applause from the audience.

It was both ridiculous and dangerous.

Following the pastor was a lawyer from Nanaimo. As Peggy introduced him, Andi recognized his name. She quickly Googled him on her phone, and after scrolling for a few seconds, found an article which linked him to Dennis Havers, the previous mayor of Coffin Cove. Havers had been a corrupt man, and Andi was sure this lawyer had made considerable sums of money over the years when Dennis had held office. Of course he'd be interested in helping the Concerned Citizens Committee oust Mayor Jade Thompson and install a candidate with more respect for the good old days.

The lawyer outlined some suggestions for the citizens, which included suing the city for misappropriation of funds, and for the Concerned Citizens Committee to form an official association. All of this he could arrange.

For a hefty fee, Andi thought. And maybe that was the pastor's motivation here too. She wanted to stand up and remind the audience that all they had to do if they felt the mayor wasn't representing their best interest was to propose a new candidate to run against her in a few months and get out and vote.

But it was her job to report the news, not be part of it. The best thing she could do was investigate this mysterious pastor and ask the mayor some hard questions. Apart from the thinly disguised bigotry, maybe the Concerned Citizens Committee had a point.

The lawyer didn't speak for long. Maybe he looked around the room at the plaid shirts and Stanfields and concluded there was little potential for a big payday here.

When it was clear the meeting was over, Andi looked around for Fred Harding, but she couldn't see him. Maybe he'd already left. Andi checked her phone. The meeting had lasted for two hours, much longer than she had expected. Professor Weber's lecture would be over soon, so she texted Harry to say she'd meet him in the Fat Chicken if he was already there.

He immediately texted back. *Large glass of wine required?* Andi quickly replied, *YES*.

"I'm so glad you came, Andi," Peggy Wilson said.

Andi looked up from her phone. She hadn't noticed Peggy standing beside her. Peggy's tone was friendly, given their exchange before the meeting.

"It's my job to report on local events, Peggy," Andi said, not wanting her to think she supported any of the sentiments expressed by the Concerned Citizens Committee.

"Well, I hope you focus on the substance, rather than the trouble at the beginning."

Before Andi could respond, she caught sight of Fred moving towards Pastor Michael, who was chatting with Cheryl and Walter at the back of the hall. Andi was too far away to hear what Fred Harding was saying, but the pastor stepped back quickly as Fred shook his walking stick in his direction. On impulse, Andi held up her phone and took a picture of the pastor, who was holding his hand out, as if to fend off an attack.

"Oh my." Peggy rushed over to rescue Pastor Michael, and Andi watched as Walter took Fred's arm and steered the old man towards the exit.

"This is Pastor Michael," Peggy said unnecessarily, as they joined Andi. She was smiling almost girlishly at the man beside her. The only indication that Pastor Michael had been rattled by Fred's outburst was a thin bead of sweat on his upper lip.

Andi noticed Peggy was wearing full make-up and lipstick, which she must have applied in between setting up the chairs and the beginning of the meeting. Peggy had also done something different with her hair, which was a mass of shiny curls.

Peggy's on the lookout for a new husband, was the town gossip, Andi remembered. If the gossip was true, Andi hoped Peggy was setting her sights a little higher than Pastor Michael Nelson.

Up close, Andi decided she disliked him. She had always tried not to form snap opinions of people, especially in her work as a journalist, but there was something about this man which rubbed her up the wrong way.

He wasn't tall, but he stood half a foot over Andi, and he adopted a stance with his chest thrust out and his head slightly to one side. He was eyeing Andi with a smile on his lips which showed yellowing teeth.

Clearly he was a heavy smoker. The smell of stale cigarettes hung like an aura around him.

Pastor Michael didn't believe in the adage that cleanliness is next to godliness, Andi thought. This man was . . . grimy. She hadn't been able to see when he was speaking, but his woollen sweater and grey pants were stained, and his shoes were scuffed. The only clean item on him was the dog collar, which merely highlighted a line of dirt around the pastor's neck.

He was older than Andi had first thought, maybe his mid-seventies, but he wasn't showing any signs of frailty and had the arrogant air of a younger man.

Pastor Michael thrust out his arm, and Andi shook the man's nicotine-stained hand. She wanted to ask him about Fred Harding, but she decided to let the pastor speak first.

"So nice to meet a representative of the Fourth Estate," he said, giving a mocking emphasis to the political term for the media.

Before Andi could reply to the jibe, the pastor continued to talk.

"It was a good turnout. Shame the mayor didn't make it. Still, she can read your report."

"I hope so," Andi said evenly. She felt like the pastor was trying to provoke her. She was both irritated and intrigued by the man. Why was he here? And why was he so determined to integrate himself into Peggy Wilson's protest committee?

"What brings you to Coffin Cove, Pastor?"

He answered immediately, as if he had a speech prepared.

"I felt Coffin Cove was one of the forgotten places where I could do the most good. So many of our rural communities have been left behind—"

Andi interrupted before the pastor repeated his entire speech.

"Yes, I understand that, but why Coffin Cove in particular? Why not Sayward, or Port McNeill? Those communities also face economic difficulties."

To her surprise, he ignored the question completely. He turned his head slightly and his gaze slid away from Andi.

"I'm surprised you're not covering the museum event tonight," he said as if she hadn't spoken. "The dinosaur lecture? Paid for by these good people?" He made a wide gesture. "They can't even get the science right. There were no dinosaurs on Vancouver Island."

"Really?" Andi didn't hide her disbelief.

"The correct term is *plesiosaur*. This entire island used to be covered by the ocean. The only remains would be from ancient sea creatures. Such a shame the lecturer is a phony."

Andi was silent for a moment. What a strange thing to say.

"Why was Fred Harding so upset with you, Pastor? Maybe he didn't agree with your interpretation of Christianity?" she asked politely.

Annoyance registered for a moment on the pastor's face, the only indication that Andi's words had landed, before he turned to Peggy and said, "You look wonderful tonight, Peggy. Shall we get a cup of tea?"

* * *

"She actually blushed," Andi said twenty minutes later. She had walked from the Community Hall to the Fat Chicken. The January night was chilly, and she'd felt the light touch of snowflakes on her cheeks.

"So the rumours are true. Peggy is hunting for a husband and she's got her sights set on the pastor," Harry said, grinning. He had Andi's glass of wine ready. She hadn't really needed a drink, but Andi was relieved to be in the warm pub. It would be cold on the *Pipe Dream* tonight.

"I do not know what she sees in him," Andi said, shaking her head. She told Harry about the evening, describing Pastor Michael, his speech and the strange conversation she had with him at the end. "He and his politics are quite unpleasant," she said.

"He didn't actually say anything racist, though," Harry commented.

"No. But the message was loud and clear. Some of the Concerned Citizens are already bigots." She told Harry about the exchange between the red-bearded man and the fisherman about Hephzibah and Ruth.

"What the hell . . ." Harry was instantly angry. "Who said that about my sister?"

"Calm down. He was made to look an idiot. But you see my point? Some people in Coffin Cove welcome this kind of crap."

"Few though." Harry was calmer now. "Most of those people are concerned about their bank balance. A lot of them are living paycheck to paycheck, and some don't even *have* a paycheck. It's a reasonable thing to question the amount of taxpayers' cash being spent on a project that doesn't benefit them, right? At least not directly. That's not racist."

"Not if the objection is purely financial," Andi agreed. "But Pastor Michael was all about the town abandoning its Christian values. It was a dog whistle."

"Wouldn't be the first time we had a preacher causing trouble in town," Harry said, draining his beer glass.

"That reminds me," Andi said. "Fred Harding was there. And he didn't seem to be a fan of Pastor Michael."

"Really? That's funny. He's exactly who I meant. He stirred up trouble back in the day. My dad said he'd come to the pub, stand on a box and tell all the loggers and fishermen they were going straight to hell. Nine times out of ten, there would be a fight. But he'd get a few recruits every week for his church."

"I'd love to know why Fred Harding was at the meeting," Andi said, setting her wineglass on the bar, and sliding off her stool. "But I'm certain he'll never tell me."

"Maybe he was checking out the competition. Warning the new pastor to stay away from his flock." Harry stood up. "Ready? Don't worry, I left the heater on. The boat is warm."

Andi smiled at him, and they both stepped outside into the first snowfall of the New Year.

CHAPTER TEN

January 6

All Katie Dagg could hear was the crunch of her footsteps and the muffled crash of waves against the steel pylons which supported the Fish Plant pier.

The dense blanket of snow smothered the sounds of Coffin Cove waking up later than usual this Saturday morning.

Katie was early. She'd walked to the museum, wanting to enjoy the undisturbed beauty of the winter morning before the city plough scraped the snow into dirty grey mounds.

Katie didn't expect many visitors to the museum today, but she had a full schedule. Charlene from the *Gazette* was dropping by.

"Just to check some details before I send my article to print," she'd said. Katie was grateful for the free publicity for last night's lecture.

It had been a success. Mayor Thompson was beaming and shaking hands with the visitors, as if she'd organized the event. Katie didn't care. The excitement on the children's faces when Professor Weber handed them real-life artifacts to handle, and his patience when answering every single question was reward enough for Katie.

A teacher had inspired her when she was very young, and she knew there were future historians and scientists in this young crowd who would attribute their careers to this very evening.

Katie paused at the museum entrance. A coffee first? Hephzibah's would be open, she was sure. No, she'd go after checking emails and writing a thank-you letter to Professor Weber. She hoped he'd reached Campbell River before the snowstorm set in.

She pulled off her gloves to fumble for her keys. The door wouldn't open when she tried it. She turned the key the other way and heard the latch click. That was odd. Could she have forgotten to lock the door last night?

Katie pushed open the door and stood in the dark foyer. She stamped her feet on the mat to get rid of the excess snow.

"Darn kids," she said out loud when she saw a dark stain trailing under the glass door into the museum hall. It stated clearly on a notice in the foyer that no food or drinks were to be consumed on the premises, but kids would be kids.

Katie knew something was wrong when she flicked on the foyer light and saw that the glass door was slightly ajar. She might have forgotten to lock the outer door, but she specifically remembered locking the inner door. She remembered holding it open for the last of the guests to leave before she turned the key and shook the door as usual. Now she thought about it, she didn't remember noticing any spilled drinks on the floor either.

Katie felt fear in the pit of her stomach. Ever since her mother had been killed, she'd suffered bouts of anxiety, but this was different.

This isn't rational, she told herself. Who would break into a museum? The artifacts were rare, but thieves could hardly sell them in a pawnshop or trade them on the internet.

Who else had a key? Just herself and her father, Lee. He'd held onto a key after he'd finished installing the lights for the new displays.

Lee had left before her in his van. Maybe he'd left some tools here. Maybe he'd spilled coffee . . .

Katie pushed open the door and called out, "Dad? Are you here?"

Then she realized his van wasn't parked outside and there were no tracks in the snow in the parking lot. It wasn't her father. When she looked down, she saw she'd disturbed the pool of spilled liquid. It clung to the last of the snow on her boot, which had turned from white to pink.

Katie's mouth went dry. Her mind didn't want to process the information in front of her. This liquid wasn't coffee.

She turned on the lights in the main hall. The stains were like large crimson brush strokes up the centre of the hall until they disappeared behind a display cabinet.

Katie's legs moved, although she didn't know how. She could only hear her heart beating. It was thumping hard against her ribcage.

Professor Weber was lying on his side in front of the lectern, which was still standing in the same place as the previous evening. His briefcase was perched beside him. One arm was outstretched as if he were trying to pull himself up.

At first, Katie was filled with relief. It looked as if the professor had tripped and fallen. Then she knew she wasn't thinking clearly at all. The professor's face was turned away from her as she approached him.

"Professor Weber? Are you all right?" She felt silly saying it. Logic told her the stains on the floor from the door to the lectern meant that the professor had lost lots of blood, and she knew the congealed pool under the professor's head indicated a massive wound. There was also a foul odour hanging in the air. But Katie continued to hope her mind was playing tricks on her, and the professor would answer or move and have some kind of reassuring explanation for this strange scene.

The last of her hope evaporated when she stepped around the prone body and saw the purple pulp and white fragments of bone where the professor's face used to be.

1958, BLAST DAY

Gerald Duffy didn't possess a watch, but he knew from listening to Doris and John that the Ripple Rock explosion was due at nine thirty that morning.

He could hear the chink of china from downstairs. His mother was taking the few bits of good tableware off the dresser, as everyone had been instructed. He could still hear John snoring.

It seemed like he'd waited for hours, and then Gerald gave an involuntary gasp and grabbed hold of the edge of his cot. The cottage was shaking. A second after the movement, Gerald heard a loud boom, which seemed to die down and then reverberate back. The cottage shook again as if the explosion were a series of enormous waves.

Then Gerald heard the clatter and crash of pots and pans in the kitchen. After that, the cottage was still and silent. The entire event was over really quickly, Gerald thought with some disappointment. He hadn't known what to expect, but he'd imagined rocks and dust raining down around them.

Then he heard a tapping on his window. He rushed over, but it was only large drops of rain.

Gerald realized he couldn't hear snoring any more. John must be awake. The creak of the wooden stairs below him confirmed it. He heard the conciliatory tone of his mother's voice. She was always like that when John had a hangover. Gerald hated it. Why couldn't she stand up for herself? Being nice never worked.

It wasn't working this morning. Gerald heard John's voice raised in anger. He couldn't make out the words, but he was probably complaining about his coffee or something.

It went silent. Then Gerald heard his mother scream. He covered his ears with his hands and shut his eyes tightly, but he couldn't shut it out. He heard a loud clatter as if something heavy had fallen. And then quiet again.

Gerald heard a loud thumping in his eyes. It was his own heart, pounding against his chest as if it might break through at any minute. He took a couple of deep breaths and clenched his hands into fists to stop them from shaking. He didn't want to leave his attic space, but knew he had to check on his mother.

In the kitchen, he found Doris slumped in a chair, her head bowed forward so it was resting on her chest. Her hair was messed up, and it fell across her face, so Gerald couldn't see her eyes. John was sitting at the table, wiping his hand across his mouth.

"The bitch tried to slap me," he growled.

Gerald ran to his mother.

"I'm all right." Doris spoke so softly, Gerald could hardly hear her. He reached out and pushed back his mother's hair, and gasped as he saw the bloody mess where her eye should have been.

He stepped back in horror. Without thinking, he turned and ran at John, screaming and flailing his fists.

"You bastard! You bastard!"

Gerald felt his body lift into the air as John's fist connected with his torso. As if in slow motion, his body made a slow arc before gravity pulled it with a rush to the stone floor.

"What's going on, Dad?"

Gerald heard William's voice coming from a long way away.

He lay there, and for a moment, struggled to get air into his lungs. The force of his body slamming on the floor seemed to have stopped everything from working. His thoughts were clear, but he couldn't breathe or talk and his legs wouldn't move.

He sensed, rather than saw, the looming figure of John approaching. The man had something in his hand and Gerald saw with horror that it was one of his mother's cast-iron pots.

John raised it above his head and Gerald opened his mouth to cry out, but no sound came. He shut his eyes and braced for the pain, but it didn't come.

Instead, he heard the rasping voice of his mother.

"Run," she said hoarsely. "Run . . ."

Gerald willed his legs to move. He forced himself upright, and then, without looking back, he did what his mother had said. He ran out into the rain, but not before he heard William laughing.

CHAPTER ELEVEN

Present day
January 7

Coffin Cove was quite beautiful in the snow, Sergeant Beth Stanton thought, as she and Inspector Diane Fowler began the descent into the town. The storm clouds had cleared and a pale-lemon sun reflected off the ocean. The blanket of white brightened dilapidated buildings and smothered neglected yards, and from this distance, an unfamiliar onlooker may have described Coffin Cove as picturesque.

Nobody had cleared the snow from the only road into Coffin Cove.

"Damn it," Inspector Fowler growled as, despite her best efforts, the rented SUV slid around a corner on the wrong side of the road.

Beth put her hand out and gripped the dashboard but kept quiet. Diane Fowler was in a foul mood, and apart from snapping at the float plane pilot and the young man who had delivered the rental car to the terminal in Nanaimo, she hadn't said a word.

Beth knew the reason for Fowler's bad mood. Yesterday evening, they had both been part of a task team poised to make multiple arrests in a series of gang-related murders on the lower mainland. They had been working on the case for months and Beth knew Fowler viewed it as career-changing. The inspector had been outwardly angry when they were both called to the superintendent's office, pulled off the high-profile case and assigned a homicide in Coffin Cove.

Beth saw Fowler's jaw set as their new superintendent handed her the file, and cheerfully said, "Good luck, girls" as they left the office.

Diane Fowler had known better than to protest and accepted the file and the patronizing remark without comment. Fowler had never hidden her ambition from the day Beth had arrived at the Integrated Homicide Investigative Team; she was playing the political game to further her career. Beth had hoped that as they were both women working in a male-dominated environment, Fowler would become her mentor. But the inspector had barely concealed her resentment that Inspector Andrew Vega, her predecessor, had recommended Beth join the prestigious team based at E Division in Vancouver. She viewed Beth as a competitor. Fowler hadn't expressed it to Beth, but she'd voiced her annoyance to other colleagues that Beth hadn't sufficiently "paid her dues" and earned her place in IHIT.

And there were uglier insinuations. Beth had worked with Inspector Vega on her first homicide in the Yukon, and coincidentally, the victim in that case was originally from Coffin Cove. Inspector Fowler had also worked with Inspector Vega on cases in Coffin Cove, yet he had never taken an interest in her career. What was so special about Beth, Fowler had wondered out loud.

"I hate this fucking place," Fowler said, the first words since they'd left the mainland.

Sergeant Matt Beaufort was waiting for them at the Fish Plant, a new building on the waterfront which had been under construction the last time Beth had been in town.

The coroner's car was parked outside, and crime scene techs, dressed in white coveralls, moved between two vans and an entrance on the side of the building.

The temperature was slightly higher at sea level, and the snow had melted to grey slush. There was a small crowd of people huddled near the building, and their attention was focused on the activity in the Fish Plant.

Matt Beaufort came forward to greet them and held out his hand to Inspector Fowler as she exited the SUV.

"Get all those people away from my crime scene," Inspector Diane Fowler snapped, ignoring the sergeant's outstretched hand.

Beth sighed. This was not a good start.

She saw Beaufort was about to say something, but he obviously thought better of it and just nodded his head. Then he moved over to the crowd of onlookers, and they reluctantly shuffled back even further.

Technically, it wasn't Inspector Fowler's crime scene. It "belonged" to the BC coroner. Even though it might be obvious how the victim died, it was only the coroner who could determine the death was a homicide. She decided the "what". Then it was up to Inspector Fowler and her team to discover the "who", "how" and "why" before justice could be done.

The coroner came over to speak to Inspector Fowler. Beth felt the wind whip off the ocean and her fingers went numb. She shoved her hands in her pockets and waited for Matt Beaufort to bring her up to speed.

Beth didn't have the same visceral reaction to this town as Diane Fowler. She'd worked well with Matt Beaufort the last time she was here. But she knew a little about Diane Fowler's history here. She'd just about been suspended because of a case in Coffin Cove, and that was the reason her career had stalled.

The gossip in the office was Diane Fowler had been thrilled to be assigned to Vega's team. He was a rising star. She had intended to hitch herself to his shirttails. But stars burn out, and Vega's trajectory plummeted downwards after he'd put citizens in harm's way during the investigation and had failed to follow protocol. Sure, he and Fowler had solved the case, but Vega had just about sunk both their careers. Vega had been a favourite of Superintendent Sharon Sinclair, and he'd narrowly escaped being fired.

Diane Fowler had been assigned to the cold case division and had languished there until the political atmosphere at IHIT suddenly changed. Sinclair announced her retirement, and Vega took extended leave and then left. The new superintendent, George Nash, had made it clear he didn't tolerate mavericks, but to everyone's surprise, he resurrected Fowler's career, and she completed the rigorous promotion process to attain the rank of inspector.

Despite having her feet back on the career ladder, Fowler was still bitter about the setbacks she'd suffered.

No wonder she didn't want to be here, Beth thought. This was going to be a tough assignment.

"It's a nasty one," Matt said, interrupting Beth's thoughts. "The side of his head is a real mess. Lots of blood."

"Who found him?"

"Katie Dagg, the museum curator. She's really shaken up."

Beth nodded. "Any information from the crime scene guys yet?"

"Not that they're telling me," Matt said. "Here comes your boss now." He gestured with his chin, and Beth saw Fowler marching towards them.

"Do we have space we can use at the detachment?" Fowler asked Matt. "We need to set up a room. I have two more officers arriving tomorrow."

Matt nodded. "Yes, ma'am, I know what you need. And I've booked two rooms at the motel. Do you need anything else?"

Fowler finally seemed appreciative. "Thank you. Excellent. Now I think the only other thing we all need is some coffee. Beth, could you organize that for us? Use the rental, and I'll get back to the detachment with Sergeant Beaufort."

Get the coffee? Seriously? She was the same rank as Matt Beaufort and part of Fowler's own team, and she was being treated like Fowler's secretary.

Beth watched Fowler get in Matt's cruiser and drive away, and then she walked towards Hephzibah's Café on the boardwalk. It was the only place to get decent coffee in town. She hoped the café would be open on a Sunday. Beth remembered Hephzibah Brown from the last time she was in Coffin Cove. Hephzibah had been burned badly in a house fire after being held hostage by an escaped convict. Beth herself had been part of the rescue team and had taken the shot which killed the convict and ended the standoff. Beth had got a commendation for her actions. But she was still the damn coffee girl.

Beth cheered up when she saw Hephzibah behind the counter. The tall, handsome woman was all smiles when she saw Beth.

"Oh, I'm so glad it's you they called. I'm happy to see you!" Hephzibah came around the counter and hugged Beth.

"How are you?" Beth asked.

"Oh, I'm fine . . ." Hephzibah smiled again, but her tone was flat.

"You sure?"

"Well, I wish we didn't have another violent crime in Coffin Cove. It's awful." Hephzibah shook her head. "I went to the lecture Friday night, and he was so much fun. The children all loved him. I don't suppose you can tell us anything?"

"Yes, any comment, Constable Stanton?" a voice said, and Beth turned round to see Andi Silvers standing behind her, grinning.

"No comment." Beth grinned back. "You'll have to try harder than that. And it's Sergeant now. Even though I'm still doing the coffee run."

"Congratulations. Inspector Fowler with you?"

Beth remembered the antagonism between the two women.

"Yes, the inspector is in charge. You'll have to ask her for comment."

Andi grimaced. Then she looked serious. "It's horrible. Katie Dagg found the professor. I've heard she's really shaken up."

"I can't say anything, Andi, I'm sorry. But it is horrible. We'll be working hard on this one, I promise you."

Beth hurried back to the car with the coffee and a large bag of muffins. *Maybe Fowler would be in a better mood when she got some food,* Beth thought as she unlocked the car.

The crowd had dispersed, and the coroner's van had gone. The crime scene tape had become detached from the museum entrance and was dragging in the slush. Beth deposited the coffee and muffins in the rental car and went over to reattach the tape.

"Officer?"

Beth swung around. "Yes?" She hadn't heard anyone approach. A woman stood behind her. She was young, maybe in her late twenties, and she had olive skin and long dark hair tied back from her face. She spoke with an accent.

"You work on this crime, Officer? You are in charge?"

Spanish, maybe? Beth thought.

"I'm not in charge, but I am part of the team. I'm Sergeant Stanton. How can I help you?"

The woman was shivering. She wasn't wearing an outer coat, just a black shirt and black pants.

"I must talk to the officer in charge." She hugged her arms around herself. "I know something."

"You know something? About this crime?" Beth asked, startled.

"*Sí,* about this crime." The woman seemed angry and her accent became more pronounced. "I see something. *Viernes por la noche.*"

Beth didn't understand Spanish, but her mood brightened immediately. A possible witness!

"What's your name?" Beth asked as she opened the door to the cruiser. "It will be easier to talk if you come to the detachment. Is that OK?"

The woman nodded and slid into the passenger seat. She waited until Beth had gone round to the driver's seat and had put the coffee and muffins on the back seat.

"My name is Juanita," she said.

* * *

Beth Stanton couldn't help but feel smug as she led Inspector Fowler into the interview room where she'd left Juanita with coffee and the bag of muffins.

"Juanita, this is Inspector Fowler. She is in charge of the investigation."

Diane Fowler took a seat facing Juanita.

"Sergeant Stanton here tells me you saw something. On Friday night? Could you tell me about it, please?"

Juanita finished her mouthful.

"I see a man fighting with the man who is dead," she said flatly.

"Where did you see this, and at what time?" Inspector Fowler asked, calmly.

Juanita shrugged. "Late. Outside the museum. The man shouts something at the professor and grabs his arm. Then he go *boom*, like this."

She made a striking motion with her arm.

Fowler glanced at Beth. A blow to the head was consistent with the professor's injuries.

"OK, then what happened?"

"The professor, he fall down. Then I run."

"Where were you?" Beth asked, getting an irritated look from Fowler.

"Near the museum." Juanita took another mouthful of Hephzibah's muffin.

"Why were you there?" Fowler was showing her impatience.

"I work at the Bistro," Juanita said, after she'd swallowed.

"The Bistro?" Fowler looked puzzled. "Where's that?"

Juanita sighed — almost dramatically, Beth thought. "Behind Fish Plant. I work until nine. Then I walk past museum to go home."

Fowler and Beth exchanged glances. They would check with Katie about the timing. Had someone stayed behind after the lecture and got into some kind of argument with the professor? More likely the professor had run into an opportunist thief and been involved in an altercation. But how had his body ended up in the museum?

"You saw this man and the professor arguing. Then the man hit the professor and then you ran. Why didn't you call the police?"

Beth was suspicious. Something was off about this woman, she just couldn't put her finger on it.

"Everyone tell me that this town is violent. Lots of crime, so I think to myself, maybe this is normal. Not my business. Then, this morning I hear the professor is dead, so . . ." Juanita shrugged.

"Can you describe this man?" Fowler asked.

"I don't have to. I know who it is. I see him before."

Juanita reached for another muffin.

CHAPTER TWELVE

"I'm the lead on this one, right?"

Andi looked up from her laptop and gazed at the young woman, who stood with her arms folded and head tilted slightly to one side. Charlie didn't usually like to work Sundays, but she'd arrived at the office an hour after Andi. Charlie was smirking a little, and her dark eyes were shining with excitement. She had got over her objections to covering the dinosaur lecture, now that the lecturer had been killed, Andi supposed.

"You mean the murder?" Andi saw the light in Charlie's eyes dim.

"Yes, the murder." Charlie was hesitant now.

"You mean the horrific murder of a seventyish-year-old professor, which will devastate his family and traumatize the community? That murder?"

"Yes." Charlie had the grace to look sheepish. Andi smiled at her.

"Look, I don't want to dampen your enthusiasm for a story, but you need to understand that the *Gazette* has a responsibility to report the facts, while being sensitive and respectful towards the victims, OK?"

Charlie stared at her. "Did you just turn into Jim?"

Andi couldn't help but laugh. "I guess I did. All right, I'm not going to scoop your story, but we are going to do this as a team, OK? We coordinate and discuss and check everything, OK? No sloppy journalism."

Charlie nodded. "All right, I promise." Then her face broke into a grin. "Where do I start? With Katie Dagg?"

Andi shook her head. "No, the police will be questioning Katie first. They won't want her to be talking to us. Let's start with Professor Weber. What do we know about him? What's his background? Let's do some digging, and later today, the police will probably do a press release."

"Can I go to that?"

Andi had caught a glimpse of Inspector Diane Fowler outside the museum. She had clashed with Fowler in the past. When Inspector Andrew Vega had been part of the Integrated Homicide Investigative Team, Andi had managed to be close to the official investigations. Fowler would never allow that.

But Sergeant Beth Stanton was in town with Fowler. She might be more cooperative.

"Yes, you go to the presser. They won't tell us much, but be prepared with questions. How was he killed? Where was he killed? Do they have suspects or leads, stuff like that. Be relentless."

Charlie interrupted, "Don't we know some of that?"

"We know he was found in the museum. We don't know if he was killed there or put there."

"Oh, right." Charlie thought for a moment. "If the police won't tell us much, why do we bother going to the pressers?"

"Because the police are part of the story," Andi said, patiently. "It's not our job to solve the murder. That's what IHIT is supposed to do. Part of our job is to hold their feet to the fire. Are they making progress? Is the community safe? Was the professor targeted, or is there some crazed killer loose in Coffin Cove?"

"I see." Charlie was looking less excited now, and her shoulders dropped.

"There are many angles to this story," Andi went on, not wanting to discourage her junior reporter, but determined to make her understand the job. "Friday night, at the Concerned Citizen's Committee meeting, there were people blaming newcomers for a rise in crime. Do they have a point? Do we need more police in Coffin Cove? You see what I mean?"

"I think so. What if someone in Coffin Cove killed him?"

Andi thought back to the previous evening and the heated rhetoric about wasted tax dollars and the museum. But why kill the professor? Unless someone had got drunk and angry?

"We report that too. And we find out why."

Andi looked at the serious face of Charlene Davis and wondered if she were ready for this story. Then she thought of Jim Peters and all the opportunities he'd given her and the trust he'd shown, even when she hadn't deserved it.

"Charlie, it's your story. You'll figure out the way you want to write it, and I'll help you."

Charlie straightened up, the smile returning to her face. "Thanks. I'll go to the detachment first and see when they're going to release a statement. It's nearly five, they must have something to say now."

"Great." Andi looked around. "Have you seen my dad today?"

"No. He was at the lecture though."

"Really?" Andi thought back to her conversation with her father on Friday evening and was surprised. He must have changed his mind.

"He was talking to Professor Weber at the end."

"You should definitely talk to Dad, then. See what that conversation was about. Did he say he was working this weekend?"

It was strange. Her father loved to be in the thick of every story. He must have heard about Professor Weber's death by now. News, especially bad news, swept through Coffin Cove like a grass fire.

Charlie shook her head. "No, I haven't spoken to him since Friday. Maybe he's resting."

Andi nodded. "Yes, that's probably it."

Bob was still receiving treatment for the smoke damage to his lungs but refused to talk about his health. He insisted on walking to the office every day, and he wouldn't let Andi or Harry drive him around, not even to hospital appointments, preferring to call a cab.

"Don't fuss. I'm fine — strong as an ox," was all he'd say to Andi.

She worried about him. Bob Hinton had always been larger than life. His booming voice and belly laughs dominated parties, and he loved nothing more than telling stories, propped up at a bar.

Lately, he'd seemed smaller somehow. He was still an impressive figure, striding through the town with his long black coat and leather hat, but Andi had caught him leaning against the wall at the top of the office stairs, struggling to catch his breath more than once.

"Do you want me to call him?" Charlie asked.

"No, he'll turn up, or I'll call him later. Off you go now. Don't let Inspector Fowler dodge any questions."

"Not a chance."

Andi watched Charlie leave the office and envied her. She looked at the pile of paper on her desk. She'd swapped the thrill of chasing a story for the tedium of running a business. There were advertising spots to fill, bills to pay and the regular columns to be completed. No wonder Jim had needed a sabbatical.

Andi resisted the urge to close her laptop and follow Charlie. Maybe she could do a little digging herself, just to help. Jim used to work the phones for Andi, getting background information from his vast network of contacts. Andi didn't have such a wide net, but she had seen one other familiar figure at the museum.

She tapped the number pad on her phone and waited for the call to connect.

"Andi Silvers, my favourite girl, how are you? I've missed you! Do you still smell like rotten fish?"

"What the hell is that supposed to mean?" Andi demanded.

Terry Pederson was a talented crime scene photographer, and one of Andi's most reliable sources.

"If you're still sleeping with that fisherman, you must smell like stinky old fish."

Andi laughed. "Well, I guess I don't notice any more."

"Why don't you ditch him and sleep with me? I smell better."

"I'll give it some thought. In the meantime—"

"In the meantime, you're after a little inside information on the Dinosaur Professor? You'll owe me a night of passion."

"Terry, I'll add it to the list of favours I owe you. I promise."

"OK, I would have come looking for you this morning, but Fowler turned up and she was indeed foul, so I couldn't risk it. The professor's head was caved in, blunt-force trauma. No weapon lying about, but oceans of blood. No splatter in the museum, just drag marks, so they're thinking he was killed outside."

"They don't know for sure?"

"It rained on Friday night and then it snowed, so most of the blood was washed away, but there were a few tiny splatters on the outside door, so he was most likely killed there and dragged inside."

"So time of death had to be after the lecture and before the snow?" Andi's mind was turning. "And the killer must have access to the museum, or Katie must have left the door unlocked."

"That makes sense."

"Anything else?"

"Not much. Fowler was tight-lipped. She was ordering the local plod around, and was mean to her very pretty sergeant, the lovely Beth Stanton. But don't expect too much cooperation from Beth. Fowler will run a tight ship. She's immune to your charm." Terry's voice was teasing.

"Well, thanks for the info, Terry." Andi was scribbling notes.

"You're welcome, as always. And when you get tired of the fish stink, there's room in my bed, and I'll—"

"Thank you, Terry." Grinning, Andi ended the call before Terry could go into any more colourful details.

Andi was about to call Charlie to give her Terry's information, when her phone buzzed and Charlie's number was displayed on the screen.

"I was just about to call you," Andi began, but Charlie cut in, her voice breathless.

"Andi, Matt Beaufort told me Inspector Fowler isn't going to release a statement until Monday morning. But get this, he hinted that they already have a lead in the case."

"Oh? What else did he say?"

"He was a bit weird, actually. He asked me if I'd seen your dad today, or if you were with him."

"That's odd. Maybe they think the professor said something to Dad? Why didn't they come to the office?"

"I don't know, he wouldn't say any more, but I'll keep on it." Charlie ended the call and Andi was left staring at her phone.

Where *was* her dad?

She had his cell phone number on speed dial. If he was grumpy about her checking in on him, she'd just bring him up to speed about the murder. He'd be annoyed to think he'd missed any action.

She listened to six rings before the call diverted to voicemail. "This is Bob," said her dad's voice. "Leave a message." There was a beep, but before Andi could say anything, an electronic voice told her the mailbox was full.

Andi thought for a moment, and then called Hephzibah.

"Hey, have you seen Dad today?"

"No, not at all. Everything OK?"

"Yeah, he's just gone AWOL."

"He might be with Ruth. You know, about her legal case? She has meetings with her lawyers all this week. She's gone in to her office to work on the case today. Give her a call, she won't mind."

"No, it's OK, I won't bother them. I'd forgotten all about that."

Andi was about to end the call when Hephzibah said, "Andi, I know you must be busy at the moment, but could we chat when you have a minute?" Andi heard an anxious tone in Hephzibah's voice.

"What's wrong? I'll come over now."

"No, no, it's probably nothing. I'll see you later. And if I see Bob I'll tell him you're looking for him."

Andi ended the call and wondered what was on Hephzibah's mind. She was usually the one listening to people's troubles.

Her phone buzzed again and Charlie's number was again displayed on the screen. At the same time, Andi heard footsteps on the stairs outside.

"Charlie? What's up?"

"Andi, did you find Bob?"

"No, I think he's with Ruth. Why?"

"Matt says there's something he should know."

Before Andi could ask her what her father should know, the door swung open.

On the phone, Charlie's voice continued, "The lead I was telling you about? It's something to do with your dad."

Andi didn't have time to process Charlie's words.

"Miss Silvers, I'm looking for Bob Hinton, your father."

Inspector Diane Fowler was standing in the doorway.

CHAPTER THIRTEEN

Inspector Diane Fowler eyed Andi and didn't bother to hide her irritation.

"This is your father's *correct* cell phone number? And address? And you are sure you haven't seen him since Friday?"

Andi bit her lip and choked back a sarcastic reply. She kept her voice even as she replied, "Yes, Inspector Fowler. Yes, to all three questions."

"And he hasn't been to the office this morning? You haven't seen him either?"

Inspector Fowler addressed the last question to Charlie, who had arrived shortly after the inspector.

She shook her head.

"Is that his desk?" Fowler asked, pointing to Bob's vacant seat. Sergeant Stanton and Matt Beaufort were with Fowler, and when Andi didn't answer Fowler's question, Fowler gestured to Stanton to move over to the desk.

"Stop right there, please, Beth. You have no right to touch or look at any of my staff's papers or belongings without a warrant." Andi was getting annoyed with Fowler's officious tone.

Fowler inclined her head. "Very well. Do you know where he is right now?"

"No. Why is it so important you speak to my father?" Andi demanded, trying hard to keep her voice civil.

"I need to speak with your father, and that's all you need to know."

We can all play that game, Andi thought as she smiled at the inspector.

"He could be any number of places, Inspector. Maybe he's visiting a friend, or working on an article for the paper, or he could be doing some shopping in Nanaimo. It's the weekend and I'm not my father's keeper. I'm sure he'll turn up and be delighted to answer any questions you have. Now, unless you have official business in my office, I'm very busy and you have a murder to solve."

As the sound of footsteps faded down the stairs, Andi spoke urgently to Charlie.

"Can you go to the band office and see if Dad's with Ruth? And then see if you can talk to Matt again, find out what lead they have, where it came from and what it has to do with Dad."

Charlie nodded and grabbed her bag.

"Call me as soon as you know something, right?"

* * *

Andi left the office in the afternoon gloom. She looked up and down the street, but it was deserted. She'd expected a police cruiser to be parked nearby, watching her movements.

Bob hadn't been with Ruth. She'd called everyone she could think of. Andi had been to the Fat Chicken, had checked with Harry and had even phoned the only taxi operator in town. Nobody had seen or heard from Bob, but a couple of people confirmed he'd been at the museum lecture.

Why had he changed his mind?

Fowler had released a press statement instead of waiting until the morning and had referred to a lead they had received from a member of the public. She had actually named Bob Hinton as a "person of interest". He'd been seen with Professor Weber after the lecture, and they needed to contact Bob Hinton as a matter of urgency.

Andi had been a journalist long enough to know what that meant. It was all so bizarre. What did Bob know, and where the hell had he gone? And who had supplied this tip to the police?

She turned right and walked briskly in the direction of the Fat Chicken. When she reached the pub, she kept walking up the hill. When she passed the turn-off to Hephzibah's cottage, she remembered Hephzibah's anxious voice on the phone.

In all the chaos after Professor Weber's death and her father's disappearance, Andi had completely forgotten.

She made a mental note to visit Hephzibah as soon as she could. But now, she had a more pressing task.

After another ten minutes of walking and a promise to herself to exercise more, Andi was standing outside Jim Peters' house. She paused for a few minutes to catch her breath.

The house was in complete darkness.

The drizzle had let up, and the clouds had parted enough for the winter moon to cast a silver light over the front yard and the covered porch.

Andi shivered. The house had a deserted, eerie feel about it.

Andi gave herself a shake. This low-slung, box-shaped house had never had the welcoming feel of a home, but it had been the perfect place for her father to rent while Jim was away.

When Jim had returned to help his ailing father with the *Coffin Cove Gazette*, it was supposed to be temporary. Then he'd realized his father was suffering from dementia, and he'd bought this house, which was big enough for the two of them.

Andi had never met Jim's father. He'd been dead a long while before Andi arrived in Coffin Cove.

She had only been to Jim's house a few times. The inside of the house was an homage to the seventies. Jim hadn't bothered to upgrade the worn kitchen or avocado-coloured bathroom.

"I always intended to sell up and move again," he'd explained to Andi. "But somehow I always stayed. Coffin Cove is like that." He'd shrugged and grinned at Andi, who declared that Coffin Cove would never be her permanent home. She was focused on building her career after a self-destructive period in her life which had resulted in a disgraced exit from a national media company. Jim had given her a humble new start at the *Gazette*.

Andi had never expected to have reasons to stay either.

She'd never expected her father to reappear in her life. Just as she felt they were getting closer and finding a mutual understanding, he abruptly leaves without saying why or where he's going? No, there was something else going on here.

What if he'd had an accident? Why hadn't that occurred to her before? She'd been so wrapped up with Professor Weber's murder and Fowler's insinuations about her father's involvement, she'd not considered that he might have fallen or had a heart attack. She'd just accepted Fowler's assertion that her father had left Coffin Cove.

She hurried to the porch, angry with herself.

"Dad?"

Andi called out as she banged on the front door with her fist.

Visions of her father lying on the floor, unable to get up or cry for help, filled her mind and she had to choke back her panic.

Had he been looking unwell lately? Why hadn't she asked him? It had only been a few weeks since he'd left the hospital.

There was no answering call, and no sounds of footsteps.

There were two other entrances, Andi remembered — a side door into the kitchen and sliding patio doors at the rear. She found the side gate and blinked in surprise as a motion light came on. Andi found the kitchen door and tried the handle. Locked.

She remembered Jim saying once that the patio doors needed replacing because the latch was broken. Andi hoped Jim hadn't had time to do the upgrade before he left.

The patio was in darkness. When Andi's eyes had adjusted, she saw with relief that the latch on the inside of the sliding doors was missing. The doors were hard to move from the outside, but Andi eased them open and then stepped into the living room.

"Dad?" she called again and then felt around for a light switch. Light filled the room, and her eyes took a second to adjust. No prone body of her father in the living room, just two armchairs and a coffee table littered with magazines and an upturned book.

Her father had been delighted with the bachelor ambience.

"Perfect," he'd said when Jim had showed him around. "Everything I need." The only belongings he'd moved in were his clothes and some boxes of books.

Andi saw the boxes stacked neatly along the wall in the living room.

"Dad?" she called out again and pulled open a door. It led to a small room which Jim must have used as an office. Her father wasn't there.

She bounded up the stairs to the second floor and flicked on the landing lights. The bathroom door was open, and she could see it was empty. Andi checked both bedrooms, taking care to walk around the beds, in case her father was lying on the floor.

Her father definitely wasn't in the house. At least she hadn't found his dead body; Andi felt some relief about that.

"OK, what next?" she said aloud.

She needed to set aside her worry and *investigate*, she thought. There must be some clue in the house, if not to Bob's whereabouts, then maybe she could figure out if he had left in a hurry. Hoping to evade the police? Andi put that thought aside.

Andi went back into her father's bedroom for a closer look. It was neat. The bed was made, and there was no way to tell if Bob slept in it the night before. A glass of water was still on the nightstand. Andi opened the closet. She recognized her father's clothes: pants and jackets hanging in a row and folded sweaters on shelves. On the top shelf, Andi found a razor and shaving foam. She left the bedroom and went into the bathroom.

A single toothbrush was in a mug with a tube of toothpaste. Towels hung on pegs behind the door, and Andi felt them. They were dry.

Andi went back to the bedroom and took another look in the closet. On the top shelf was a large suitcase.

If her father had left, he had packed nothing.

Andi took a quick look in Jim's bedroom again, but judging from the layer of dust on the tallboy and nightstands, nobody had been in there for a while.

Andi checked the kitchen last. There was a good deal of food in the fridge, as if Bob had recently stocked up on groceries. In the sink was a lone mug. The coffee machine was off and had half an inch of cold coffee in it.

Andi stood for a few minutes, trying to make sense of it all.

It looked as if Bob had left the house for the office, fully intending to come back. It seemed to Andi that her father hadn't returned to the house at all since the lecture. She went over the timeline in her mind. She had left the office thirty minutes before the lecture started. Charlie said she'd seen Bob at the end of the lecture. That would have been what? Eight thirty, nine o'clock? He didn't stop at the pub, he didn't take a taxi, and it was a twenty-minute walk back to the house. Had he been attacked on the way home? Was his body in a ditch somewhere? But surely he'd been found by now? It was almost two days since the lecture.

Andi shook her head, as if to dislodge those thoughts. She closed her eyes and continued her mental assessment of everything she knew.

According to Inspector Fowler, her father was seen with Professor Weber outside the museum. Who had given

Fowler that information? Was it possible there had been an accident? Could Bob have just panicked and run?

It was so unlike her father. And if he was seen outside the museum, how had the professor's body ended up inside? If her father had been in a frantic state, it was even more unlikely that he'd have manhandled the professor's body into the museum and then ran. Ran where?

None of this made sense. Her father had a lot of flaws but he wasn't a killer.

Andi wandered back into the living room. She stared at the empty chair again, imagining her father reading. She felt a hollow feeling in her stomach, as if she hadn't eaten recently. She'd felt like this years ago when she was a child. There was a vague recollection of sitting on a rug with her mother. It was a sunny day, and her toys were scattered about. Andi remembered being happy. Then a shadow loomed over her. It was her father. She stretched out her arms, but he ignored her. Her parents started arguing. She couldn't recall what happened next, but she remembered a sharp pain in her leg. Had a bee stung her? She must have cried out, because her mother had gathered her in her arms to soothe her. When Andi's tears had dried, her father was gone.

Bob Hinton had mostly stayed out of Andi's life. She'd preferred it that way. She always expected her father to leave eventually, and he'd never disappointed her. But this was different. The hollow feeling wasn't abandonment, she realized. It was fear. Fear that she didn't know Bob Hinton at all.

The sound of a car engine and a siren's single whoop made Andi jump. She went to the window and squinted her eyes as blue light filled the room.

There was a firm rap on the front door.

"Police! Open up."

Inspector Fowler stood in the front porch.

"Ah, Miss Silvers. What are you doing here?"

"What do you think, Inspector? I'm looking for my father."

"And is he here?"

"No."

"Can we come in? We'd like to see for ourselves, if we may?"

Fowler's tone was flat and professional. Andi considered refusing but decided there was no valid reason to stop Fowler from entering. It would do her no good to be combative with the inspector. The police had considerably more resources than she did, and she wanted to find her father as much as they did, albeit for different reasons.

She stepped aside.

A sheepish-looking Sergeant Matt Beaufort followed the inspector into the hallway.

"The living room is that way," Andi directed them.

"This is James Peters' house, is that correct? Your father was renting?"

"He is renting," Andi corrected. "Well, house-sitting, I suppose."

"You have a key?"

"No." Andi explained how she had entered the house.

"I see." Fowler pursed her lips.

"I was worried my father may have had an accident. Fallen down the stairs or something."

Under Fowler's gaze, Andi felt herself get flustered. "I was concerned for my father's safety," she said, although her words sounded defensive.

"Of course."

"You have it wrong about my father, Inspector. I'm afraid something's happened to him."

Fowler's face was hard to read. She gave a theatrical sigh. "You know what, Miss Silvers?"

"What?" Andi stared at the inspector.

"The simplest explanation is usually the right one. I think *you people* spend far too much time looking for conspiracy theories in every dark corner." The inspector's sarcasm was far from subtle. "A person was murdered. Your father was in the vicinity. Now he is nowhere to be found. I don't believe in coincidences, do you?"

Andi tried to hide her irritation. The problem was that the simplest explanation wasn't apparent until you had all the facts. Andi hadn't spent her career chasing conspiracy theories. She pursued the truth, however strange it might be. It seemed such an odd thing for Fowler to say. It felt like she'd rehearsed this speech, hoping for an opportunity to provoke her. Did she despise all journalists, or just Andi?

Andi tried to keep her voice level.

"I don't believe in coincidences either, Inspector. My father has vanished. I don't know why or how, but I know you have no evidence that he murdered Professor Weber or was even involved. All you have is a sighting of my father with Professor Weber after the lecture. It's still usual for *you people* to follow the evidence, isn't it?"

Fowler's face darkened. She didn't hide her anger and opened her mouth to speak. Andi heard Matt Beaufort clear his throat. So far, the sergeant hadn't said a word, but before Fowler could respond to Andi's sarcasm, Andi continued.

"I have a question for you, Inspector. How do I report my father as a missing person?"

"It's far too early for . . ." The inspector stopped, realizing the point Andi was making.

Sergeant Beaufort leaped in.

"Should I get on with the search, Inspector? We've been here a while."

"I'm aware of the time, Sergeant," Fowler snapped. Just then, her cell phone chirped. Glaring at Matt and then at Andi, she walked away from them and entered the living room.

"Don't worry, Andi," Matt said earnestly. "We'll get to the bottom of all of this." His words were kind, but Andi ignored him. She was straining to hear Fowler's conversation. All she could make out were a few curt words: "Yes. Yes, I see. Campbell River. Right."

The phone conversation ended, and Fowler reappeared in the hallway.

"Sergeant, look around, please. Then report back to me at the detachment."

Matt nodded and looked as though he was about to ask a question, but Fowler brushed past him, obviously not wanting to say anything in front of Andi.

"Have you found my father, Inspector?" Andi asked, as Fowler stepped out of the house. She sensed the inspector had received some significant information.

"No, Miss Silvers. But we will."

It took ten minutes for Beaufort to confirm Bob Hinton was not in the house. Andi watched as the cruiser made a U-turn in the road and roared away.

What did they know?

Andi's phone buzzed. It was Harry.

"Did you find him?"

"No," Andi said, and started to cry.

CHAPTER FOURTEEN

January 8, morning

"Ready for coffee?"

Andi opened her eyes. Harry was standing at the foot of the bed. His tone was sharp. As Andi moved her head and a thumping pain behind her eyes caused her to wince, she knew why.

"Water first, please."

Harry disappeared into the galley and returned a minute later with a glass of water. He watched as Andi drank it down, his arms crossed.

"Thank you." She waited for Harry to speak.

"You really tied one on last night, Andi. What were you thinking?"

"I don't know," she said weakly. She'd been upset. Harry had bought her a glass of wine at the Fat Chicken and had listened to her as she poured out her worries about her father. Then she'd had another glass of wine. And then another. And then she remembered nothing.

"I'm sorry," she said.

Harry wasn't finished.

"You know, getting drunk isn't the solution. If you're going to find your dad, you need a clear head."

"I know that. I was stressed, OK? I had a couple of glasses too many, Harry. I said I'm sorry." Andi was irritated now.

"I can't help you if you can't control your drinking," Harry continued.

"I didn't ask you to help me!" Andi winced at her own raised voice. "I'm not one of your goddamn lame-duck projects."

"What the fuck is that supposed to mean?" Harry's face had darkened with anger.

"I mean, I'm supposed to be your girlfriend, and if I'm just here because of your *saviour complex*, then I'd rather leave." Andi swung her legs and got out of bed. Her head swam a little, but she reached for her clothes. "And you know what? This boat is fucking freezing and I don't have room to work or think. I can't live like this."

She knew the words hurt. They'd come out her mouth and now she couldn't get them back. Harry stood silently for a moment and then turned to leave.

"Where are you going?" she asked, wanting him to stay. "I'm—"

"To help Ike," he said over his shoulder before she could finish. "He doesn't care about my fucking *saviour complex*."

Andi felt the boat sway as Harry stepped onto the dock.

"I'm sorry," she said to herself. "Shit." And she lay back down on the bed and closed her eyes.

Her phone trilled from somewhere in her pile of clothes. She grabbed it, hoping it was Harry.

"Andi, I've found something. I think Bob did talk to Professor Weber on Friday night," Charlie said, excitement in her voice.

* * *

Andi arrived at the office fifteen minutes later.

"Bob went to see Professor Weber because he found this on the wire," Charlie said, waving a piece of paper as soon as Andi came through the door.

"Go on," Andi said, ignoring her headache and sitting down. "What did he find?"

She knew Bob subscribed to various official websites where journalists posted press releases. Every evening, he'd check all of them. It was old school, but he liked to keep up to date with the latest breaking news across Canada.

Charlie handed the piece of paper to Andi.

It was a press release from the *Campbell River Tribune*. Andi remembered Fowler's phone call. She'd said something about Campbell River, hadn't she?

Andi read through the release and immediately understood. "Weber? This must have something to do with Professor Weber."

Charlene said, "I know it is. I've done some checking. Randolph Weber is . . . well, *was* Professor Weber's father. I think Bob read it and was going to ask Professor Weber about it. That's why he waited to talk to the professor alone."

Andi read the press release again. The body of one-hundred-year-old Randolph Weber had been discovered in his cottage on Quadra Island on Friday, 5 January. Randolph had been due to move into a nursing home in Campbell River, and his long-time health worker, Sylvie Hamm, arrived at his home to find Randolph's battered body. The coroner had declared the death a homicide.

"Who would want to murder a one-hundred-year-old man?" Andi wondered aloud.

"Someone who was robbing him?" Charlie said. "Maybe he disturbed someone, and they attacked him."

"And you're certain Randolph Weber was Professor Weber's father?" It was an unnecessary question. Why else would Fowler get a call about this homicide if it wasn't likely connected to the professor's murder?

Charlene nodded. "Yes. I contacted the journalist at the *Tribune*. They were about to call us. They had just seen the press release about the professor's murder."

"Professor Weber can't have known about his father's death. I bet Dad was going to break the news. He'd have thought it was the right thing to do. Nothing worse than finding out about a loved one's death in the newspaper. It explains a lot."

"At least we know Bob didn't kill the professor's father," Charlene said. "He hasn't been to Quadra Island."

"He didn't kill anyone!" Andi snapped, her head throbbing harder. "This tip or lead the police has, it must be a mistake."

"I meant, the police don't have anything to link him with the Quadra Island murder, and now we have a reason for him wanting to be with the professor alone," Charlie said in a small voice.

Andi immediately regretted her tone. "Yes, of course. You're right. Sorry, I'm just worried."

"Would you like me to see what I can find out about Randolph Weber? It can't be a coincidence that both he and his son were murdered just days apart, can it?"

Andi realized she'd stopped thinking like a journalist.

"No such thing as a coincidence. Maybe Dad was just in the wrong place at the wrong time. Maybe the same person who killed Weber Senior was waiting to kill the professor and my father got in the way."

Charlie nodded. "But, if Bob was in the way, why wouldn't the killer just have . . ." She stopped and looked at the floor, colour rising in her face.

"Why wouldn't they have killed Dad too?" Andi finished for her. "Charlie, they may have."

She struggled to get those words out, but she continued.

"We don't know yet. Maybe the forensics will turn up something at the scene. Maybe Dad saw the professor's murderer, and he got scared and ran." Even to herself, Andi didn't sound convincing. If Bob had seen something, he would have helped or called the police. No, something had made him run, or . . .

Andi pushed her worst fears aside. There was only one way she could help her father now. When they had all the facts, the simplest explanation would reveal itself.

She picked up the press release and walked over to the wall. It was still covered with the Halwell investigation. She looked at Charlie.

"Help me clean this off," she said. "It's a story we'll never publish. We need to get to work on the story we have now."

CHAPTER FIFTEEN

Ruth Cloutier had never seen Mayor Jade Thompson as agitated as she was right now. The mayor's normally pale complexion was flushed, and she was twirling a pen in her hand around and around. Every so often, she would glance down at the manila folder on the desk in front of her.

Ruth and Chief George Timms of Lhihw Xpey, Three Cedars First Nation, had accepted the mayor's offer of coffee. Ruth could tell that Jade would have preferred they refuse her hospitality and proceed with the meeting immediately by the perfunctory way she made the offer, but Chief George never liked to rush. They sat quietly, waiting for their coffee.

The meeting was about the Hope Island Redevelopment Project. The previous year, buoyed by the progress of the Fish Plant development in Coffin Cove, the conversion of the abandoned hub of the local fishing industry to gleaming store fronts, the new Coffin Cove Museum and six apartments, Mayor Jade Thompson had signed a Memorandum of Understanding with the chief and Three Cedars. The "spirit" of the agreement was for an economic partnership between the city and Lhihw Xpey. The Three Cedars Band would build a language and cultural centre on the island, and the city would develop and promote tourism opportunities.

It sounded good.

Already, Ruth had heard the mayor refer to the agreement as a "reconciliation project". Jade Thompson had become a shrewd politician. She was keenly aware of the current political climate, and Ruth was sure the mayor would use it to bolster her chances for re-election later in the year.

A stain upon Canadian history, politicians were saying now, as they discovered more and more graves on sites of old residential institutions.

It was hard not to be cynical. Savvy operators like Jade were making it part of their "platform". Truth and reconciliation equal native votes, Ruth thought bitterly, as she watched Jade twirl and tap her pen.

But Jade was in between a rock and a hard place. Already some of her constituents were pushing back against the Hope Island Project. They didn't want a cultural and language centre. They didn't mind a few totem poles and ceremonial dancers for the tourists, but why not fishing charters and kayak tours? Businesses that weren't specifically "native".

Part of Ruth wanted to give up. "Why are we trying to educate white people if they don't want to be educated?" she'd said to the chief before the meeting. "Most white people still think of stereotypical 'Indians' fighting the cowboys in western movies. They're disappointed if we're not wearing feather headdresses and hurling tomahawks!"

She'd glared at the chief, who looked at her gravely, nodding his head. He was a quiet man, and popular with his band members. He'd run unopposed in the last three election cycles and was affectionately known as Chief George. He was a big man who didn't smile often and could be an intimidating presence.

"Do you think I should dust off my loin cloth?" he asked in a serious tone, and Ruth couldn't help laughing. He'd wagged a finger at her in mock severity. "Stop that. It's not nice to poke fun at ignorant people."

Their quiet presence in Jade's office had unnerved the mayor, judging by her fidgeting. Ruth was sure they were about to get unwelcome news.

Ruth bit her lip. The Hope Island redevelopment was far more than just another project for her. The remains of her lost sister, Essie, had been discovered on Hope Island. Ruth had wanted to honour her sister's memory, and all the other lost native children. A language and cultural centre was a fitting tribute. She didn't want to give it up.

A young woman came into the office carrying a tray with two mugs. The mayor waited a few moments for Ruth and Chief George to take their coffee, and then she plunged straight into the meeting.

"I don't have good news," Jade said. "This project is not going as well as I hoped. In fact, it's turning into quite the shitshow." She tapped the folder in front of her with her pen.

Ruth kept her face impassive. Mayor Jade Thompson's directness was part of her appeal for the community. She prided herself on being down to earth and getting right to the point.

Jade flipped open the file and continued.

"Let me summarize. The 'Concerned Citizens Committee' has sent me a letter—" she picked it up and waved it — "requesting a 'seat at the table' for the redevelopment of Hope Island. They say that the island belongs to the city, and as such, it is outside our mandate to allow the land to be developed by Three Cedars' band. There's some other legal stuff in here, and I'm uncertain any of it is relevant, but the fact remains that the committee is against the project and intends to protest it in any way possible."

Ruth shrugged. "Just because they threaten legal action doesn't mean they will win."

"No, that's true. But any kind of legal action will hold up the project. It might take months to get it back on track. And then there's the optics."

Ruth nodded. "The optics . . . I see." It might severely hamper a re-election campaign. Ruth left those words unspoken.

"And now we have a murder investigation on our hands." The mayor sighed as she threw the letter on the desk. "This wasn't the start to the new year I was hoping for."

"Neither did the professor, I imagine." The words came out more sarcastically than Ruth had intended.

Jade looked at her without speaking for a moment and then nodded her head. "You're right. I didn't mean to sound callous. It's just that the Concerned Citizens Committee also mentions an increase in violent crime during my tenure. It's hard to argue against that when the coroner's parked in front of the museum all weekend."

Ruth asked, "What is it you want from us?"

"I think we need to shelve this project — just for a while. Then, maybe we can consult with this committee and incorporate some of their suggestions, come to a compromise."

Ruth knew what Jade was really saying. It would be a failure for her, a black mark against her tenure as mayor, if the Concerned Citizens Committee successfully blocked the Hope Island Project. It would be another issue to be exploited by an opposing candidate.

Again, Jade paused.

"Do either of you have anything to say? Any comments, at least?"

Ruth said calmly, "I believe we have a legally binding Memorandum of Understanding."

Jade's nostrils flared. It was the only outward sign Ruth had got under her skin. It didn't change the situation, Ruth knew, to deliberately antagonize the mayor, who had been an ally of sorts for the Three Cedars Band.

"We do. I was hoping you would understand my situation and work with me on this."

"What is it you are asking us?" Ruth said bluntly. "Or should I say, what is it that the committee want?"

It was as Ruth suspected. The committee proposed scrapping the cultural centre and selling a substantial portion of the island to private developers, who would build a fishing lodge and cabins.

"They say that the new museum can showcase First Nations culture," the mayor finished, and looked at Ruth and Chief George.

"We are not dinosaurs," Chief George said quietly. "Despite the best efforts over hundreds of years, our people are not extinct. We do not belong in a museum."

Ruth said, "I and the other band lawyers will look at the Memorandum of Understanding. We will have a meeting to determine our legal standing."

Jade nodded her head. "I think it's in all our best interests if we find a compromise with the Concerned Citizens Committee."

Chief George spoke again, his face expressionless. "Your best interests, Mayor Thompson."

Jade fidgeted in her chair. "You don't understand, Chief. These people could hold up the project for months. And if they run a candidate against me and I lose, then they will just throw out the MOU anyway. Your best way forward is to compromise."

The chief said nothing. He stood up, showing the meeting had finished. Ruth followed suit.

"There is another way, Mayor," Chief George said mildly as he reached the door.

"And what's that?" Jade asked, an edge in her voice.

The chief turned around. "We will run our own candidate for mayor of Coffin Cove."

* * *

The parking lot at the band office was empty when Ruth and Chief George arrived back after the meeting with the mayor. Schools didn't open for another few days, so many of Ruth's colleagues were still on vacation.

Ruth had worked for Lhihw Xpey for nearly a year. She was a lawyer herself and had passed the bar, but had taken a position as economic development officer, using her legal knowledge to negotiate contracts on the band's behalf. She thought of the list of projects she was working on, and her own personal civil case against her sister's killer. It was a mountain of work.

"I'll contact the lawyers," Ruth said to Chief George before returning to her office. He had been quiet on the journey back. Ruth wanted to ask if he was serious about running a candidate against Jade in the next election cycle. She hoped he wasn't thinking that she should be the candidate. It would be an uphill battle, Ruth thought, and she had plenty of battles to fight before then.

Ruth's footsteps on the granite floor tiles echoed around her, amplified by the vaulted ceilings. The building was in the logistical centre of the reservation, which also happened to be the site of an abandoned coal mine. It had taken many millions of federal dollars to complete just the engineered foundation, so it didn't collapse into the myriad of old mine shafts which crisscrossed the land.

There had been an outcry, of course. The Coffin Cove community — even before the formation of the Concerned Citizens Committee — had complained bitterly that the band was getting a handout for a huge, state-of-the-art office, while they had to spend their own tax dollars on redeveloping an eyesore on the oceanfront.

It would definitely be an issue for a Lhihw Xpey mayoral candidate, even though the office building had been funded by a federal grant. For some people, it didn't matter where the money came from or why. They just needed someone to blame for their own financial situation.

Ruth saw that her office door was open and frowned. She was sure she'd closed it when she left for the meeting. She always kept her desk clear, but she had sensitive legal documents in her filing cabinets.

Someone had been in her office. There was a white envelope with her name in block capitals written across the middle.

Ruth picked it up. Maybe someone saw it at reception and delivered it to her office instead of dropping it into her pigeonhole with the rest of her incoming mail.

She opened the envelope and read the words printed on the single sheet of paper, and then dropped it as if it were on fire.

CHAPTER SIXTEEN

"Peace offering?"

Harry held out a coffee and a brown paper bag.

"It's a bacon sandwich. I hear greasy food is good for a hangover."

Andi smiled at him from behind her desk. "Peace offering accepted, thank you. And I'm sorry about this morning."

Harry pulled up a chair and sat beside her. "No, I'm sorry. You're an adult and I treated you like a child. It's just that—"

"Drowning my sorrows in a bottle of wine won't change anything?" Andi finished for him. "You're right. I don't know why I did that."

Harry pulled her gently towards him and kissed her. "Let's move on, OK?"

"There is one thing," Andi said. "I'm going to stay at Jim's house for a bit. Until Dad turns up. I can't tell you why . . . it's just I need to be there . . ." Her voice trailed off. She couldn't put this feeling into words, this need to stay somewhere her father had been recently, the need to feel a connection.

Harry bent his head. "I understand," he said after a moment's silence.

"But there's something else you should know. Something far more important," Andi said, changing the subject, and she told Harry about the murder on Quadra Island and the connection to Professor Weber.

Shock registered on Harry's face. "The professor's father was murdered? That can't be a coincidence, surely?"

"We don't know much at the moment, but Charlie has been talking to the reporters at the *Campbell River Tribune*, and one of their sources is saying Weber Senior had been dead for a while before they found him. The police think it was a robbery gone wrong."

"So your dad saw the press release and went to break the news to Professor Weber?" Harry frowned. "But that doesn't explain the tip the police have. Sounds like they actually suspect him of killing the professor. It makes no sense."

Andi sighed. "None of it makes any sense at all. If the professor had reacted badly, and there'd been some kind of tussle, then Dad would have called the police. He wouldn't have run away and hidden. And if he'd seen something, he'd have tried to help. But at the moment, it's the only connection we have."

She gestured at the wall. "We have two victims, obviously connected. Charlie is on her way to Quadra Island now to dig up background on both our victims."

She paused and looked at Harry.

"It's easy to draw a line between the two murders, but we need to keep an open mind. I suppose coincidences happen. So we'll work the story from all angles, and hopefully along the way, some connection to Dad will shake out."

"What connection would your dad have with Quadra Island?" Harry asked. "Has he ever been there?"

"No connection, as far as I know. But we'll see what Charlie digs up."

"You think she's ready for this? It's a big story."

Andi sighed. "I think so. I *hope* so. She's tenacious and she can sniff out a story. Plus, she has a contact on Quadra Island. Her Auntie Delia lives there. I've made Charlie promise to call in at the end of every day so we can talk it through. I would go with her normally, but with Jim gone and now Dad gone, I need to be here to keep the *Gazette* going."

"At the risk of displaying my saviour complex, is there anything I can do to help?" Harry grinned at Andi.

Andi laughed and held up her bacon sandwich. "You're already helping."

Harry looked at the wall. "You've taken the Halwell case down."

"We've got more urgent investigations at hand," Andi said firmly. "Dad and Ruth will understand. It's not forgotten, just on the back burner for a while."

Harry nodded. "Why do you have the Concerned Citizens Committee poster up there?"

"It's something Dad taught me. Don't just focus on the facts you have at hand, look around the incident, whatever it is, and try to see anything out of place. It could be anything or anyone. Just trust your intuition. The Concerned Citizens Committee meeting was on the same night as the lecture and the murder. There were several angry people at the meeting, and who knows? Maybe they took out their anger on the professor."

"Or maybe one of them might have seen something?" Harry said. "I can't believe that someone would take their grievances out on the professor."

"You weren't there. It got heated at the end."

"I see you have Pastor Michael's picture up there." Harry got up and looked closely. "It is weird that this guy just showed up and immersed himself with Peggy's committee."

"Right? There's something off about him. And you know what else has been bothering me?"

Harry looked at Andi. "What?"

"The reappearance of another 'eccentric' pastor, Fred Harding. Why on earth was he at that meeting? And why was he so angry with the pastor?" She picked up her phone and scrolled to the picture she'd taken and showed Harry.

"These two people have just appeared in Coffin Cove. I need to find out more. And I need to talk to Katie Dagg. I can't think of anyone else who could have given that tip about Dad to the police."

Harry thought for a moment. "You know, there's someone else who's just turned up in town. It's a long shot, but you know Ike has been badgering me to collect moorage fees?"

Andi nodded. "The new boat? Hasn't the owner turned up?"

Harry shook his head. "Not yet. But it might be worth finding out about him — or her. The boat showed up a day or two before the murder."

"OK, I'm leaving that one for you. You're now officially part of the team."

Harry looked serious. "I'm used to being the skipper. Maybe I should be team leader?"

"Don't push it," Andi laughed.

CHAPTER SEVENTEEN

Inspector Fowler's face was stony.

Beth had listened to the earlier morning news report and guessed Fowler had done the same. The IHIT team in Vancouver had made multiple arrests of gang members and charges ranged from homicide to possession of illegal weapons. A massive haul of all kinds of street drugs were on display for the public, and the press officer emphasized the months of dedicated police work it had taken to make Vancouver's streets safer for the public.

Commendations were likely. Superintendent Nash himself made a short statement praising the efforts of his "elite" team.

When Beth arrived with the morning coffee order, the makeshift murder room was filled with the low hum of phone conversations, the clatter of the ancient photocopier and the sound of fingers tapping on keyboards. The rest of the team had arrived on the first ferry and were already hard at work. Despite the activity there was only one name scrawled across the whiteboard at the front of the room: Bob Hinton.

Fowler stood beside the whiteboard and glared at her team until the noise subsided.

"On Friday, the body of a one-hundred-year-old male was found dead in his home on Quadra Island," she started.

"Shocker," someone murmured.

"He had been bludgeoned to death, according to the coroner; he was the victim of a homicide."

"Isn't that Campbell River's problem?"

Fowler took a deep breath and ignored the interruption. Instead she scrawled on the whiteboard and stood back for her team to see.

"Randolph Weber — yes, he was related to Professor Gerald Weber, our victim. He was Professor Weber's father. So, it's *our* problem. Major Crimes in Campbell River has got the case, but Sergeant Stanton here will be joining them to ascertain if there is any connection between Weber Senior's death and that of his son. In the meantime, maybe someone could bring me up to speed with the hunt for Bob Hinton?"

The officers fidgeted in their seats and cleared their throats or looked intently at their computer screens as if the answer to Bob Hinton's whereabouts might pop up in an email.

"Inspector Fowler?" *What the hell?* thought Beth. She was being sent to Campbell River to babysit a case that Major Crimes were perfectly equipped to handle, so what if she managed to piss off Fowler before she went? It was clear to Beth that her mere presence was irritating to her boss.

Fowler looked at Beth, not bothering to hide her annoyance. "What?"

"Do we still think Bob Hinton is the top of our list?"

Fowler looked at her as if she were an idiot. "He's the only lead we have."

"I'm not sure about Juanita," Beth ploughed on. "Her story seems a little . . . too convenient, I suppose."

"Too convenient?" Fowler narrowed her eyes. "Convenient how? For whom? She came forward with information on her own accord. She checks out. Her story checks out. Katie Dagg also saw Bob Hinton with Professor Weber. What exactly is your problem?"

"Lack of physical evidence?" Beth pointed out. "Literally no physical evidence tying Bob Hinton to the scene, either outside or inside the museum. Plus, Katie Dagg didn't see an altercation between Bob Hinton and Professor Weber, and then there's the mystery of the unlocked doors. And even if there were some kind of misunderstanding, why would Bob Hinton disappear? He's attended thousands of crime scenes as a reporter and knows the procedure. Wouldn't he have just called the police?"

Fowler's voice became harsh. "We have no way of knowing Bob Hinton's state of mind, or what he's capable of—"

"But why drag the body into the museum? It doesn't make sense. And who is this Juanita? Shouldn't we be looking at everyone at the lecture that evening, rather than pouring our resources into looking for one man . . ."

Beth knew she had completely overstepped the mark. The room fell silent and the officers who had been following the exchange suddenly found their laptops and desks very interesting indeed.

Fowler's voice was quiet and dangerous.

"Sergeant. Thank you for your input. Your point of contact at Campbell River is Sergeant Vaughan. I suggest you work with him, rather than attempt to tell him how to do his job. Maybe don't treat the locals like idiots. You never know, you might learn something. Please gather your things, and get out of my murder room."

Beth did as she was told.

* * *

Matt Beaufort smiled at Beth as she left the detachment. "Good luck." He winked at her.

"Stanton, a minute before you leave." Fowler followed her out the door and they stood in the chilly morning air.

"I don't know what you think you're doing, but if you ever undermine me like that again, I'll make sure you are out of IHIT and directing fucking traffic in some no-name shithole in BC, you understand me?"

Beth felt a hot flush work up her neck. "Sorry, Inspector, I just—"

"You just thought that because Andrew Vega took you under his wing, you're somehow the smartest and the best. Well, take a look around you, do you see the great Andrew Vega anywhere? No? You don't, because Vega fucked up big time and nearly screwed up my career as well as his own. I will not allow that to happen again. So remember this, *Stanton*—" Fowler practically spat her name out — "you work for me. You do what I tell you to. And if you do that, we'll get along just fine. Oh, here's the file on the Campbell River Weber case. Your job is to find connections with our case, if any. Got that?"

"Yes ma'am," Beth said, looking Fowler directly in the eye.

"'Yes ma'am' is the correct response," Fowler said as she spun around and walked back to the detachment.

* * *

Sergeant Vaughan had a high-pitched voice, and as she talked to him on her cell phone, Beth imagined him as a pimple-faced youth. He wasn't at Campbell River detachment when she arrived there, two and half hours after leaving Coffin Cove. The constable on reception was expecting her, at least, and Vaughan had left a message for Beth to call when she got to the detachment.

He made no attempt to hide his displeasure at her arrival in Campbell River.

"I don't know why IHIT would be interested in this case," he said. "I interviewed the lady who found him, and she says he was shaky on his feet and could have fallen. There was nothing taken, according to her. The coroner got this one wrong if you ask me."

* * *

Beth took a deep breath. Inspector Fowler had made it clear she was to work with the locals and not alienate them. *Don't treat them like idiots*, she'd said. Beth's first thought had been about kettles and black pots. She'd seen Fowler's mere presence rub colleagues the wrong way, not to mention her abrupt and condescending manner.

"I've seen the preliminary coroner's report. She determined the cause of death to be blunt-force trauma to the head. He'd been dead several days. And then there's the matter of his son's murder a few days later."

"Yeah, the old man's skull was cracked like an eggshell. But the dude was a hundred years old. His bones were as brittle as dry twigs."

Beth bristled at Vaughan's dismissive tone, and he hadn't even commented on Weber's son.

"Well, the coroner called it and here I am. So, what's the plan?" She kept her voice brisk but polite.

Vaughan explained he'd arranged for the constable stationed on the island to meet Beth the next day and show her the crime scene — "if that's what it is".

"Just one more question," Beth asked, before finishing the call. "How did the lady you interviewed know that nothing was missing?"

Vaughan gave a theatrical sigh, as if Beth had asked the dumbest question he'd ever heard.

"Sylvie Hamm was his Community Health worker. She visited him every week for ten years."

"Right. Thank you. I'll need your interview notes and I'd like to talk to Sylvie Hamm myself. Does she live on the island?"

Vaughan sighed again. "All the notes are in the file at reception. But if you want to talk to Sylvie Hamm, you can visit her tomorrow. Her contact details are also in the file."

"What an arrogant ass," Beth muttered as she finally ended the call. But she couldn't help wondering if Vaughan was right. The coroner determined whether a death was a homicide, not the police. But the coroner had been wrong before.

There was little that Beth could do until the next day, so she decided to get something to eat and then check herself into a hotel. At least she could read the file again and make some notes for the next day.

* * *

"Ideal Café," the constable at the reception desk told Beth, as she handed her a manila file. "It closes at four, so you'll have to hurry. But it's the best place to eat in town."

The Ideal Café was tucked away on an industrial estate, between a mechanic's workshop and Wiltshire Trucks. The café was empty and the waitress made a show of checking the clock when Beth walked in.

"You just made it," the waitress said.

"Sorry, I know I'm late. I was told this was the best place to eat in town," Beth said, and was rewarded with a smile.

"Take a seat, honey. Hope you're OK with a burger, because that's all we have left."

"Sounds wonderful."

While she was waiting for her burger, Beth flipped open the file and started to read.

* * *

Charlie parked her car outside the Terminal Café. Her Auntie Delia had told her the owner knew everyone and everything that happened on Quadra Island.

Charlie thought of Hephzibah and how Coffin Cove's only café was the place to go to tune into local gossip. The only problem, as Andi kept reminding her, was sorting out the fact from fiction.

It's a start, Charlie thought as she pushed open the door. Besides, she was hungry.

The café was deserted except for a small lady with dark hair behind the counter.

"Are you Christie?" Charlie asked.

"I am. Do I know you?"

Christie had a wide smile and welcomed Charlie enthusiastically when she identified herself and her family connection.

"I love your Auntie Delia! She always helps out at the Christmas Craft Fair. Now, take a seat, what would you like to eat?"

Charlie ordered soup and a sandwich and sat down at a table by the window and watched the ferry ease away from the dock and glide back towards Campbell River.

Christie arrived with her food and two cups of coffee. She took a seat opposite Charlie.

"So, what brings you to Quadra? Just visiting?"

Charlie explained. "I'm a reporter with the *Coffin Cove Gazette*. I'm here to cover the murder of Randolph Weber."

"Oh, that poor old man." Christie's face clouded over with sadness. "What a terrible thing. It's really upset the whole community."

Charlie continued, "Yes, and unfortunately his son died two days ago in Coffin Cove. It was a violent death too."

The woman's eyes widened. "He was murdered? Oh my God."

Charlie told her the details in the press release.

"You think the deaths are connected?" Christie asked. Before Charlie could answer, a bell jingled and the door opened. A tall woman wearing bright yellow rain gear came in shaking droplets of water from her shoulders.

"Another downpour, and it's started blowing out there," she said. "The ferry schedule will be shot." She looked at Charlie and Christie. "That soup smells good."

Christie gestured for the woman to join them. "Monica, you'll never guess what's happened now. Go on, tell her," she said, nodding at Charlie.

Monica took off the jacket and pulled a chair up to the table. "What's going on?"

While Charlie told Monica the whole story, Christie got up to get Monica a bowl of soup.

"Oh my. That's awful." Monica looked at Charlie in horror. "I can't believe it. Poor Gerald." She sat silently for a moment, and then looked at Charlie. "At least Randolph didn't know about Gerald. He would have been devastated. Who would do such terrible things? Do the police think it's the same person?"

"We don't know yet. They're investigating, of course."

"And that's why you're here? To get the scoop?" Monica sounded irritated.

"Monica, Charlie is Delia's niece. She'd just doing her job," Christie called from the kitchen.

"I'm here to get some background about Randolph Weber and his son. I'm not going to write anything disre-spectful. But two violent deaths in one family, maybe it's more than a coincidence. And it's my job to find out." It came out a little more defensive than Charlie had intended, but Monica nodded and relaxed in her chair.

Quadra Island was a close-knit community, much like Coffin Cove. Auntie Delia had warned her that some people wouldn't want to talk to her.

Charlie pushed on. "I'd like to talk to anyone who knew Randolph Weber and his son—"

"Did you speak to Sylvie Hamm yet?" Monica inter-rupted. "She's been telling everyone who'll listen that Randolph had an accident. But I don't trust that woman as far as I can spit."

"Sylvie Hamm found Mr Weber, is that right? Was she close to him? I'd like to speak to her while I'm here," Charlie said, hoping it would prompt some good information.

Monica threw back her head and barked out a humour-less laugh. "Sylvie Hamm was at that old goat's cottage at least once a week. The local gossip was she was trying to get him to marry her — you know, a rich older husband, just about to croak." She winked and then her face fell. "Oh, I don't mean any disrespect to poor old Mr Weber. But she definitely knew him well. She didn't pay half as much atten-tion to her other clients."

"How well do you know Sylvie Hamm?" Charlie asked.

Monica looked at Charlie suspiciously. "I don't want to be quoted in your newspaper."

Charlie decided to come clean. "We think . . . that is, my editor and I think the two deaths might be connected. And there's also a missing person who could be connected to the deaths, we don't know."

She fished in her pocket and pulled out her phone. She scrolled through the pictures until she found one of Bob at the New Year's Eve party.

"Have you ever seen this man? Maybe on the ferry?"

Monica took the phone and looked closely. "No, I don't think so. But it doesn't mean he hasn't been on the ferry. I only work three days a week now."

Christie arrived back at the table, and Charlie showed her Bob's photo.

"No, he's never been in here, who is he? You think he has something to do with Randolph Weber's death?"

Charlie shook her head. "No, but he disappeared about the same time. His name is Bob Hinton and he's my editor's father."

"Wow, that is weird," Christie said. "Well, what do you want to know?"

"I want to know all about Randolph Weber and his son. I thought Sylvie Hamm could help me. She was Randolph Weber's health worker, right? And she reported his body?"

Monica nodded. "Sylvie is the only Community Health worker on the island. She's . . ." Monica looked at Christie. "Help me here, what can we say about Sylvie Hamm?"

"You said a minute ago that you thought she was trying to marry Mr Weber?" Charlie prompted them both.

Monica rolled her eyes. "It's just silly gossip. Randolph was devoted to Inga, his wife. Inga died about twenty years ago. But Sylvie is *odd*. She was strange when we were children, really quiet and didn't mix much. She looked after her parents when they both got sick, so I wasn't surprised when she became a health worker, and for years she did a good job — wouldn't you say, Christie?"

The café owner nodded her agreement and then chimed in, "Sylvie was married for a while, and she has a son. Her husband divorced her because she couldn't stop spending. She filled up their house with . . . *stuff.*"

"What kind of stuff?" Charlie asked. "She collected things?"

"Not like normal collections. You know some people collect ball caps or antiques or something? Sylvie collects everything. Magazines, books, old furniture people put beside the road. Her yard is full of the stuff she can't fit in her house. Her husband worked at the oil patch in Alberta, and when he came home one summer, she'd spent all his paychecks on her crap, and none of the bills were paid. So he took all the boxes of stuff to the dump, divorced her and got custody of Cody, their son."

Charlie could think of many old-timers in Coffin Cove who refused to let go of collections of old wheelless cars resting on concrete blocks, or rusting farm equipment gradually devoured by creeping brambles. Even Clara Bell, Katie Dagg's elderly assistant curator, was famous for her trailer surrounded by her "treasures", including a life-sized plastic horse she called Trigger.

Clara had once told her, *If you grow up with nothing, you see the value in everything. Even if it looks like junk.*

Christie continued, "Nobody has been in her house for years. I can't imagine what it's like in there."

Monica said, "People talked about Sylvie, but she was basically harmless, until she started taking things."

"You mean stealing?" Charlie asked. "From her clients?"

"She said it was just misunderstandings. She took a trinket or something from an elder in Heriot Bay. The lady had been Sylvie's client for years and liked her. But a trinket went missing — nothing particularly valuable — and Sylvie swore black was white that the old girl had given it to her and forgotten. But then she stole from my mom."

Monica's face darkened. "Mom had surgery and Dad needed help, and I couldn't be there every day, so Sylvie came in. It went OK, until she got fixated on a little ceramic mug that I made for Mom when I was little. Mom loved it, there was no way she would give it away. Anyway, Sylvie kept looking at it, and saying how pretty it was, and one day it was gone."

"She took it?"

"We don't know. But she was the only person apart from family who had been in the house. Mom was really upset and didn't want to make a fuss, but I made a complaint to Sylvie's supervisor in Campbell River. Nothing happened though. Nobody could prove she stole it."

"Her supervisor didn't do anything?" Charlie asked.

"No — I think because her son Cody stepped in and threatened to report them to the Employment Standards office if they fired her."

Monica sighed. "I don't blame Cody. I'm sure it's been really hard for him. But he must care about his mother, because I see she has a brand-new truck, and I'm sure she couldn't afford it without his help."

Charlie sat quietly for a minute, absorbing the information and wondering if any of it was relevant to her story. A thought struck her.

"You said that Sylvie's been telling people Randolph's death could be an accident? Do you think . . ."

She left her thought hanging there, uncertain how to say what was on her mind, without making a baseless accusation.

"I don't know about that," Christie said, immediately picking up what Charlie meant. "It seems very confused. The police said Randolph disturbed an intruder. I can't believe Sylvie would get violent, especially towards Randolph. She's been visiting him for years."

"An intruder? Out there?" Monica seemed unconvinced. "It's isolated. Someone would have to know the island. My mom lives out there."

She hadn't reacted to Charlie's musing, so Charlie decided to move on. "Your mom lives near Randolph's home? Did she know him well?"

"They were neighbours forever," Monica said. "Poor Mom — first Dad, then Randolph and now Gerald. She'll be so upset."

Charlie hesitated. "I don't want to upset your mom, but if she knew the Weber family well . . ."

Monica pressed her lips together. "If you promise to be respectful and not be sensational or anything like that, then you can speak to Mom, *if* she wants. But I have to be there. I suppose it's better she talk to a reporter who has some connection with us Islanders. Is tomorrow OK? In the morning? I have to work in the afternoon."

"Yes, that would be awesome, thank you," Charlie said, and then quickly added, "I really do appreciate it, and I promise I'll show you the article before we print it."

Monica smiled. "OK, then."

* * *

Charlie was sure Sylvie Hamm's cottage was once an attractive home on a desirable lot, right at the end of a no-thru road near Heriot's Bay.

It was the kind of property investment people would love to get their hands on. If someone was prepared to spend a few thousand dollars to clear the land of the piles of junk partially hidden under tarps, the black garbage bags which spilled out onto what once was the lawn, and to move or burn the old furniture which was heaped in precarious pyramids, then it might be a prime piece of real estate.

It was lucky for Sylvie's neighbours that her house was nestled out of view behind tall firs planted in a row.

Charlie parked her car behind a red truck which stood out like a gleaming beacon in the sea of debris, and then got out.

Charlie stood looking at the truck for a moment. She recalled that Monica had mentioned Sylvie recently acquired a new truck. Why would a son indulge his mother with a new truck, but not really help her face her issues? It didn't make sense. Maybe it was easier to throw money at a problem rather than solve it.

At least she knew Sylvie Hamm was at home. But would she agree to an interview?

Charlie suddenly felt overwhelmed. Maybe she should come back with Andi. She'd never knocked on anyone's door before and asked for an interview, especially someone who'd recently had a traumatic experience. What if her questions upset Sylvie? Monica and Christie had painted Sylvie as someone who was mentally unstable, or at least fragile.

The front door was partially blocked by damp cardboard boxes which had sagged and split open, exposing the contents, which looked to Charlie like art supplies — half-finished oil paints and canvases, now irreparably damaged by the elements.

Charlie looked back at her car, still undecided, when she heard a creaking sound.

"Who are you?" a voice asked.

Charlie, startled, turned back to see Sylvie Hamm standing in the doorway. She had a long, fleshy face with wide blue eyes and a small mouth. Her cheeks were rosy, as if she'd been sitting by the fire. Her expression seemed a little vacant, Charlie thought, as if she were focused on something in the distance, and her voice had a childlike quality.

Sylvie Hamm's most striking feature was her hair. It grew up and out from far back on her forehead, and then it hung down beyond her waist. It was thick, like long strands of steel wool. It was impossible to tell if Sylvie was fat or thin, because she was wearing a strange layer of clothing. A black skirt covered her feet. Charlie could see a shapeless grey tunic, a wool sweater and a long sleeveless cardigan. All the garments looked tired and grimy.

No going back now, Charlie thought.

"Mrs Hamm? My name is Charlene Davis, and I'm a reporter for the *Coffin Cove Gazette*. I was hoping you wouldn't mind answering a few questions about Randolph Weber?"

"Randolph? He's dead." Sylvie spoke in a flat tone.

"Yes, I'm sorry for your loss. I understand he was a long-term client of yours?"

Sylvie didn't reply, but her eyes didn't leave Charlie. After a moment, she nodded. "I don't want to talk to the papers."

She stepped back and started to close the door.

Charlie pushed on. "I'm sorry to tell you that his son, Professor Gerald Weber, also died. In Coffin Cove, two days ago."

Sylvie Hamm stood still. Was there a flicker of interest in her eyes?

"Who will get his house?"

Charlie wasn't certain she'd heard correctly. "I beg your pardon?"

"His house? Gerald was his only child, so who will get his house and his things?" Sylvie asked the question in a calm tone, as if it were a completely reasonable query in light of the bad news.

Charlie shook her head. "I'm sorry, I have no idea."

"Oh." Sylvie continued to stand in the doorway, her face expressionless, but her eyes not leaving Charlie.

"So . . . would it be OK to ask you a few questions about Randolph Weber? And maybe Gerald, if you knew him? The police think the two violent deaths are connected, and maybe you have some information which might help? Maybe we can figure out who gets his house?"

Charlie didn't know what the police were thinking, and she felt a stab of shame at the lie. But Sylvie's eyes widened at her words, and she stepped back from the doorway and gestured for Charlie to follow her.

CHAPTER EIGHTEEN

"Katie, I'm so sorry. It must have been awful."

Andi handed Katie Dagg a mug of coffee and sat down opposite her. She had asked Katie to meet her at Hephzibah's because the police still had the museum taped off as a crime scene. Police cruisers were still parked out front, and crime scene investigators dressed head to toe in protective gear were moving in and out of the Fish Plant building. Even the restaurant was closed.

Katie looked tired and pale.

"Thank you. It was . . . terrible. So much blood. I've never seen anything like it." She looked at Andi, her eyes filled with tears. "I didn't think until now how horrible it must have been for you. When you . . ." She bent her head down.

Andi knew what she meant. It was Katie's mother, Nadine, that she had found outside her old apartment. The horror of discovering her mutilated body had forced Andi to move.

Andi reached out and took Katie's hand. "It will get better, I promise. Look, I know this is a bad time for you, but you know my father has disappeared?" She felt sorry for Katie, but she needed information.

Katie nodded. "Inspector Fowler seemed to think Bob had something to do with it. She called him a 'person of interest'. But your dad had never met Professor Weber before the lecture, had he?"

"No. We think he wanted to talk to him alone, though." Andi told Katie about Randolph Weber.

Katie looked at Andi, her mouth open in shock. "His father? Dead too? Oh my God."

"Yes. So I need you to tell me everything you know about Professor Weber. It might help me find Dad."

Katie rubbed her face with her hand and appeared to pull herself together.

"Well, I didn't spend much time with him. We had a coffee to chat about the lecture. He was tired, he'd come straight from the airport, and he wanted to have a nap before the evening."

"Did he seem anxious or worried about anything?"

"Not at all. He was excited to get back on the lecture circuit. He said his research meant he spent a lot of time alone, and he said he wanted to get out of the Ivory Tower, as he put it." Katie looked at Andi and smiled. "You missed the lecture. He made it fun. The kids love dinosaurs, but even the adults were taking part."

"I wish I had been there instead of the Crazy Crackpots Committee meeting."

The joke made Katie giggle. "Was it that bad?"

"Worse." Andi described the meeting, exaggerating a little to make Katie laugh again. "The pastor was a self-righteous idiot, but Peggy Wilson is all gaga over him. I think the rumour of her husband-hunting is true."

Katie smiled, but she frowned as if trying to remember something. "You know, I met the pastor."

Andi was instantly interested. "Where?"

"Here. I didn't actually meet him then. He was with Peggy Wilson. I think they were handing out flyers for the meeting. He was odd, I thought. He took one look at Professor Weber and me and immediately left."

"That's weird."

"I thought nothing of it until I was in the museum office with Professor Weber. I heard someone walking around and I got up to see who it was, and it was Pastor Michael."

"What was he doing?"

"Nothing really. He was just wandering. I told him we were closed, but it was strange. He must have heard me, but he just ignored me. He looked right through me."

"He did that to me," Andi said. "It was as if he didn't like what I was saying, so he chose not to listen. What did you do?"

"Nothing. He was just looking, so I left him there and went back to my office. But a few minutes later, I noticed him hanging around outside again. The door was open, and it seemed like he was trying to get a glimpse of Professor Weber."

"Did you confront him?"

"I just asked him if he needed help, and then he came right into my office and just stood in the doorway. He looked at Professor Weber and said, 'So this is the famous Dinosaur Professor,' but it was kind of rude, really."

"Did he tell you that 'dinosaur' is the incorrect scientific term? The exhibit is actually a 'plesiosaur'?" Andi used a mocking tone, but Katie stared at her.

"No, he didn't, but that's exactly what Professor Weber and I were discussing. I was worried he would be mad because I'd called the lecture and the exhibit 'Dinosaurs of Vancouver Island' because, technically, the exhibit is not a dinosaur. It's an Elasmosaurus — a plesiosaur, as you say. He was lovely about it, and agreed with me we would get far more kids coming to a 'dinosaur' lecture. It's marketing." She shrugged. "He said it doesn't matter what gets them through the door, it's what they learn when they are here."

Andi told Katie what Pastor Michael had said at the meeting.

"So he must have overheard our conversation and repeated parts of it, but why?"

Andi shook her head. "I have no idea. How did you get him to leave?"

"I just told him we were busy. I had to be blunt. Finally, he walked away, and I locked up the door behind him. It was . . . unsettling."

"How did Professor Weber react?"

"I apologized, and he said not to worry. He came across more and more people who didn't believe science, including religious zealots, but he was quieter after that."

Religious zealots. The words struck a chord.

"Anything else I can tell you?" Katie finished her coffee.

"Was the professor rich? I'm trying to think why someone would want him dead. Money is one of the main motives for murder. Did he earn a lot from his research?"

"God, no. He was definitely against anyone making money from scientific research. You've heard of dinosaur hunters?"

Andi thought for a moment. "You mean like people who go out and dig up dinosaur bones and then sell them?"

Katie nodded. "Yes. Ever heard of the T-Rex called Sue?"

Andi said slowly, "Yeah, I think I've heard about it."

Katie went on. "It was a high-profile clash between scientists who believe these discoveries should be donated to museums and commercial hunters who sell to the highest bidder. There was a long legal battle over Sue's discovery in South Dakota. The owner of the land, the scientists who found her, the federal government — everyone wanted to make money. In the end, the Chicago Museum bought Sue for millions of dollars. Professor Weber helped with the legislation in Canada which prohibits the sale of some prehistoric finds, prompted by that case. He wrote several articles about it."

"So he never profited from it?"

"Not at all. When I was in university, we had an entire semester about the ethics of scientific research. That's when I found out about Professor Weber, after reading his papers."

She looked at Andi sadly. "If I'd never invited him to come to Coffin Cove, he'd be alive right now."

"Katie, stop. The person who's responsible is the person who killed Professor Weber, nobody else," Andi said firmly.

Katie didn't look convinced, but she'd got some colour back.

Andi asked a few more questions, but she didn't feel any further forward by the end of the meeting. But one thing Katie had said kept echoing in her mind.

Religious zealots.

* * *

Jim Peters had left his truck for Andi to use while he was away. She drove it out of town towards the main highway. She passed the small strip mall and trailer park at the edge of Coffin Cove, the newly painted *Thank you for visiting, come back again soon* sign and then crossed the bridge over Coffin Cove River.

Then she took a sharp right onto a gravel track. There was a sign, partially obscured by brambles, which read *The Valley*.

The track descended at a steep incline, and just as the river came into view, Andi braked and swung the truck left so she was travelling upriver towards mountains in the distance.

The torrent of brown water rushed past. In places, the river had burst its bank, and Andi had to slow to a crawl to cross flooded parts of the rutted track.

Andi remembered the first time Jim had brought her to the Valley.

"See those brown patches on the mountainside?" he'd said. "Clear cutting. That's why this valley regularly floods and nobody lives here anymore."

Almost nobody.

Andi passed the decaying Quonset huts and crumbling buildings which used to be the Coffin Cove hatchery.

The track inclined upwards and, in the distance, rising out of the swamp grass, was the black silhouette of a dwelling. Andi couldn't distinguish the outlines, but she knew there were three buildings, not one. As she got nearer, she could see a cross on one building and a thin plume of smoke rising from a chimney.

Fred Harding refused to leave the Valley. In the days before the Valley flooded, the Harding family was part of a thriving farming community. The last time Andi had been here, she'd seen other old farmhouses with sagging roofs and rotting doors. Just three years later, and these buildings had all but slumped into obscurity, the last jagged edges of rooftops virtually hidden by spindly alder trees.

Andi stopped the truck beside the old farmhouse. The place was tidier than she remembered, although the mildew still grew on the outside of the house, evidence of frequent flooding.

As Andi got out of the truck, she saw a child's swing. It belonged to Sarah, Fred Harding's long-dead granddaughter. Andi's probing into the cold case — interference, as Fred had seen it — had resulted in Sarah's killer going to prison.

People working in the justice system liked to talk about closure, Andi thought, but even in those cases where justice was served, closure was just a myth. A murder was like casting a stone into a millpond. Nothing was ever the same after the calm was shattered. The ripples were always there, even if they became less noticeable over time. Fred Harding had never thanked or even acknowledged Andi's work. Why would you thank someone who reopened painful wounds?

"What do ya want?"

Fred Harding had materialized beside her, his bent frame resting on his cane.

"I brought you some diesel," Andi said.

"Why?" the old man demanded, his fierce eyes visible under white bushy eyebrows.

"Jim Peters brings you diesel, but he's away. So I brought it instead."

Fred grunted. "Thought it was Jim's truck. Where'd he go?"

"Vacation."

Fred grunted again. Andi doubted he'd ever left Coffin Cove. She had already decided that directness with Fred Harding was the best strategy.

"But I want something from you," she said, "in return for the diesel."

"What?" he demanded.

"Information."

"About what? I don't know nuthin' about nuthin'," Fred muttered.

Andi walked around to the back of the truck to untie the jerry cans from the truck's bed. "I want to know why you were at the Concerned Citizens Committee for starters," she said.

"None of your business. Maybe I'm *concerned*," Fred sneered.

"Bullshit. You haven't been 'concerned' about Coffin Cove for years. Not since Sarah—"

"You keep her name out of your filthy mouth." He raised his voice. "I can go to any meeting I damn well like!"

"Fred . . ."

"That's Mr Harding to you," he growled.

"Mr Harding. You heard about the murder, didn't you?" He nodded, and Andi went on. "What you don't know is that my father is missing. The police think he's connected with the murder, but I don't. I think something happened to him."

"Nuthin' I can do about that," Fred said, but his voice was lower. "Maybe he's guilty. Guilty men run."

"Guilty men sometimes stay in plain sight. Sometimes guilty men deceive us," Andi said. She hoped a veiled reference to his granddaughter's case might prompt him to say more, but he was silent, so Andi tried again.

"What do you know about Pastor Michael Nelson, Fr . . . I mean Mr Harding? And what did you say to him at the meeting?"

"You fool!" Fred Harding bellowed without warning. Andi backed up, startled by the ferocity in the old man's face. "Fools, every one of them. All around you." He shook his cane at Andi and seemed to straighten a little.

"Mr Harding . . ." Andi began, but Fred Harding ignored her. He seemed to forget she was even there as words tumbled out of his mouth and he raised his face to the sky.

"'And he laid hold on the dragon, that old serpent, which is the Devil, and Satan, and bound him a thousand years, and cast him into the bottomless pit, and shut him up, and set a seal upon him, that he should deceive the nations no more, till the thousand years should be fulfilled: and after that he must be loosed a little season . . .'"

He was preaching, Andi realized, as the old man's voice roared and then fell.

"'. . . And when the thousand years are expired, Satan shall be loosed out of his prison, and shall go out to deceive the nations which are in the four quarters of the earth, Gog, and Magog, to gather them together to battle: the number of whom is as the sand of the sea . . .'"

Andi sighed and reached into the truck and pulled out the jerry cans.

Fred Harding was paying her no attention at all. His frail body shook and his voice cracked with emotion.

"'. . . And the devil that deceived them was cast into the lake of fire and brimstone, where the beast and the false prophet are, and shall be tormented day and night for ever and ever . . .'"

* * *

"Fred Harding was still preaching to his imaginary congregation when I left there," Andi said when she got back to Coffin Cove.

Harry was waiting for her in the Fat Chicken. Andi ordered a soda water.

"So nothing helpful?"

"No, he kept spouting Bible verses about the devil walking among us and something about being cast into fire and brimstone."

"Sounds like Fred. I bet he kept the diesel, though." Harry grinned.

"Yep. Doesn't mind gifts from sinners, I suppose."

"What about Katie?"

"She's really shaken up, which is not surprising. And she's beating herself up for even inviting the professor. She says she saw Dad talking to Professor Weber after the lecture. They were standing outside the museum. She locked up, and they were still talking when she walked to her car. She says she couldn't hear anything, no loud voices and definitely no waving arms or anything. She told the police as part of her statement, but it couldn't be construed as a 'tip'. So, still more questions."

"She's sure the door was locked when she left?"

Andi nodded. "She's certain. She remembers seeing Professor Weber outside. She turned back to lock the inner door and then the outer door, and then waving a hand at the professor and Dad before walking to her car."

"Whoever killed the professor must have picked the locks. Katie didn't say there was any damage to the doors?"

"No. She says everything looked fine when she got to work in the morning, except for the unlocked doors and blood smears and, of course, the dead guy in the museum," Andi said grimly.

"Any word about his father?"

"No. I'm expecting Charlie to call. But she might not have got much yet. It will take a while. How did you get on this afternoon?"

Harry shrugged. "Not much. Ike caught sight of the owner, but by the time he got out of his office, the guy had disappeared again. I looked at the boat. It's in crappy shape, and the owner's name is Captain Ron."

"Captain Ron? How do you know?"

"Because it's painted on the side of the boat."

"That's hardcore investigative work," Andi commented.

"Yep, and that's not all. Captain Ron runs a salvage company."

"Also painted on the side of the boat?"

"Yup." Harry raised his beer glass in a toast. "Now, who do I talk to about a raise?"

Andi laughed and finished her soda water. "Nice try."

Harry put his empty beer glass on the bar. "You heading up to your dad's place?" He got off the bar stool and squeezed her shoulder.

Andi nodded and then looked up at Harry. "You know, you could stay over."

He leaned over and kissed her. "No. You need your space. Besides, there's probably some *Gazette* rule about not sleeping with the boss." His voice was gentle, and he smiled. "You can fire me when this is all over and Bob is safely back at home."

"I'll definitely do that."

CHAPTER NINETEEN

Charlie was feeling claustrophobic and nauseous.

Sylvie had led the way through walls of cardboard boxes, plastic totes and piles of paper and clothing. There was barely room for Sylvie to squeeze past, and she had to turn sideways to avoid toppling the piled clutter.

If it fell over, Charlie thought, *Sylvie could lie buried for days, unable to move.*

The stench was overpowering. Charlie fought the urge to cover her nose and mouth with her jacket. There must be dead rodents among the mountains of junk. Maybe a dead cat or dog.

It was impossible to tell how many rooms were in the small house, as all the doorways were obscured. The only way to navigate through was to follow the narrow trail in the gloom.

Eventually, space opened up and there was a table and a couch visible.

Sylvie nodded at the couch and Charlie sat down. The space was lit only by a bulb hanging from the ceiling, and it took a moment for Charlie's eyes to adjust.

Sylvie had her back to Charlie and seemed to be clearing something off the table. Charlie watched her as she dug into an open box. Her movements were furtive, and Charlie wondered what Sylvie didn't want her to see.

Charlie cleared her throat and tried not to breathe too deeply.

Sylvie swung round. "You want some tea?"

"Er . . . no thanks," Charlie said. She hadn't seen a kitchen, but if there was one, she didn't want to drink or eat anything that came out of it.

"How did Gerald die?" Sylvie asked suddenly.

"I'm afraid he was murdered," Charlie said gently, not sure how this strange woman would react.

"He never visited," Sylvie said. "I visited Randolph every single week. He liked me."

"You knew him well? What was he like?" Charlie asked, quick to jump on an opening in the conversation.

Sylvie nodded. She was still standing, and it was making Charlie uneasy.

"He liked me," she repeated.

Charlie felt sweat building on the back of her neck. This had been a mistake.

"You know what?" she said brightly. "I'd love a glass of water."

Sylvie stared at her and then nodded. She eased her body around a stack of magazines, which reached nearly to the ceiling and disappeared out of sight.

Charlie got up and walked over to the table. Sylvie had been keen to keep something out of view. What was it? She'd have a quick look, and when Sylvie came back, she'd make her excuses and leave.

Beside the table was a shoebox full of cigarette lighters, the shiny Zippo kind. Charlie moved them around and found a small polished wooden box. This must be what Sylvie was hiding.

Charlie picked it up and opened it. Inside were two gold bands nestled in red velvet. One was large and plain, the other smaller with what looked like inlaid diamonds. Wedding rings. Charlie gently pulled the bigger one out.

On the inside of the band were two engraved intertwined letters.

R&I.

The other one was the same. *R&I.* Randolph and Inga?

Charlie didn't hear the whoosh behind her. She was so intent on examining the rings, she didn't see the shadow behind her either until it was too late. When the blow came, it was completely unexpected and Charlie's legs buckled. She was momentarily paralyzed from the pain in her head. As she collapsed on the floor, she moaned.

"That's mine," she heard Sylvie say from a long way off. Charlie's fingers uncurled from the ring she was holding, and she didn't resist when she felt Sylvie grab it.

"Sylvie . . ." she said weakly and tried to sit up. The blow from Sylvie's foot to her stomach expelled all the air from Charlie's lungs, and she fought for breath. Her vision went with a kick to the side of her head, but cleared momentarily as Sylvie Hamm's blurry face came into focus. The last thought Charlie had before she blacked out was that Sylvie looked terrified.

CHAPTER TWENTY

January 9

Andi woke to a bleeping sound and a light flashing in the darkness. She patted around on the bedcovers and found her phone. It told her it was six thirty. She still hung on to the hope she'd see her father's number, but no. Worry overtook her momentarily. Bob had been officially missing for over 72 hours.

Banishing the thought from her head, Andi opened the message, which said in true Harry style:

Morning, Boss. Hep and Ruth need help. Coffee in half an hour?

That was enough to get Andi out of bed. What help did Ruth and Hephzibah need? She hoped it wasn't anything to do with the Concerned Citizens of Coffin Cove. She remembered the ugly comments made by the man at the meeting. These self-righteous idiots were now blaming the "lack of morality" for Professor Weber's murder. Damn, she'd been so caught up in the murder and Bob's disappearance, she'd completely forgotten about Hephzibah. And then she'd wallowed in self-pity and wine. Andi stood up and stretched. It was nice to be warm and have a little space, although she missed Harry's body next to her. She must have slept well, because her head was clear and she felt refreshed. Harry was right about one thing: drinking herself into a stupor never helped. If she was going to find her father, she needed to hold herself together and focus on her work.

She'd been unfair to Harry. He didn't deserve to bear the brunt of her frustration or her hangovers, not that she intended to have another one anytime soon.

Andi glanced at the pile of clothes she'd left in a heap at the side of the bed. She would have to get a change of clothes from the boat, but in the meantime, she had time for a shower.

She picked up her jeans and gave them a good shake. Her socks fell out and one rolled under the bed. Andi crouched down and felt around and found the sock, but her fingers found the smooth surface of what felt like a book.

Andi pulled it out. It wasn't a book, but a pad of paper — one of the legal pads her father favoured for taking notes and drafting articles in longhand.

Across the front, in her father's handwriting, was one word with eleven numbers underneath.

Walrus
54-11-410-7985.

Walrus? Someone's name? Was that a telephone number? It looked like an overseas number. Her father had many contacts and friends abroad, and preferred phoning rather than sending emails, so that was likely. Was it significant? Could her father have left the country? Andi had no idea. It was probably nothing, just her father contacting an old friend, but she folded it up and slid it into her pocket. She'd do some digging later. She glanced at her phone. Time to get going. Harry would be waiting.

Hephzibah was pouring a mug of freshly brewed coffee for Andi as she walked through the door. Harry was already sitting with Ruth in the easy chairs at the other end of the café. Both of them looked up as Andi came in. Andi had always found it hard to read Ruth, because she rarely had her emotions on display, but this morning, her mouth was a tight line, and her dark eyes were hard.

Harry was leaning forward, his hands clenched, and anger emanated from him like an electric current.

"What's going on, Hep?" Andi took the mug in one hand and gratefully received a warm morning glory muffin in the other.

"Come and sit down. We'll tell you all about it." Hephzibah touched Andi's arm and lowered her voice. "Why weren't you with Harry last night? Is everything all right?"

Andi heard the anxious tone in her friend's voice.

"Everything is fine. I stayed at my dad's place last night. I just need a little space at the moment. Harry understands. All is well, I promise."

Andi settled herself in a chair and looked around. "What's the story?" she asked, and took a bite of her muffin.

"I should have told you or Harry immediately, but I thought it was best to ignore . . ." Hephzibah started, but Ruth put her hand out and took Hephzibah's hand.

"There's no blame here," she said softly. "But we can't ignore this. Especially with everything that's been going on."

"Ignore what?" Andi asked.

"Hephzibah received a note," Harry said, and handed Andi a piece of paper.

"And then I received one," Ruth said.

Andi read the words, written in simple letters.

Leviticus 18:23 Do not have sexual relations with a SAVAGE and defile yourself with it. A woman must not present herself to a SAVAGE to have sexual relations with it; that is a perversion.

Leviticus 20:13 If a woman has sexual relations with a woman, both of them have done what is detestable. They are to be put to death; their blood will be on their own heads.

Andi immediately dropped the piece of paper on her lap.

"This has to go to the police," she said. "We can't touch this anymore."

"It's all right," Ruth said. "I made a photocopy, and the original is in here." She held up a Ziploc bag. "My note says exactly the same, and it's in here too. I was the only one who touched it. I'm taking them both to the detachment afterwards. We just wanted you to know."

Andi sat back in her chair. She felt like the breath had been knocked out of her.

"I don't want to say it, but the last part is almost certainly a death threat."

Hephzibah put a hand to her mouth and looked as if she were about to cry, and Andi wished she could take back her words. "I'm sorry, Hep. I'm sure this isn't serious, it's just a cowardly act by a bigoted asshole who wants to scare you. But it's against the law to send hate mail. And this is definitely hate mail. I'm so sorry."

"When I find who sent this filth, they won't be writing anything for a long time," Harry growled.

"Oh Harry, it's best left to the police." Hephzibah composed herself. "I wish I'd said something earlier. It's just, I didn't want to worry Ruth . . . and . . ."

"When exactly did you get it?" Andi asked.

"It was on a table with a bunch of flyers. I found it when I was clearing up."

"So someone left it while you were here?"

Hephzibah nodded. "But I was busy and lots of people could go in and out without me noticing."

"When did you get your note?" Andi asked Ruth.

"At work when I was at a meeting. It was on my desk."

"Didn't the receptionist see who dropped it off?"

Ruth shook her head. "No. Anyone could have walked in. They would have to find my office, but there aren't many staff at work at the moment, so anyone could wander around."

Andi said, "The person who wrote this knows Bible scripture. Does it narrow it down?"

In her mind, she saw Fred Harding spouting scripture verses the day before. But then she thought of the angry young man who'd insulted Hephzibah early in the meeting.

Ruth shrugged. "Maybe. But if you look, you can literally find a verse in the Bible that supports any point of view. They're not just attacking our relationship. The word 'savage' is directed at me. They even wrote it in capital letters."

Ruth's tone was matter-of-fact, but her eyes remained like polished granite. She continued, "There is one thing that could be a coincidence. Someone called me a savage just recently."

Hephzibah's head shot up. "Who? When?"

"New Year's Eve at the restaurant. You remember the server? The one who spilled wine on me?"

"Yes. I thought she said something to you," Andi said. "She called you a savage?"

"She said something in Spanish, and I didn't understand it. When I saw this note, I looked it up. She said to me, 'I'm so sorry, *bárbara*.' It sounded a little sarcastic, but she seemed genuinely sorry, so I thought I was being overly sensitive. But the word *bárbara* means 'savage', or literally, 'barbarian'."

"What conceivable motive would she have to write a note like this?" Andi said, her mind racing.

"Racist bigots don't need a motive. It's what they do," Ruth said simply.

"Let's have a chat with her," Harry said.

"Not you," Andi said. "You're too angry. Let me go. I'll get more out of her. I'll tell her I'm writing profiles of newcomers to Coffin Cove or something."

"What do we do now?" Hephzibah asked.

"Give the original to Matt Beaufort. He might get fingerprints. Then I'll write a report in the *Gazette*. At least the person who did this will know it's under investigation. And I'll mention it to Juanita when I interview her."

"Are we sure we want to do that?" Hephzibah looked anxiously at Ruth. "It will bring so much attention to us."

Ruth leaned forward and spoke deliberately. "I'm tired of turning the other cheek, Hephzibah. I'm ready for 'an eye for an eye'."

* * *

When Ruth had left and Hephzibah was busy with a customer, Andi and Harry sat together.

"You look rested," Harry said. "Good sleep?" His voice was gentle.

"Yes." Andi sighed. "I've been thinking about what you said about . . . my drinking. It's a . . . a habit I need to break." She stumbled over her words. Her father had been a heavy drinker in the past and there were still times he overdid it. She wondered briefly if that had anything to do with his disappearance, and then dismissed that thought.

Harry leaned over and kissed her. "You know what Hep and I went through with my dad, Andi. If you're one of those people who can't stop, it's a slippery slope. And there are never any answers at the bottom of the wine bottle."

Andi nodded. "I know. I need answers, Harry. For everything: Dad, Professor Weber and his father, all the crap with the Concerned Citizens, and now Ruth and Hephzibah."

Andi shared her thoughts about the notes.

"I thought about Fred when I read that note. He's the only person I know who quotes the Bible. Plus, he's all 'Old Testament', so he probably isn't at all open-minded about same-sex relationships."

Harry shook his head. "Fred would come into the café and rant at Hephzibah. He wouldn't write a note. Someone was deliberately trying to scare them."

"That's why it's important to get it out in the open." Andi checked her phone. "I need to write this article today if I'm going to meet the deadline for the next edition."

She folded the photocopied note and opened her bag.

"Oh, I nearly forgot," she said, pulling out the note-pad she'd found that morning. "What do you think this is?" She handed the pad to Harry and told him where she'd found it.

"Your dad's handwriting?"

She nodded. "Yes. The numbers could be a phone number. Not sure what 'walrus' means."

Harry shrugged. "Sorry, it means nothing to me. One way to find out, though. Dial the number, see who you get."

"I will." Andi checked her phone again. "Talking about phone calls, I haven't heard from Charlie yet. Maybe I should call her."

"Give Charlie a little room," Harry said. "She'll get back to you when she's got something interesting."

CHAPTER TWENTY-ONE

Beth Stanton was awake before her alarm sounded. She had a full day ahead of her.

The previous evening she'd studied Sergeant Vaughan's case notes. At first, she'd been inclined to agree with him. Randolph Weber struggled with his mobility, which was to be expected at his age, and he was very frail. There was little evidence that anyone had been in the house apart from Randolph, no sign of a struggle, and all the fingerprints had been identified.

But there was something odd about Sylvie Hamm's statement. She told Vaughan her schedule was to visit Randolph Weber every Tuesday. So why had she left her visit to Friday? Especially after the long holiday weekend. Sylvie was also adamant that nothing was missing in the house. But how would she know? Did Randolph have valuables hidden away?

Beth noted that Sylvie Hamm's supervisor, Juliette Parsons, worked at the Community Health office in Campbell River. She would visit Juliette before she went to Quadra Island. There was a tickle at the back of her mind. She wanted to know everything about Sylvie Hamm before she interviewed the lady herself.

Juliette Parsons was a small mousey woman, dressed in a grey suit with sensible black shoes. Her grip was firm, and she looked Beth directly in the eye when she introduced herself. Beth got the impression that Juliette was a practical, down-to-earth woman, and likely to do things by the book.

Her first impression of Juliette Parsons was correct. Juliette was polite and invited Beth to her office, but was reluctant to share any information.

"I can't give out confidential information about our clients without the proper legal work," Juliette said, after gesturing for Beth to take a seat in her cramped office. "So I'm not sure if I can be of any help." She smiled at Beth.

Beth frowned. "Mr Randolph Weber is dead."

Juliette continued to smile.

Beth tried another angle. "I believe Mr Weber was due to go into a nursing home, because of his mobility issues. It was public knowledge, his neighbours and Sylvie Hamm confirmed it, so I'm wondering why he wasn't moved sooner? He could hardly walk, I understand?"

The implication was clear, and Juliette's face became hard. "I can't give out information from our files. As a general observation, I can tell you that moving elderly people from their homes can be a traumatic event in their lives. We do everything possible to make sure our elders are ready. Sylvie would have worked closely with Mr Weber for many months before the move."

"Sylvie has been Mr Weber's Community Health worker for some years?"

Juliette nodded. "That's correct."

Was it Beth's imagination, or did Juliette just get defensive?

"I'm wondering, how often would a Community Health worker visit their elderly clients? Is there a set schedule?"

"Most of our workers in the field set their own schedules. Each client has different needs. But once or twice a week would be normal."

"And given that Mr Weber could hardly walk, it makes sense that Sylvie would be there regularly, correct?"

Juliette had ceased to smile. "You would have to check Sylvie's schedule."

"I did. Sylvie found Mr Weber on the fifth of January. Her statement says it was the first visit of the new year. It seems a long time between visits, doesn't it? Especially as it's winter and Mr Weber was on his own."

"We can't be in our clients' homes twenty-four seven, Sergeant Stanton. And Sylvie Hamm was here on the fourth of January for her quarterly appraisal."

"Would you say Sylvie Hamm is good at her job? She cares for her clients?"

"She's worked for Community Health for many years, Sergeant," Juliette said, but Beth noticed the caution in her voice and the way she evaded the question.

"You've known her a long time?" Beth pressed.

Juliette sighed. "No, Sergeant, I haven't. I'm new here. I've only been Sylvie's supervisor for a few months."

"How often have you been out to Quadra Island?"

Juliette Parsons flushed. "I'm due to go out on the eighteenth."

"So you've met none of Sylvie's clients?"

Juliette shook her head, still red-faced. "Look, Sergeant, it's very busy around here. I have—"

Beth held up a hand. "I'm sorry if these questions are inconvenient. But an elderly man, your client, was murdered or had a terrible accident under your watch. I would have thought you would want to cooperate in any way you can."

"I don't see—"

Beth ignored her. "Have you had any complaints about Sylvie Hamm?"

Juliette sat and looked at her hands, which fidgeted in her lap. Beth waited. Finally, Juliette raised her head. "There have been several complaints about Sylvie recently. From clients. She doesn't answer their calls, and she said she'd lost her cell phone. And . . ."

"And . . . ?" Beth prompted.

"There was a complaint made a while back, that Sylvie had stolen an ornament from a client. She claims it was a mistake. Apart from that, Sylvie is a little . . . eccentric. She can be volatile. That's why I have an appointment booked to visit her. I don't usually do that. But there was a phone call yesterday . . ." Juliette hesitated.

"A phone call? From a client?"

"No. It was from a truck dealership. A salesman was following up on a loan agreement Sylvie just signed. He wanted to verify her employment. It's just . . . well, I thought it was odd because Sylvie doesn't earn much. It's really none of my business, but Sylvie had given incorrect information for her loan." Juliette looked back at her hands.

"Incorrect how?"

"Wrong address, and she'd lied about her salary," Juliette said quietly. "I think that's fraud, isn't it, Sergeant?"

* * *

Wiltshire Trucks was next to the Ideal Café.

Beth looked longingly at the small establishment, imagining how good their breakfast menu would be, but she was running out of time before she had to catch the ferry to Quadra Island.

The dealership wasn't open, but Beth could see a man sitting at a desk at the edge of the showroom. He was peering at a computer screen.

Beth rapped on the glass door. The man lifted his head and pointed at the *Closed* sign in the window. Beth fished in her purse for her identification and held it up for the man to see.

His head dropped as if in resignation, and he got up from the desk and walked over to open the door.

"Can I help you?"

The man was little more than a boy, Beth decided. He was lanky and wore an ill-fitting suit. The jacket was too short in the arms and it exposed his thin wrists. He had dark hair which fell over his eyes and hid most of his pale face. When he brushed his hair back in a nervous gesture, she could see black smudges under his eyes.

She smiled at him. "I'm Sergeant Beth Stanton. I'd like to ask you a few questions about a recent transaction. Do you have a few minutes?"

He nodded, but looked uncertain. "Do you want to come in?"

"Yes," Beth said firmly, still smiling, but she stepped forward before he could answer. He automatically stepped back.

As she got close to him, she smelled something acidic and noticed a yellow stain on his shoulder. A glance at his left hand and she confirmed to herself that he was probably newly married with a baby.

"Let's sit, shall we?" Beth took the lead and walked over to his desk. There was a chair which he presumably used for customers, so she sat down and waited for him to take his seat.

"What's your name?"

"Gord. Gord Wiltshire," he said, the last part of his name coming out as a heavy sigh.

"Oh? As in Wiltshire Trucks?" Beth asked brightly.

"My dad," he said without enthusiasm.

Beth got to the point. "I'm here about a sale you made to a Sylvie Hamm. A few days ago, in fact."

His face fell, and he brushed his hair back. "Oh God, has she smashed it up?"

"No, but why do you say that?"

Gord Wiltshire rubbed his face. Another nervous gesture. He also looked at the door as if he were expecting someone.

"She, er . . . she seemed a bit . . . flaky."

"And yet you sold her a fifty-thousand-dollar truck?"

Panic slid across his face. "I shouldn't have sold it to her. She wasn't really qualified, but I needed the commission badly. My dad only pays commission, and it's shitty, and I have a new baby." He looked as though he might cry.

Beth felt sorry for him. "You phoned Sylvie Hamm's supervisor, right?"

He nodded. "Yeah. She told me what her real salary is. She lied about that." He stopped and looked at Beth. "Is that why you're here? Because she lied on her loan application?"

Beth took a deep breath. She really shouldn't be asking any of these questions. She couldn't imagine what Inspector Fowler would say if she found out.

"No. My investigation is about something else, but Sylvie's name came up. Look, if it makes you feel any better, it wasn't your fault that she lied on the application form. You didn't do anything wrong."

"Tell that to my dad," he muttered. "What do you want from me, anyway?"

It was a good question. Beth was aware she was on a fishing expedition, and worse than that, working on her intuition. She could almost hear Fowler's rebuke in her mind.

"Would you mind if I had a look at the file?" she asked.

Gord Wiltshire looked at her, a faint cloud of suspicion in his eyes. "Does my dad have to know?"

Beth shook her head. "No. He won't find out anything from me."

Gord's shoulders slumped. "He'll find out sometime," he said gloomily.

Beth held her breath. Then Gord stood up. "I'll make you a copy of that file."

CHAPTER TWENTY-TWO

A foghorn sounded and the loud blast wrenched Beth from her thoughts, which were focused on the mysterious Sylvie Hamm. The ferry shuddered as it docked, and Beth joined the line-up of foot passengers waiting to disembark.

It wasn't raining, but Beth's hair was dripping from the clinging fog in just the short walk to the ferry terminal parking lot.

"Sergeant Stanton?" An RCMP officer was waiting for her, standing beside a marked cruiser parked in front of a café.

"Hello, yes, that's me. You must be . . . ?" Beth had completely forgotten the name Vaughan had given her that morning.

"Constable Sorensen, ma'am," the young man said, a little self-consciously, as he held the cruiser door open for her.

"It's Beth, Constable, if you're OK with first names."

"Suits me, ma'am . . . I mean Beth. I'm Peter." He grinned at her and seemed to relax.

"Great. Now, Sergeant Vaughan tells me you're up to speed and you can show me around?" The cruiser windows were steaming up. Beth would have loved a coffee but wanted to get going.

"I was first on the scene after the call came in," Peter said. "It was awful."

"Your first?" Beth asked, remembering her first homicide when she was a rookie, in Whitehorse, up in the Yukon.

He nodded. "There was so much blood. And the smell . . ."

"Yes. I know. Well, the best we can do for the victim is find out the truth."

"Yes, ma'am. Oh, I got you a coffee." He gestured to one of two travel mugs wedged between them. "I didn't know if you took cream or anything."

"Bless you." Beth smiled. "Black is good."

Constable Peter Sorensen turned onto the only road leading from the ferry terminal. He explained it was a twenty-minute drive to the victim's cabin on the west side of Quadra Island.

"How many at the detachment here?" Beth asked.

"Four of us. But we cover Cortes Island, Read Island and Maurelle Island."

"Busy?"

"Hardly any homicides, if that's what you mean." He gave a nervous laugh. "It's busy in the summer. Drunk tourists mainly. In the winter it's quiet. The odd domestic. Petty theft."

"And Mr Weber, was he well-known in the community?" Beth wanted to know as much as possible about the victim.

"Everyone knew who he was. I mean, he's one of the oldest residents and lived here for over sixty years. But for the last few years we've hardly seen him out, except for a talk he did for the Historical Society last year. He was sharp as a tack, but I think Sylvie Hamm had persuaded him to go into a home in Campbell River. Not sure if this end was better for the old guy."

"Did you know him? Personally, I mean?"

Peter shook his head. "I met him at the talk. But we only exchanged a few words. It was just before his hundredth birthday, but he was really interesting. He was one of the engineers who worked on Ripple Rock."

"Ripple Rock?"

"You've never heard of Ripple Rock?"

Beth shook her head.

"The Ripple Rock explosion was the largest controlled explosion in Canadian history. Ripple Rock was an underwater rock formation — more like an underwater mountain really, with two peaks, and it caused some treacherous currents in Seymour Narrows, just north of Campbell River. Lots of fishermen lost their lives trying to navigate the currents. So the government blew it up."

"To save the fishermen?"

"More like clear the passage to make trade easier," Peter said with a smile. "But the explosion took chunks out of the rock and made the waters safer for everyone."

"How on earth did they do it?"

"That's what Randolph Weber's talk was about. He was one of the senior engineers. They drilled down into the rocks and made dozens of little tunnels like rabbit warrens. They filled them with explosives and then boom!"

"Amazing."

"Yes. It took three years, from 1955 to 1958. Quite the feat of engineering."

"Did Randolph come to Quadra Island because of Ripple Rock?"

"I don't know. His neighbour would know more about his history. Mrs Drummond her name is."

Beth dug into her bag and pulled out her notes.

"What about the community worker who found the body? Sylvie Hamm?"

Constable Sorensen pulled a face. "Sylvie Hamm is . . . odd," he said slowly, as if carefully choosing his words. "She's been the Community Health worker on Quadra for years. But she's definitely eccentric."

"She says that nothing was taken from the house, and from the interview notes, was adamant that Mr Weber had an accident. How would she know nothing had been taken?"

"She visited Randolph every week, sometimes more. There was gossip she was trying to get into his will."

Beth turned to look at him. "Is that possible?"

The young constable shook his head. "It's only island gossip."

He slowed the cruiser. "If we take that road, we can stop at her place if you'd like to talk to her first?"

Beth nodded. "Let's do that." She had questions for the mysterious Sylvie Hamm.

* * *

Charlie opened her eyes and a searing pain stabbed in her forehead, so she closed her eyes again. Her mouth and lips were dry, and her senses seemed jumbled. Could she hear voices? It took a moment for her to unscramble her thoughts and remember what had happened. It came back to her in flashes. The blow to the back of her head. Sylvie kicking her in the stomach.

She had a vague memory of being dragged by her arm, and then Sylvie wrenching something from her hand. "They're mine," she'd said.

The little box with the rings in it.

A rush of fear cleared Charlie's mind. If Sylvie had Randolph and Inga's wedding rings, did that mean she killed Randolph? A blow to the head, like the one she delivered to Charlie, would have killed an elderly man instantly. And what would she do with Charlie?

After a moment, Charlie forced her eyes open and tried to ignore the pain. She was lying on stained carpet. She looked up, and towering above her were more of Sylvie Hamm's boxes. Her body was jammed between them and a door.

She gingerly moved her arm and gasped as her shoulder refused to cooperate at first. She tried again and managed to push herself into a sitting position. Then realized she was still clutching something in her hand. It was a cigarette lighter. She dropped it on the floor and then tried to quell her rising panic.

She took a breath to calm herself. And then she pushed one leg under her body and reached out with her good arm to steady herself. The other leg was next, and even though her vision blurred and her head throbbed with pain, she was standing.

The first thing she did was feel in all her pockets for her cell phone. Damn it, she'd left it in the car. Then she tried to open the door. It didn't feel like it was locked, and the handle turned, but when Charlie tried to push it, it was jammed shut. She imagined Sylvie must have piled boxes or furniture on the other side.

Now Charlie was upright, and her eyes had adjusted to the gloom. She could see grey light filtering through gaps between the boxes and piles of debris.

It had been late afternoon when she'd arrived at Sylvie's, and it was getting dark. If it was light outside now, then she'd been here a whole night. As if to confirm, her stomach rumbled. She hadn't eaten since her sandwich at the café with Monica and Christie.

A thought struck her. Auntie Delia would have missed her! And she had a meeting arranged with Monica and her mother that morning, and she'd promised to call Andi. Charlie felt better. It wouldn't take them long to figure out where she was.

At that moment, she heard a vehicle approaching the house. It was muffled, but she was certain she heard two car doors slam. A moment later and she heard banging at the front door. Whoever it was must have seen her car. Charlie couldn't hear Sylvie moving. Surely she'd have to open the door?

Then Charlie heard voices. Still, she didn't hear Sylvie open the front door. There was silence. Why didn't they break in? In desperation, Charlie began thumping at the door. Her voice was hoarse and reedy, but she shouted as loud as she could.

"Help! Help me!"

Nothing. Then she heard the vehicle's engine start and then fade away.

"Be quiet!"

Charlie tensed. "Sylvie, you must let me out. Those people are looking for me. They will come back, and you'll be in trouble. But if you let me out now, it will be OK, I promise."

Charlie couldn't help it; tears were coming, and her voice cracked. "Sylvie, please. I won't tell anyone about the rings."

She could hear breathing. Sylvie must be just outside, but the woman didn't answer.

"Sylvie, please. You can't keep me here,"

Charlie heard shuffling outside, and she hoped Sylvie was moving boxes. But then the noise stopped, and Sylvie said two words.

"They're mine."

* * *

"I'm certain she was in there," Beth said. "We can't call her cell phone. She's lost it."

They were on their way to Randolph Weber's house and the crime scene.

Peter Sorensen nodded. "It's been a long time since I've been out here. It's got worse. That truck is new, though."

"Stands out, doesn't it? That junker behind it looks more at home here than the truck. And the other car looked in fairly good shape. Why would one person need three vehicles? They were all insured."

Beth thought of her chat with Gord Wiltshire. She would definitely ask Sylvie Hamm how she was financing her truck purchase.

Sorensen said suddenly, "I could phone Cody, her son. I went to school with him. Maybe she has a landline still? I could ask him to call and say we're doing a wellness check."

"Good idea. Do it," Beth said.

The constable slowed the truck.

"This is it."

"It's isolated," Beth said, "especially for an elderly person living on their own."

The constable had turned onto a gravel track. Branches brushed the cruiser as the vehicle bounced over potholes, partially filled with ice.

When the cruiser stopped, Beth was looking at a wooden cabin with a wrap-around deck which reminded her of TV shows she watched when she was little, like *Little House on the Prairie*, or *The Waltons*.

The exterior wood was faded and paint was peeling off the window frames, but overall, the structure looked well maintained. To the left was a lean-to half-stacked with wood. A carpet of soaked sawdust lay around a stump with an axe leaning against it. There were mounds of snow piled against each structure, sheltered from the rain by the trees which surrounded the clearing except for a trail opening up to the right.

When Beth got out of the cruiser, she could hear waves crashing on the shore.

"Let's get on with it, then," Beth said briskly. She reached back into the cruiser and grabbed the file. Peter Sorensen hadn't moved. Beth was getting the impression that he didn't want to go inside. She couldn't blame him.

The only clue to the ugliness of recent events was the yellow police tape across the door. The constable produced a key and unlocked the door.

"After you," he said with a quiver in his voice. "I'll make that call to Cody."

Beth had been right. Constable Sorensen didn't want to relive that day. She left him outside to make his call.

The first thing Beth noticed was the smell. It was metallic, mingled with cleaning chemicals. After the coroner and forensics team had done their job, the body had been removed. Then a hazmat team had been called to clean up. They were good, Beth thought as she surveyed the floor where Randolph Weber's corpse had lain for several days, but it would take days of airing out this cabin before the stench of death would recede.

Beth didn't expect to find anything significant. The officers before her were professionals. But now it was Beth's job to look at the circumstances of the death with fresh eyes.

The living room was small, but Beth could see it had been cosy and welcoming. Bookcases lined the walls beside the fireplace. Assorted rocks and knick-knacks were arranged on a coffee table and along the mantel. There were old sepia photographs of family groups and several of a handsome woman whom Beth assumed was Mrs Weber. From her notes, Beth knew Inga Weber had died of cancer some twenty years ago.

There were pictures of Randolph Weber's son too, the now deceased Professor Gerald Weber. He was a thin child with large eyes looking at the camera with a sorrowful expression, Beth thought. Pictures of a graduation and one of Randolph and Gerald showed a much more robust young man, although he stood almost a foot shorter than his father. In these pictures, the son was smiling. There was one with Inga Weber. This time, Gerald was older and Inga was leaning on a walking stick. *It must have been the start of her illness*, Beth thought. There was a large window on the right side, and now Beth could see the ocean through the trees.

Beth wandered into the kitchen. It was old-fashioned with a mustard-coloured stove and matching fridge. Another window looked out at the same beach view from the kitchen sink. There was a mudroom off to one side with a modern stack washer and dryer in one corner.

This must have been the door that Randolph used most, Beth thought as she looked at the collection of outdoor coats hanging beside a door. There were rows of footwear under the coats — work boots, gumboots and a pair of dress shoes. No slippers, but he may have been wearing those when he died. Beth made a mental note to check the photographs.

She opened the door and saw a gravel pathway leading to the woodshed. There was a neat stack of wood and kindling just outside the door under a tarp.

Beth closed the door. Something was bothering her, though she couldn't decide what it was. She went back to the front door and found Constable Sorensen standing inside.

"Did Randolph chop his own wood?" she asked.

Peter Sorensen shook his head. "No. John Simpson delivered a load of wood in October, and he came out before Christmas to chop and stack some for Randolph. He said the old man was having trouble even walking to the woodshed and was very upset about it. Apparently, Randolph said it was time he went into a home if he couldn't look after himself. John said it was the first time he'd ever heard Randolph talking like that, but figured he was probably right. It was time he had someone to look after him."

Beth went back to the mudroom, pulled out her phone and took a picture of the small stack of wood outside the door, and then the assorted shoes and coats. She didn't know what she was missing, but maybe if she had a visual image, it might prompt something later.

Beth walked back through the kitchen and the living room and took a picture of each of the family photographs. There was something on the edge of her mind, just out of reach.

"Did you reach Cody?" she asked.

"Yes. He said he'd call his mother and get back to me," the constable answered. He hadn't moved from the front door.

Beth opened the file she was carrying. She wondered if it was possible Randolph had fallen. She should consider all the possibilities.

Beth leafed through the file until she found the photograph of Randolph Weber lying dead on the floor. She went up the stairs halfway and turned around. She walked down, checking each step. They were wooden, polished to a high gloss. Randolph may have been wearing his slippers, but still it was plausible that the old man had lost his footing. But where would he have hit his head? And how would he have ended up face down, with half his body in the living room?

She closed her eyes to imagine what might have happened. If he had been attacked, it must have been in the kitchen or at the foot of the stairs. The blow to the head could have spun him around and the force would have propelled the body backwards.

Beth agreed with the coroner. It was hard to conclude his death had resulted from an accidental fall.

"OK, I don't think there's anything else to see here," Beth said, as she closed her file. "Oh wait. What's this?"

She pulled out a photograph of a coffee table. Beth looked around the room and located it beside the fireplace. At first, she didn't know why the photograph was included in the file, but when she looked closer, she saw there was a distinct dust-free patch. A perfect square, as if a box or other object had been removed recently.

When Beth examined the table, she saw that someone had cleaned off the dust, probably the hazmat team sent in when the forensic officers had finished.

"Yes, that was strange," the constable admitted. "But we asked Sylvie Hamm and Mrs Drummond if they could recall what was there, and neither of them could. Besides, Mr Weber's wallet was on his bedside table. Whatever was there could have been moved at any time."

Beth understood what the constable was saying. There wasn't enough evidence pointing to a robbery being the motivation for the attack.

"I'd like to see his bedroom. And then, I'd like to talk to Mrs Drummond, and we'll try Sylvie Hamm again."

Randolph Weber's bedroom was sparsely furnished but tidy. It was a masculine room, Beth decided. There were no ornaments or throw pillows or anything to suggest the man had once been married, except for a black-and-white picture on the bedside table of Mr and Mrs Weber standing in front of the cabin.

They were not young in this picture. Inga Weber was smiling, but it looked strained, and she was leaning on a cane. Randolph was holding her around the waist with one hand and had a walking stick in the other. He wasn't smiling.

Beth wondered if Gerald Weber had taken the picture.

She swallowed hard. The whole family gone, all three deaths violent in their own way. Beth's own mother had died after a long battle with cancer, and she knew it wasn't a peaceful way to end a life. Now Inga's husband, after surviving years alone, was dead at the bottom of a staircase with a cracked skull, and their only son murdered.

Strangely, it felt to Beth as if the Weber family had been punished. But for what, and by whom?

She shook her head. Now she was being too emotional. Inspector Fowler had warned her about that.

We don't work on intuition and feelings, Stanton. Just evidence.

Just as Constable Sorensen had said, Randolph Weber's wallet was on the bedside table beside a lamp. There was a book on the nightstand about engineering. It had been well-thumbed and there was a bookmark halfway through. Beth flicked to the last marked page. It was full of mathematical equations, well beyond Beth's understanding.

"Anything interesting?"

Beth jumped. She hadn't heard Peter Sorensen come up the stairs.

"No. I haven't found anything."

As Beth descended the stairs and Peter Sorensen locked the door behind them, the feeling she'd had before gnawed at the edge of her mind. There was something missing from the house. Something that should have been there but wasn't. Beth pushed the thought away. No use dwelling on it now. It would come to her eventually.

There was a buzzing sound, and Peter Sorensen pulled out his phone and tapped the screen.

"Hi Cody . . . OK. Yes, she said she lost it . . . Oh, right. OK, then. Thanks."

He ended the call. "Cody says Sylvie's not answering the landline. He's going to try her cell again, but doesn't expect her to answer."

Beth nodded, and right at that moment, heard a phone ringing. She looked at Sorensen. "Yours?"

He shook his head.

"It's not mine either."

Beth looked around and walked towards the sound. It was loudest near the front door of the cabin. She bent down and began scraping away at a small mound of snow just as the ringing stopped.

Under the snow and half trodden into the damp dirt was a cell phone. Beth pulled it out carefully and looked at the cracked screen.

"What's Cody's number?" she asked. "Quick, the battery's about to die."

Peter read out the numbers. It was the number still displayed on the screen.

"When did it snow?" Beth asked.

"Tuesday night," he said. "It was still snowing a bit on the morning of the third. Why?"

"For this cell phone to be under the snow, Sylvie must have dropped it before it snowed. She lied about the time she was here."

Beth felt her own phone vibrate in her pocket.

"Officer Vaughan? Charlie Davis? Yes, she works for the *Gazette* in Coffin Cove . . . What? We're headed to Sylvie Hamm's right now. I'll call you when we get there. She lied about the time she found Weber's body. I'm bringing her in for more questioning."

Beth ended the call and looked at Peter Sorensen. "Remember those two cars outside Sylvie's place? One of them might belong to a missing journalist."

* * *

Charlie heard banging, followed by moaning. The sound of the phone ringing had been the start of it. Sylvie must be getting agitated.

Charlie's legs were aching now. She'd been standing for some time in her cramped space. She was getting anxious too. What if her Aunt Delia had just assumed Charlie was coming another day and hadn't raised the alarm?

She needed a plan.

The room had got brighter. The stacks of boxes must obscure a window. If she could move the boxes, one by one, she might be able to climb up and escape through the window. It would take a while because there was no room to make another stack. It would be like moving pieces in a chess game. First a box, then her body. She also risked burying herself under Sylvie's stuff, never to be seen again. Charlie pushed that thought aside.

Carefully, Charlie moved one box. It was covered with dust and made her sneeze, but thankfully, not heavy. She placed it down beside her and only had enough space left on the floor for her feet.

"Don't you touch my stuff!"

Charlie heard Sylvie's voice outside the door.

"Let me out, then," Charlie called. She was getting angry now.

"Leave my stuff alone. It's mine," Sylvie repeated.

Charlie ignored her and moved another box and then another. She had to climb up to the space she'd just made. As she moved her feet, she caught sight of something on the floor. It was the cigarette lighter. A thought formed in her mind, and she squeezed her body around so she could bend and pick it up.

She could still hear Sylvie shuffling around outside the door.

Charlie continued to move boxes, ignoring the ache in her shoulders and thighs.

Sylvie was making a strange moaning sound again. "Leave my stuff alone. It's mine. It's mine . . ." And Charlie could hear thumping. Was Sylvie clearing the doorway? What if Sylvie attacked her again? Charlie worked quicker. She had to be careful. Some boxes were falling apart, their contents spilling everywhere, and she risked losing her footing and being crushed by falling debris.

Sylvie was shouting now. "Leave my stuff alone! Don't you touch it!"

Charlie could see the window. Just two more boxes and she would be beside it. She grabbed one of them and instead of placing it gently beside her, she hurled it. There was the sound of breaking glass and then a howl from Sylvie Hamm.

Charlie saw the door handle move and heard Sylvie strain to open the door a crack.

The window was single pane and had a rusty lock. Charlie frantically tried to prise it open, but it was jammed tight. She looked back and saw Sylvie attempt to squeeze her body through the gap between the door and the boxes.

The woman was strong, but Charlie had a plan.

"You stay away from me," Charlie shouted in her most commanding voice, "or I'll burn all your stuff."

Sylvie's red face appeared and miraculously her body followed. She was standing at the foot of the path Charlie had cleared.

Charlie held up the cigarette lighter with one hand, her eyes on Sylvie. With the other hand, she felt around for something heavy to force the rusty lock, or if all else failed, break the window.

Sylvie had stopped moving, her eyes on the lighter.

"It's mine," she snarled again. "Don't you touch my stuff."

"I don't care," Charlie shot back. "I'll burn it all up if you try to hurt me again."

Her hand closed around a wooden object. It was a lampstand.

With her free hand, she hammered at the lock, and finally it moved slightly. One more thump and the window would be open. Charlie had to take her eyes off Sylvie for the last effort, and as she did, she heard Sylvie lunge towards her.

In simultaneous moves, she flicked the lighter on and tossed it at the nearest box then pushed the window with all her might.

It gave way, and Charlie was falling. As she hit the ground, her lungs pushed out air and she struggled to take a breath. She heard a loud wailing sound and smoke started billowing out the window above her. Charlie hauled herself upright and forced her legs to move.

She staggered, righted herself, and then took unsteady steps, hanging on to the building walls to keep from falling. She was sobbing now and could hardly see her breath coming in rasps.

Then, her body bumped into something and she screamed.

"It's all right," a calm voice said, "I'm a police officer."

1958, BLAST DAY

"That boy is on the beach again."

Inga Weber stood at the window.

"He must be freezing. It's pouring out there."

Randolph heard the worry in his wife's voice. Despite them promising one another that they'd always communicate in their adopted tongue, she'd never lost her German accent, and it was more pronounced whenever she was anxious.

He stood beside Inga at the window and watched the thin boy run along the beach as if he were being chased by wolves.

"Dear God," he murmured.

"Oh Randolph, go and get him. I'll give him something to eat. He looks so thin."

Randolph smiled down at his slender, dark-haired Inga, who looked up at him with anxious brown eyes. He patted her shoulder.

"I'll see if the boy is all right. But Inga—" he squeezed her shoulder — "we can't interfere. The boy has a mother."

"Not much of a mother," Inga said, anger replacing the worry in her voice.

He sighed. "Inga . . ."

"I know, I know. Just make sure he is all right. Take a coat."

"A coat?"

"Yes." Her voice was firm.

Randolph hesitated, studying his wife's face for a moment. She gave him a small nod.

"If you are sure."

He left Inga by the window and climbed up the narrow stairs to the second floor of their cabin. On the left side was their bedroom. The door was open a crack, and he could see Inga had made the bed as usual. She'd taken the pictures down as they had been instructed in case the Ripple Rock blast shook them off the walls. They were still stacked neatly against the wall. The other bedroom door was firmly closed. It had been nearly a year since Randolph had been in this room. Even when he'd heard Inga sobbing quietly, he couldn't bring himself to go inside. But now, she wanted him to get a coat for a child she only knew by sight. A boy they barely knew. Randolph wasn't sure if this was a good thing or not. But if it made his wife happy, he'd go into his dead son's bedroom, take a coat from the closet and give it to the shivering child on the beach.

He hoped he was doing the right thing. For both Inga and the boy.

Randolph walked down to the beach in the rain, carrying the coat over his arm, aware of Inga watching him from the window.

She'd watched him many times before.

He remembered the first time he'd seen the boy on the beach. At first, he'd thought his eyes were deceiving him. Since Theo had died, Randolph had lost count of the number of times he'd thought he glimpsed his son in the yard, or at the window when he came home from work.

But this boy didn't look like Theo. He was thin, with blond hair and pale skin.

The beach was deserted almost every day. Randolph had walked his dog and played with Theo in the summer on the sand while Inga propped herself up against the driftwood and read her book. If Randolph closed his eyes, he could hear Theo's laughter and feel the warm salt air against his cheek. But now both the dog and Theo were gone. Randolph rarely ventured down the narrow trail from the cabin to the sand dunes.

Randolph would have turned from the window and ignored the solitary figure had he not recognized the boy. He was certain the child was the one he'd caught hiding out at the mining camp a few days earlier. He'd been angry — not with the boy, but with his parents. Why was the boy not in school? He felt the same anger rise as he pulled on his boots and set off down the path to the beach.

When he got there, he couldn't see the boy at first. Then he saw the small figure crouched over a rock pool. As Randolph approached, he saw the boy had arranged pieces of driftwood and a collection of rocks and shells. The boy seemed not to hear Randolph and didn't look up until the man was towering over him.

"Shouldn't you be at school, boy?" Randolph tried to keep his voice soft. He didn't want to frighten the child again.

The boy sat back on his haunches and looked up at Randolph. He held a stick in his hand, and with a tug on his heart, Randolph remembered Theo's fascination with the crabs he'd found in rock pools.

"Well?" Randolph asked again. "Why aren't you in school?"

The boy's cheeks burned red, and he hung his head.

"Too stupid for school," he muttered.

"Is that right, eh?" Randolph said. He was silent for a moment. At the camp, he'd not noticed the dark circles under the boy's eyes. He looked hungry, and again, Randolph had felt the knot of fury in his stomach. Some people didn't deserve children. It wasn't fair.

He noticed the fear in the boy's face, and he forced himself to smile. Randolph gestured at the boy's pile of treasures.

"What do you have there?"

The boy shrugged. "Just rocks."

Randolph crouched down. "Can I look?" His tone was gentle.

The boy nodded.

"Well, let's see here . . . you know what this is?" Randolph held up one of the boy's rocks. It was flat, but it had a raised swirl on one side.

The boy shrugged again, not meeting Randolph's eyes. "Just a rock."

"No, it's not just a rock, it's a fossil. You see this here?" Randolph ran his finger over the raised swirl. "This used to be a living thing."

He'd got the boy's attention. The boy stared up at him, suspicion on his face.

Randolph laughed. "You never heard of fossils?"

The boy shook his head.

"A fossil is the preserved remains of living creatures. You see this here?" Randolph held up the boy's rock. "A long time ago, this island was underwater. It was covered by the ocean. This creature here—" he touched the swirl on the rock — "this creature died and sank to the bottom of the ocean. Over millions of years, layers of sand and earth covered the creature and eventually turned into rock. This creature — or parts of it — turned into rock too and formed this. This is called a fossil. There's lots of them on this beach if you know what you're looking for."

He could see the boy was intrigued. He continued, "I have a book at home. I'll lend it to you if you like."

The boy stared at the ground again.

"Can't read."

"Never mind. I'll help you. What's your name?"

Randolph became a regular visitor to the boy's beach sanctuary. He discovered the boy's name was Gerald, and after making discreet enquiries, he found out Gerald was the son of one of the camp cooks, Doris Duffy.

Doris was popular with the men. Randolph had watched her flirt with one man in particular, John Jennings. John was an ex-con, a charmer with a mean streak. Randolph heard rumours that John and his son William had moved in with Doris.

It explained, he thought, the misery he saw in Gerald's eyes.

"What will become of the boy after Blast Day?" Inga had asked. Every day, she inquired after Gerald, although she never mentioned him by name, and never accompanied Randolph to the beach.

"I don't know."

Randolph knew the question which hung in the air between them. They could not have any more children after Theo.

And now today was Blast Day.

Everyone should have sheltered inside. Randolph was one of the chief engineers on the project, and he knew there was little chance of injury or damage to property when the explosives were detonated, but the government officials had wanted to discourage gawking crowds.

Residents on Quadra Island had been ordered to stay home and keep the windows closed.

The blast had been successful. Randolph had observed the controlled explosion from a bunker with the other engineers and invited VIPs.

For the last three years, Randolph Weber and his team had supervised a three-shift operation of about a hundred men who drilled tunnels into the twin peaks of Ripple Rock, inserting over twelve hundred tons of explosives into a warren of tunnels.

At 9.31 a.m. that morning, the blast had propelled thousands of tonnes of rock into the air. It had been an impressive sight. It had also been a success.

In the hours after the explosion, divers had reported that the peaks of Ripple Rock, so long the nemesis of sailors, had been reduced in height, now laying a safe fifty feet underwater.

There had been cheers and clapping in the bunker. Randolph could have stayed for the speeches and champagne, but he wasn't one for the political backslapping. He was glad it was over. When he'd first heard about the ambitious project to remove the enormous underwater mountain from

Seymour Narrows, he'd been excited. The notorious stretch of water had claimed many lives and was described as one of the "vilest stretches of water in the world". Randolph had been proud to work on the complicated project.

But since Theo was gone, he'd lost his enthusiasm. Maybe if he and Inga had never come here, their child would have survived. Randolph was a logical man; he didn't believe in fate. But sometimes, he felt like the "vile narrows" had claimed one more life. He gave himself a shake. He was just tired. He had opted to walk home. His contract was over and the job was completed successfully. Besides, he should be grateful. His engineering skills were now revered around the world — he'd never be without work. The miners and other staff who had run the camp were out of a job, including Gerald's mother and her boyfriend. The camp was empty. Randolph knew the miners had got their last paycheck the night before. Many had already left, some of them leaving most of their cash in the pub by the ferry terminal.

Randolph had walked along the man-made trail that connected Maud Island to Quadra Island, and he turned towards the road that lead to Plumper Beach. He and Inga would stay on Quadra Island. Theo was buried here. Inga would never leave him, so Randolph would travel for work, he thought. He hoped his wife could bear his absences.

Heavy droplets of rain had dampened Randolph's shoulders as he walked, and he was soaked when he arrived home to find Inga anxiously staring out the window, watching the boy on the beach.

Randolph carried Theo's coat to Gerald's hideout.

From a distance, it looked as though Gerald had curled up to sleep. When Randolph got closer, he could see the boy's body was folded into the foetal position and was trembling all over.

"Well now," Randolph said as he crouched down. "Did the explosion scare you?" He was worried. As his friendship with the boy had blossomed, he'd become accustomed to Gerald's smiling face as he approached.

He put his hand out and lightly touched Gerald's shoulder. The boy shuddered, and Randolph realized the boy was sobbing.

"Tell me," Randolph said. "Tell me."

Gerald gasped and seemed to try to control himself. He turned his face to Randolph, his pale skin even whiter in the gloom of the rainy afternoon.

"He's killing my mother."

The words were spoken so softly, Randolph could hardly hear them over the sound of the rain beating down on the driftwood.

"Come," Randolph said and held out his hand.

Wordlessly, the man and the boy hurried along the beach, leaving Theo's coat behind them in the sand.

CHAPTER TWENTY-THREE

Present day
January 9, afternoon

Bob Hinton opened his eyes. It was pitch black. He let out a groan as the drill hammer started pummelling in his head again. Even in his disorientated state, he felt someone nearby. He felt something rough against his face, and then the blackness gave way to a blinding light. It pierced his senses, and he groaned again. Instinctively, he went to move his hand to cover his eyes, and a shaft of pain up his arms and soreness in his wrists told him his hands were still secured somehow behind his back.

It took a moment for his eyes to adjust. He was strapped to a chair, his ankles bound to the front legs and his hands behind his back. His head ached from a blow he'd received earlier, and his mouth was dry. He felt nausea rising from his stomach, and then drips of sweat formed on his upper lip.

A shaft of sunlight illuminated a small room with wood-panelled walls, ceilings and floors. An old sack lay on the floor beside him. He'd obviously had his head covered — which accounted for the smell of animal feed — but who had taken it off him?

"He's going to puke."

A man's voice came from above him somewhere, answering his question. The man was right. Bob's stomach heaved, and he deposited the contents on the floor beside him, vomit splashing over his legs.

"Water," Bob rasped, the weakness of his voice surprising him.

A figure stood in front of him, silhouetted in the sunlight. The figure, a man, maybe the same one who'd correctly predicted Bob's puking, had his face covered with a black ski mask. He thrust a plastic bottle to Bob's lips and held it so Bob could drink. Cool water flowed down his throat. He felt better, less disorientated.

"Where am I?" he asked, attempting to sound authoritative. "Who are you?"

The figure chuckled.

Bob had asked this every time he'd received water or food. The last time, his questions had resulted in a blow to the side of his head. This time the man walked past him, and Bob heard metal scraping, a door creaking and then footsteps as the man — or men, Bob assumed, even though he only heard one voice — left the room. The door creaked shut, and then Bob heard the rattle of metal again, as Bob supposed they locked the door behind them.

"Hello?" he said. He couldn't be sure he was alone. No answer came. They — whoever they were — can't be worried about noise, otherwise he'd be gagged. So, he must be far away from other people.

They had taken him to the bathroom several times. The walls were logs, and it looked like he was in a cabin. He had strained to hear something. Traffic? Anything to give him a clue to his location. But there was nothing except the chirp of birds and the soft rustle of a breeze through leaves. Or maybe that was the sound of waves? Was he still in Coffin Cove? He'd sniffed. He wasn't certain, but he thought he detected the faint briny scent of the ocean.

Dear God, what had happened? Panic surged through his body, and he struggled to free his hands again. Something hard bit into his skin. It was no use. His captives, whoever they were, had him tightly bound. Bob forced himself to focus and think clearly. He needed to piece together the last hours and days. The only way he could monitor time was by meals, but he couldn't be certain how often he was being fed. He was sure he'd been here for more than two days, maybe three.

If he could figure out who was holding him captive and why, maybe he could negotiate with them. At least, he reasoned with himself, if they'd wanted him dead, they'd have killed him by now. Maybe he had something they wanted? But what?

Tell the story, he told himself. *What do you know for certain? What clear memories do you have? Then connect the dots. Figure out what they want.*

It had been the evening of Professor Weber's lecture, he remembered. Andi had already left the office. Charlie had been there finishing up an article, and he recalled her standing at the office door, reminding him it was nearly time for the lecture to start. He told her he wasn't going. He didn't feel like it. He hadn't felt like doing much lately. But he changed his mind. Why?

Before he closed his laptop, he'd checked the wire as he always did before leaving the office. What had it been that had made him change his plans? Something had caught his attention.

Bob's head was still pounding as he closed his eyes and willed his subconscious to offer up the information.

That's right! He'd been stunned to find the press release about elderly Randolph Weber found battered to death in his cottage on Quadra Island. His reporter's senses were alert, and he instinctively knew the name was not a coincidence. Sure enough, a simple Google search revealed that the unfortunate victim was indeed Professor Weber's father.

Surely the lecture was cancelled. He'd hurriedly printed out the press release and left the office. It had been a rainy January evening, and in his haste, he'd forgotten his hat and gloves. When he got to the museum, he'd been surprised to find Professor Weber animatedly delivering his lecture. *He can't possibly know about his father*, Bob had thought, and he'd been angry at whoever it was who'd released the information without notifying the professor first.

Maybe someone had tried but couldn't reach him? It happened. A press release was no way to find out about the death of a loved one, Bob had decided, especially when they'd suffered a violent death. He'd break the news to the professor.

Even as Bob processed this detail in his present predicament, he felt a pang of guilt. He hadn't been interested in the professor's feelings; he'd sensed a story. He knew from all his experience as a journalist, in the first throes of grief, people often reveal interesting snippets of information. That's what had got his attention. Maybe his situation now was punishment from God or the universe for all those times Bob had invaded someone's tragedy just to get good copy. But there wasn't time to think about that now. Bob pushed the guilt aside.

What had happened next? He forced himself to return to the story.

When the lecture ended, he'd waited while the attendees filed out, until only Katie Dagg and the professor remained.

When the professor had finally collected his belongings and was walking towards the door to leave the museum, Bob had stepped forward and introduced himself. He'd walked out with the professor and Katie had locked the door and left.

The professor was a small man, Bob recalled, and he could see in his mind's eye the professor's delicate hands, with papery skin and bluish veins. They were the main indication of Weber's age, as his face was free of wrinkles except for laughter lines around his intelligent blue eyes.

Professor Weber had listened intently as Bob broke the terrible news.

"Dear God," he had stuttered. "Are you sure it's my father? He was due to move into a nursing home . . ."

Bob had shown him the press release.

"Dear God," the professor had repeated. "Who would want to do this to my father? He wasn't a rich man."

"Maybe you should speak to the police?" Bob had suggested gently. "They may have more information."

"You're right, of course." The professor had turned to hurry off, but then had stopped.

"Thank you so much, Mr Hinton, so kind of you . . ."

Bob had waved it off, and with another stab of guilt, had promised to help in any way he could.

Bob felt another wave of nausea rise in his throat as he struggled to focus on the next few minutes. They were the key to unlocking the mystery behind this, so he tried to summon up all the memories embedded in his senses.

He'd shivered, he remembered, aware again that he wasn't wearing his hat. It was raining hard. The museum was shrouded in darkness and he was standing alone outside the door. What had he done next?

He had plunged his hands into his pockets, searching for his cell phone to call Andi. She'd been at the Concerned Citizens Committee meeting and he was sure she'd want to know this news. He'd left his phone at the office.

Undecided, he'd waited a moment before walking in the direction of the office.

Had the blow come while he hesitated? He'd felt the rush of air behind him and heard a grunt just before his brain seemed to explode into a firework display of stars and lights and a pain so powerful that he'd dropped to his knees. Just before he blacked out, he'd heard a voice he recognized, but from where?

"Got him."

And then he was gone into the dark.

As Bob closed his eyes with the effort of dredging up this sequence of events from his fractured memories, he had another thought which made him straighten up in the chair with panic, ignoring the tearing of his shoulder muscles and soreness of his wrists.

"Andi!" he mumbled.

What would Andi think? Would she be worried and look for him? Or would she assume he'd just walked out of her life as he'd done so many times before?

This realization, even more than the danger he was in, caused frustration to swell up inside of him. After all the progress they'd made with their relationship, he couldn't leave her hating him for letting her down yet again. No way. Not while he had an ounce of life left in him.

"Hey!" he shouted, jerking his bound hands, ignoring the warm trickles of blood he felt on his palms and fingers. "Hey! You bastards! Get in here and tell me what you want!"

But nobody came.

A wave of despair washed over him, and he slumped forward as far as his restraints would allow. It was no good. His only hope was his daughter and her investigative instincts. It was all up to her now.

CHAPTER TWENTY-FOUR

"Charlie's OK, thank God."

Andi looked at Harry and rubbed her face. She was exhausted, and it was only four o'clock in the afternoon.

"What happened?"

"After her Aunt Delia called me, she found out where Charlie was headed yesterday. Apparently, she was talking to locals in the café and had asked a bunch of questions about Sylvie Hamm, so she figured, correctly, that Charlie was probably there. Thank goodness she called the police first, because when they got there, Sylvie Hamm's house was on fire and Charlie had busted out through a window."

Harry's eyes widened. "Holy shit! Now there's two of you I have to worry about."

Andi ignored him. "It's all a bit jumbled, but from what I gather, the police are also questioning Sylvie Hamm about Randolph Weber's death. Charlie was at the hospital, but she'll call later."

"Hospital? Is she hurt?"

"A bit bruised. Sylvie Hamm attacked her, but there's no real physical damage."

Andi rubbed her face again. "It's my fault. I should never have let her go on her own. It's a homicide investigation, for God's sake. What was I thinking? Dad's already missing, what if . . ."

"What if nothing," Harry said firmly. "Don't do that, Andi. It doesn't help. Charlie's OK, and she's learned a valuable lesson. Maybe she even learned more than you ever do."

Andi managed a weak smile. "Let's hope she's smarter than me."

Harry grinned. "It's part of your charm." Then he got serious. "I don't suppose she found out anything about your dad?"

Andi shook her head. "She didn't say, and I'm sure she would have told me right away. A dead end as far as Dad's concerned."

"What now?" Harry asked.

"Well, first I'm going to call this phone number and find out what or who 'Walrus' is. Then I'm going to find Juanita and have a chat about the notes which Ruth and Hephzibah received." Andi checked her phone. "The Bistro is open for dinner at four, so I should catch her before her shift starts. What about you?"

Harry stood up. "I should see Ike about the mysterious Captain Ron, the salvage guy. Oh, I nearly forgot in all the excitement. I have news of a development."

"What's that?"

"Pastor Michael Nelson is collecting donations for the Committee fund," Harry said.

"The Committee fund? Fund for what?" Andi sat back in her chair. "This is all getting weirder, if that's even possible."

"You've got that right," Harry said, and he came around the desk to kiss her.

* * *

"Hello, this is the Walrus Club. How may I help you?" The man's voice had a cultured British accent.

The phone had been answered on the first ring. Andi felt her heart leap. Maybe she was on to something.

"My name is Andrea Silvers," she said. "These may sound like strange questions . . ."

"Try anyway," the man said, sounding amused.

"Can you tell me what the Walrus Club is and where you are?"

"Ah. The Walrus Club is a private gentleman's club, and we are located in Buenos Aires. Does that help?"

"Argentina?" Andi was surprised, but something clicked at the back of her mind.

"That's correct. Anything else?"

Andi knew her father had travelled all over the world. Maybe this was just a call to an old acquaintance.

"Does the name Bob, or Robert Hinton, mean anything to you?"

"I'm afraid we keep our member's details confidential. I cannot confirm or deny if Mr Hinton is a member of the Walrus Club."

"I see. Would it make a difference if I told you Bob Hinton is my father, and he's missing? And the only clue I have is the Walrus Club's telephone number scrawled on a piece of paper. Please, can you help me?"

Her voice cracked a little. It was a long shot, but it was all she had.

There was silence at the other end of the line. Andi was thinking someone had cut her off when the man spoke again.

"Please wait for a moment," and then the line went quiet.

A full two minutes later and she heard an inaudible murmur before the man returned. "Miss Silvers? Considering the situation, I have found someone who may help you. Please hold."

Before Andi could thank him, the line was quiet and then another voice said, "Andrea?"

"Yes, it's Andrea Silvers here. I'm Bob Hinton's daughter. Do I know you?"

The voice was gravelly, probably with cigar smoke and whiskey, Andi thought.

"You won't remember me. You were just a baby when I saw you last."

"Are you a friend of my father?"

"Not exactly. I worked for a rival newspaper back in the day. But your father was a fine journalist, and I respected him."

"He's missing," Andi said. "Did he talk to you recently?" She was aware the man had not given her his name.

"I don't want to get involved in this hare-brained investigation your father is obsessed with," the voice said. "But I spoke to him on New Year's Day. He wanted some information."

"About what?" Andi asked.

"Not what — who," the man said. "He wanted to know about a woman named Juanita Romero."

CHAPTER TWENTY-FIVE

"Hey, Harry!"

Harry was already heading towards Ike's office. He looked up and saw Ike waving his arms as if he were guiding an aircraft in to land.

"Harry, come here, man."

Ike's voice was urgent.

When Harry got there, Ike was behind the desk, tapping urgently on his keyboard. He didn't even look up as Harry entered. His face was flushed red. With annoyance or excitement, Harry couldn't tell. It wasn't like Ike to be this agitated.

"Harry, man, look at this." Ike gestured at Harry to come round the desk and look at the computer monitor.

"I got this email this morning," Ike said. "What do you think?"

Harry read the email, which was from a private marina owner on the Sunshine Coast.

The subject of the email was: *Salvage Boat Dumping Garbage.*

The marina owner said that a man, claiming to be the owner of a salvage company, was collecting garbage and junk for a fee from shipyards, and then taking the loads out to sea in his little boat and dumping them. The marina owner did not have proof to support his claims and had emailed hoping someone else had seen the shady salvage boat and had pictures or could get some hard evidence, so the boat owner could be reported.

"Keep scrolling," Ike said.

Harry did and saw a chain of emails replying to the original. Yes, one harbour master replied, he'd seen that boat, and it was towing an old tugboat. Another tugboat owner said he'd seen the boat piled up with black garbage bags. There was even an out-of-focus picture.

"Well? It's the same boat, isn't it?" Ike demanded.

"Looks that way. Where is it now?" Harry looked out the office door and saw the troller tied up in the same spot. He could see a pile of black bags on the deck.

"The boat's there, but 'Captain Ron', or whoever he is, isn't on his boat. I saw him this morning, but that new pastor came into the office to ask for a donation and I missed my chance to talk to the slippery son of a bitch."

"Pastor Michael?"

"That pastor who's involved in Peggy Wilson's new committee. The Concerned Citizens, or whatever they call themselves. I'm not giving money to that crowd."

"You're not 'concerned', Ike?" Harry smiled, gently teasing his friend.

"I am concerned," Ike said hotly. "Concerned about some asshole who doesn't pay his moorage and dumps crap into the ocean."

"He probably went into town for supplies. He'll be back."

"I hope so. He's been sneaking around when I'm not here."

"Must have been avoiding you."

Ike grunted. "That's the weird thing. It wasn't me he was avoiding this morning. He took one look at that pastor and hightailed it up the boardwalk."

"Maybe he heard the pastor was collecting donations," Harry said. "What do you want me to do?"

"If Captain Ron comes back, have a friendly chat. See if you can get some information. And my moorage fees."

"I can do that. I want to chat with him anyway."

"Thanks. I'm thinking about closing up. Looks like snow again. I promised the wife I'd shovel the driveway."

"No problem." Harry grinned. He was certain Ike would be warming himself with a brandy at the Fat Chicken.

As he was about to leave the office, Ike said, "I haven't seen Andi for a couple of days. You two break up?"

"No," Harry said evenly.

"You can't have a woman like that live on a boat, man. Especially in the winter."

It irritated Harry. "What's wrong with the boat? I've lived on the *Pipe Dream* for years. It's comfortable."

"For you, yes. You've lived on boats for the best part of your life. But it's no place for a lady." Ike shook his finger. "You've been single far too long, and you've forgotten how to treat a woman. If you're not careful, she'll run off after that inspector who was all over her a few months ago."

Harry stared at Ike. Why couldn't people mind their own business?

He was about to tell Ike he wasn't going to take relationship advice from someone who spent more of his free time on a barstool than in the company of his wife, but he thought better of it.

"I'll bear it in mind, Ike."

"Good man." Ike nodded approvingly, obviously missing Harry's sarcastic tone.

* * *

Ike was right about one thing. Clouds hung heavy over the ocean, and the temperature had dropped. Snow was on the way again. Harry checked the forecast. Snow, then a warm front which would bring wind and rain.

Harry busied himself on the boat for a while. There was always maintenance to do. He lowered himself in and out of the engine room, checking the bilge pump and oil levels in the engine. Every so often, he'd glance over to the troller to check for signs of life, but there were none. Oh well, Captain Ron would have to make an appearance sometime.

When Harry finally stood on the deck of the *Pipe Dream*, after putting away his tools, the wind stung his face. White caps were scuttling across the cove, and the winter skies were as dark as night.

Harry thought briefly about joining Ike in the Fat Chicken, but he'd promised to hang around. He was tiring of the atmosphere in the bar just lately. He used to enjoy a quiet pint, and the odd conversation about hunting or the weather, but these days, there were too many heated arguments about local politics and griping about newcomers and the Fish Plant.

He pulled out his phone and tapped in Andi's number, and then clicked it off before the call went through. She'd call him if there was news about Bob. An early supper and a movie on his laptop, he decided. Later on, he'd check the troller again.

Harry stood in his heavy jacket, waiting for the oil stove to warm the galley. It was quiet without Andi. He could see into the stateroom and her hoodie and a wool blanket were still strewn on the bed.

It took half an hour before it was warm enough that he couldn't see his breath anymore. Maybe Ike had a point. Summer evenings on the deck watching the sun go down were romantic. Freezing winter evenings were plain miserable. He'd got so used to this life, he hadn't thought about it from Andi's perspective.

He slipped off his jacket and was reaching for a jar of stew to warm in a saucepan when he heard the chug of a diesel motor.

Surely the troller wasn't leaving the dock now? But then, if Captain Ron were about to ditch garbage, what better time than a dismal winter evening?

Sighing, he pulled on his jacket and opened the galley door. Harry could see the belch of exhaust fumes surrounding the troller, and a man crouching on the dock, loosening tie-up lines.

"Hey!" Harry shouted. "Hey, can you hang on a minute?"

The figure straightened up, and in the gloom, Harry thought he saw him glance over his shoulder, but he didn't acknowledge Harry. Instead, he hopped onto the troller, and in a few seconds, Harry heard the engine rev.

"Shit."

He should let the troller go and report back to Ike in the morning. But Harry felt the frustration of recent days boil up, and he made a decision. He'd follow the troller and see for himself if Captain Ron was dumping garbage.

It only took moments to untie the *Pipe Dream*, and Harry was in the wheelhouse, easing the boat away from the dock.

CHAPTER TWENTY-SIX

"She's not working here anymore." Paul Brecon looked at Andi. "Look, I'm sorry. I have no idea where she's working now."

He was distracted. "Andi, we open in a minute or two, and I'm short-staffed."

"This is important," Andi insisted. "I need to know everything you know about Juanita Romero. Let's start with how and when you hired her."

Paul Brecon sighed and scratched his head. "You know, she just kinda showed up. Before we were open and setting up the kitchen, she just appeared."

He thought for a minute, and Andi waited patiently.

"I asked her if she'd replied to my ad online, and I don't even remember what she said. She just gave me her references, and they looked good, so . . ." His voice trailed off. "We were really busy, and to be honest, being a server isn't rocket science and I needed bodies. I just figured if she didn't work out, then . . ."

Andi suppressed her irritation. "Did you check her references?"

Paul looked sheepish. "No, I guess I didn't . . ."

"OK, do you know where she was living?"

"Uh, I didn't ask."

Andi snapped, "Did you know *anything* about her?"

Paul's attitude changed. "Look, she was a pretty good server. I paid her for New Year's Eve and the next couple of days, and then she didn't turn up. I hire lots of servers. Sometimes they don't turn up, OK? What's with all the questions, anyway?"

Andi sighed. "Paul, I'm sorry. You've probably heard my father has gone missing, right?"

Paul didn't meet her eyes. "I, er, heard the police wanted to talk to him about the professor."

"Yes, well, I think Juanita knows something about my father's disappearance, and who knows? Maybe something about the professor. All I know is that she went missing about the same time my father went missing, and I don't think it's a coincidence. So I'm trying to find out as much as possible, that's all."

"All right." Paul's tone softened. "The only thing I can tell you is I overheard her talking to another server one evening. She was asking where Juanita was from, and she — Juanita — said she was originally from Argentina and that she'd come to Canada to be near her brother."

"Did she say what her brother's name is? Or where he lives?"

"Er, Steven, or something like that, and no, she didn't say where . . ." He stopped and thought for a minute. "She said he was a security guard or something like that, and he'd worked in Ottawa. Yes, that's it."

Andi stared at the manager. It all clicked into place.

"Thank you," Andi said and turned to leave.

"Hang on, there is something else," Paul said. "She asked to be your server. At your table on New Year's Eve, I mean. I thought nothing of it at the time, but it was a bit odd, I suppose."

CHAPTER TWENTY-SEVEN

Ruth's eyes felt gritty. She sat at her desk and tried to focus on the laptop screen, but even to her keen legal mind, the words were not making sense anymore.

There was a gentle knock at the door.

"Are you nearly done for the day, young lady?"

Ruth smiled at Chief George, who stood in the doorway.

"Yes. I've had enough of all this, for one day." She gestured to the documents covering her desk.

"All 'lawyer talk'?"

"I'm afraid so," Ruth said, "but I'm getting through it. I've finished the grant applications at least."

"I would be happy if I never heard lawyer talk again," he said dryly. "But lawyers are a necessary tool for modern battles, I suppose."

"That's the problem." Ruth sighed. "These are old battles, and we're still losing them."

"No. We are holding the line. You are our secret weapon, Ruth, but you are tired. You must go home and sleep well. It will all look better tomorrow." His tone was kind, and Ruth was touched by his confidence in her.

She closed her laptop. "You're right. I am exhausted."

"Can I walk you to your car?"

She thanked him and refused. The chief said goodnight, and a moment later, Ruth heard the front entrance door swing open and closed. Ruth didn't like leaving the place in a mess, so she busied herself tidying her desk and took a collection of half-finished coffee mugs to the small kitchenette which all the staff in the band office used for their lunch breaks.

The building was empty again. Ruth felt nervous and wished she had taken up the chief's offer. She thought about the note which had appeared in her office and felt a knot of fear grow in her stomach. She was used to bigoted remarks, but the words in that note were full of hate.

It was hate born of ignorance, Ruth knew. This band office was an example. Not one dime of city funds had been used. It had been built using a federal grant, but the government had made creating division between white and indigenous people an art form. Ruth wished she could sit down and show the committee the original blueprints Lhihw Xpey had submitted when applying for the grant. A member of the band council had made detailed drawings of four log cabins to house the eight departments which made up the governing structure of the band and one larger "big house" for ceremonies and meetings. The total cost, including the installation of communications technology, would have been a fraction of the cost of building this ostentatious structure. The grant had been agreed, but the blueprint rejected. Instead, the architect was appointed by the Department of Indigenous Services and this office building was the result. The options had been clear — this building or nothing.

There were fifteen offices, a boardroom, a conference room, and a lobby which would have been appropriate for a high-end hotel. This was the first winter the band had used the office building, and already three receptionists had quit because the building was so cold. Instead of wood stoves, the architect had designed thermal underfloor heating, which failed after only three days of operation. There were only two electricians on the entire island qualified to repair the system, consequently the entire office staff came in bundled in layers and only stayed the absolute minimum time required.

"Waste of money," the Coffin Cove residents had said. "Nobody is ever there. Do they ever work?"

Instead of outright murdering the indigenous population or legislating away their culture, the government now set them up to fail, Ruth thought.

Her grandmother Nora had told her, "White people have many ways of lying to us. One way is to bury us with incomprehensible contractual documents and wear us down with 'lawyer talk'."

The thought of Grandma Nora made Ruth smile through her exhaustion. Whenever she had a decision to make, Ruth imagined herself sitting at the kitchen table and holding her grandmother's calloused hands, and she asked Nora, "What would you do?"

Grandma Nora would have approved of Hephzibah and would have encouraged her to move forward with the legal case against Elizabeth Halwell for the wrongful death of Essie George, Ruth's sister. All Grandma Nora had wanted was to find her missing granddaughter. The loss had broken her.

"She wants to be found," Grandma Nora had told Ruth, and Ruth had promised to find Essie. Nora was a realistic woman, and knew in her heart Essie must be dead, but all she wanted was for Essie's spirit to be at peace. Ruth had found Essie long after her grandmother was gone, but Essie still was not at peace. Not until there was justice for her murder. Ruth hadn't fulfilled her promise yet, and there was much work to do. Ruth wasn't particularly spiritual, but she believed her grandmother walked with her, giving her strength for the uphill battle to come.

Ruth removed her copper bracelet and filled the sink with soapy water. As she washed the mugs, her stomach growled, and she realized she'd only had coffee since breakfast that morning. Hephzibah would have a delicious meal waiting for her, she knew. Either leftovers from the café, or something from her pantry or freezer.

Our pantry or freezer, she corrected herself. It had been a long time since she'd shared a home with anyone — not since Grandma Nora when she was a teenager — and it had taken a while to get used to sharing her space with another human being. *But Hephzibah wasn't just any human being*, she reminded herself as she slipped the copper bracelet back on her wrist and again admired the faded but intricate carving of the raven symbol. Hephzibah was her soulmate.

It was freezing outside. The piles of dirty snow had been cleared to the sides of the parking lot, but the walkways were treacherous. As Ruth was the last person to leave the building, she flicked the light switch as she left the lobby and then locked the doors using the light from her phone.

"Stupid idiot," she said out loud, as the parking lot was now in complete darkness. The sky was clear though, so Ruth waited for her eyes to adjust and then she could make out the shape of her car ahead of her.

Ruth could hear the crunch of her footsteps through the crust of the frozen snow until she reached the cleared tarmac of the parking lot. Thankfully, she was wearing boots with decent tread on the soles. The sound of her movements echoed in the still of the night and it unnerved her. She stood for a moment, and then almost screamed as a loud shriek pierced the air. Then she heard a rustle from overhead and laughed.

Damn ravens. They could make blood-curdling cries, like the one she'd just heard, and then other times they made sounds like a baby crying. They weren't known as tricksters for nothing.

Ruth waited for her heartbeat to settle a little and finally reached her car without slipping. She stopped. What was it that made her hesitate?

Something wrong. Something wrong. SOMETHING WRONG.

Ruth heard the voice in her ear. Maybe it was Grandma Nora, maybe it came from within her own intuition, but as she reached out her hand to unlock the door, she was aware of another presence in the darkness.

"Hello?" Her voice sounded shaky, and she fumbled with the key, but before she could open the car door she felt heat, like someone's breath on her neck and then an arm clamped around her neck and pulled her backwards.

She tried to get her legs under her again, to regain some balance, but the backwards movement was too fast and her heels dragged helplessly along the ground. She tried to scream, but the arm around her throat was choking off her airway, and she couldn't breathe and make sounds at the same time.

Fight back, fight back, her brain told her and she attempted to struggle, her arms and hands making contact with the silent person dragging her.

Then they came to a stop. Her captor loosened his grip and, quick as a flash, Ruth twisted away and forced her legs to move. Then a sharp pain in her head jerked her to a stop. Her attacker had a fist full of her long dark hair, and she was going backwards again.

"Bitch."

One word, uttered in a low growl, and then a punch to the side of her head. She heard, more than felt, the crack as her cheekbone shattered, then there were pinpricks of lights dancing and swirling in her brain and she could taste her own blood. Finally she heard the hideous laughter of a raven fading away in the darkness.

CHAPTER TWENTY-EIGHT

The wind had picked up, but Harry and the *Pipe Dream* had fished in the unforgiving waters near to the Alaskan border. Sometimes he'd peered through green water as the seemingly bottomless troughs had swallowed him between mountainous waves. He adjusted his course a little to cut efficiently through the swell.

Harry expected the troller to swing to the left as it came parallel with the mouth of the cove, but to his surprise it kept straight on.

Hope Island. *Of course.*

Contractors had been clearing the land for the new development. They had moored a barge on the north side of the island and had been filling it with debris from the building site. Nobody would notice a few more bags of garbage.

Ruth had told him that the contractors had stopped work until either the city or Three Cedars Band paid them, so there wouldn't be anyone to see Captain Ron's garbage runs for a while.

At least he wasn't dumping it into the ocean.

Harry decided to keep following until he'd confirmed his speculation, but he throttled back a little, hoping Captain Ron wouldn't see he was following.

Sure enough, the troller made a north turn as it got close to the island and skirted the rocky coast until it disappeared from sight.

Harry knew the troller would have to slow right down to navigate the rocks concealed just a few feet below the surface. It would take the little boat another fifteen minutes, at least, before it reached the dock.

He kept his distance, so he didn't have to worry about the rocks. The *Pipe Dream* needed deeper water than the troller to manoeuvre.

He'd follow at a distance, take pictures if he could see anything, and then head back to Coffin Cove. It would be pitch black soon, and as experienced as he was, Harry didn't want to be out here in the dark. Even with running lights, there was always the possibility of hitting drifting logs which had come loose from a boat on its way to a sawmill.

As he steered around the island, he saw the small boat moving slowly towards the dark shadow of the barge, until it was swallowed in the darkness.

It would be impossible to see anything from this angle, Harry realized, so he gave the island a wide berth and pushed the throttle forward a little.

Captain Ron would think the bigger boat was bypassing the island completely.

Harry could just see the troller come alongside the barge when the dock was directly to his right. Harry slowed the *Pipe Dream* until the engine was idling, and he picked up his camera. It always had a telephoto lens fitted for long-range wildlife shots.

Harry pushed open the sliding window. He took a sharp inward breath as the cold air hit his face, but he trained the camera on the troller and then swore. There wasn't enough light left for a decent picture, even with the boat lights on. But the lens was as good as binoculars, so he kept the camera pointed towards the barge and the troller.

He could see a dark figure on the deck. He was about to press the shutter just in case when he heard a noise. Was that someone shouting? Noise travelled a long way on the water, but Harry was sure it came from the shore. He swung the camera up and was surprised to see the outline of another smaller vessel tucked in on the other side of the dock. It looked like a speedboat, maybe a Sea Ray.

The contractors must be on the island, or maybe they had a caretaker looking after their equipment.

This made everything a lot easier. If the contractors caught Captain Ron dumping garbage on their barge, that was all the evidence Ike would need to report the bogus salvage operation.

Then Harry felt foolish. What was he doing out here chasing around in the dark? He'd promised to help Ike collect his moorage fees, not act as some kind of environmental vigilante. What was it Andi has said? That he was determined to "fix" everything?

But he didn't know how to be any other way. Greta, his mother, had told him on the day she left to live on this very island with his baby sister, that he was man enough to look after himself and his drunken, abusive father. He had been ten years old, and he believed her. He had taken care of his father, even when Ed didn't deserve it, and he'd taken care of Hephzibah too. Harry was furious with the cowardly asshole who sent that disgusting note to his sister and her loyal and beautiful partner. Hephzibah deserved happiness. How dare someone threaten her?

He clenched his fists in frustration. Andi may be right about some of it, but it was his responsibility to look after the people he cared about. He tried to look after his estranged daughter, paying regular deposits into her bank account, even though they hadn't spoken to each other for over two years. And now there was Andi herself. Impulsive, brilliant, passionate Andi. He'd never met anyone like her, and he did not know how to be in a relationship with her. But he sure as hell didn't want it to end.

According to Ike, he wasn't doing a good job of taking care of Andi. Maybe it was time to think about moving off the *Pipe Dream*.

He suddenly wanted to talk to Andi very much. Enough of this. He'd report to Ike in the morning, and he could do what he wanted with the information. He turned to look back at Coffin Cove. The familiar lights of the town looked welcoming and friendly.

Then he saw a flash of light coming from the island in the deepening darkness. He trained the camera back on the shoreline. There were three small orbs of light bobbing up and down.

Men carrying flashlights, Harry guessed. The contractors must still have a crew over here.

Captain Ron must have seen the approaching lights because Harry heard the troller's engine burst into life, and then start chugging away from him.

Harry had to leave too. He'd been here far longer than he'd intended. The winter night had descended like a black curtain around him. Clouds obscured the moonlight and stars, so he reached to click on his running lights when he saw another flash from the island. A split second later, he heard a sharp crack, like a branch snapping from a tree.

Harry was just processing what he'd just seen and heard when it happened again.

There was no doubt now. Someone was firing at the troller. The troller was moving at speed now, back toward Coffin Cove.

What the fuck was going on? Who in their right mind would fire at someone for dumping garbage? Harry grabbed his radio and was about to hail the coastguard when he saw the lights again, but this time bobbing away from him until they disappeared into the undergrowth on Hope Island.

Did that really happen? Maybe he'd been mistaken.

There was only one way to find out, so he pushed the throttle forward. Hopefully, Captain Ron could tell him what the hell just happened out here at Hope Island.

CHAPTER TWENTY-NINE

Someone pulled the cloth sack roughly from Bob Hinton's head. The sudden light blinded him and he struggled to focus. He must have dozed off because he hadn't been aware of anyone entering the room. His exhaustion had finally beaten out his fear. His senses adjusted. First, he noticed the sour smell of his own sweat. The taste in his mouth was metallic. In his fear, he'd bitten his own tongue, and now he felt dried blood congealed on his lips.

As his eyes got used to the light, which now came from a bare light bulb and not sunshine, he could see four people standing in front of him. Two men, still wearing ski masks. Hired thugs? Probably. They both had crew cuts and tattooed arms. They wore black denim jeans and steel-toed boots and, Bob noted with dismay, had the bulge of what must be firearms tucked in their waistbands and covered by black hoodies. They were standing upright with their feet apart, and Bob wondered briefly if they were military men.

The women he recognized.

"Bob. Long time, no see," the older of the two said cheerfully. She was wearing jeans too, perfectly tailored to her slender figure, and an expensive leather jacket zipped to her neck, which was covered by a silk scarf. Her hair was an ash blonde, and her fine-boned face was barely covered with make-up. She would have been beautiful if it wasn't for her thin lips and hard blue eyes.

Bob understood now.

"Elizabeth, lovely to see you again," Bob managed in a hoarse voice. "Of course, I should have known this was all about you. You always were very theatrical."

"Shut up, you bastard," the other woman said with passion. If he hadn't recognized her face, Bob would have certainly known her accent. It was the server from the Cove Bistro.

"Juanita, is it?" Bob said. "What are you doing here? Didn't I leave you a large enough tip?"

Juanita visibly bristled. "You'll pay for what you've done, you son of a bitch."

Elizabeth laughed. It was a tinkly sound, like ice cubes in a glass.

"Juanita, my dear, calm down. Bob, you look confused. Never mind, you're a smart man. You'll figure it out soon enough."

"Not that smart, otherwise I wouldn't be here. I'd be facing you in a courtroom."

"Ah, Bob. Now, you know I would never let that happen. I've spent considerable amounts of money over the years making sure that powerful people keep me away from all that public nastiness."

"So why am I here? Why not write another check?" Bob felt a kind of calm come over him. This woman had no problem killing people. Bob had researched Elizabeth Halwell for years. People who would talk to him, off the record, said she actually enjoyed taking lives. The act of murder invigorated her, as if she were feeding off the life energy of her victims. Bob didn't believe in that voodoo nonsense, but he knew fear when he saw it.

If Elizabeth Halwell wanted to end his life, she'd do it without a second thought. So why not get some answers while he could? At least he'd get some closure in the last moments of his life.

"I had planned to. But would you believe that our pathetic government is actually yielding power to the damn natives? Everyone is so darn politically correct these days. Now, if an Indian whines, then everyone listens." She sounded genuinely bemused by this, Bob thought.

"So you thought a civil case might expose you for the murdering bitch you are?" Bob asked, regretting it a moment later when one thug stepped forward and punched him in the side of the head.

Bob saw a myriad of flashing lights as pain exploded in his head. He heard a howl and realized a moment later, when his brain synapses eventually fired, that it was his own voice.

From far away, he heard the two women laugh.

Bob's body slumped forward. He felt the restraints dig into his wrists. He felt a hand grab his shoulder and pull him upright.

He heard a door open behind him, and then the sounds of footsteps merged with guttural sounds. To Bob's disorientated brain, it sounded like a trapped animal.

"Don't let him faint," he heard Elizabeth order. "He has to be awake for this."

A chair scraped on the floor. Bob turned his head and saw the two thugs shove another body into a chair. With horror, he knew who it was.

"Fuck you," Bob spat out. "Fuck you. You have me. Why don't you leave her alone?"

"But she's the cause of all my trouble." Elizabeth smiled, clearly delighted at Bob's reaction. "Aren't you, Ruth?"

Ruth lifted her head. One of her eyes was swollen almost shut. The other was dark and as hard as flint.

"As my colleague just said," Ruth spoke calmly, "fuck you."

One man raised a hand, but Elizabeth said, "No, no, not yet. Pull the chair over here. I want her facing Bob."

When this was done, Bob looked at Ruth and then at Elizabeth.

"Look, you have me. Kill me, but let her go. She'll retract her legal case and, as you said, what does it matter what an Indian says, right?" He knew there was a desperate note in his voice, and it amused Elizabeth greatly, because she laughed again.

"You're gonna die anyway," Juanita said. Bob had forgotten about her.

"Shut up, Juanita," Elizabeth snapped. The laughter was gone in an instant. Bob felt the room get very small as the woman's mood changed.

"Get him up," she ordered.

To Bob's surprise, both men stood behind the chair. One held him by the shoulders, while the other cut the hand ties. Then, one thug grabbed him under the armpits and hauled him to his feet. Bob felt the muscles in his thighs scream after being cramped in one position for so long.

"Now," Elizabeth uttered the one word.

"What . . ." Bob started to say, as one man grabbed him by the wrist and forced something heavy into his hand. Then Bob knew what was happening.

"No . . ." he tried to shout, but the words were strangled at the back of his throat. The thug manipulated Bob's fingers, and then he was holding a gun with his finger on the trigger. The thug's gloved hand held his hand in place. Bob strained to move his arm, move his fingers, but the man was too strong.

Bob was pointing a gun at Ruth's head.

"No, no, please, God, no . . ." The words came as a whisper, as the thug squeezed down on Bob's trigger finger. Bob shut his eyes and felt his arm jerk, and then the gun fired.

The blast deafened Bob. He could smell an acrid aroma. Tears were running down his face. In the distance, he heard screaming, and as his ears cleared, he dared to open his eyes. He felt a hand push him back into the chair and re-tie his hands.

Laying in front of him, in an ever-expanding pool of crimson, was Juanita. Her death mask — at least the half of her face that remained — was one of shock. Bob's forced shot had struck her head. Brain matter was splattered on the wall behind her body.

It was Ruth screaming. In one stride, Elizabeth Halwell was beside her, and she slapped Ruth across the face.

"Enough," she said.

The room fell quiet except for Ruth's gasping breaths.

"Well," Elizabeth said cheerfully, "I hate loose ends." She wrinkled her nose. "That's the problem with dead bodies. All the shit."

Bob looked down. Mingled with the blood was a brown stain. In death, the body had relaxed all its muscles, and internal fluids were draining from Juanita's corpse. The stink was filling the room.

"You crazy bitch!" Bob said, not bothering to keep the panic out of his voice any longer. "What the fuck are you going to do with us?"

"Kill you," Elizabeth replied, unconcerned by the insult this time. "But better than that, kill all your family and your legacy."

She said the last word with mock reverence.

"What are you talking about?" Bob didn't think he could be any more scared of this woman, but fear was burning like acid in his stomach.

"Sometimes fate intervenes," Elizabeth said solemnly. "My plan was just to kill you and Ruth and dump you both into the foundations of this ridiculous cultural building, or whatever it's supposed to be." She waved her hand.

She hesitated for a split second. Even in his panicked state, Bob noticed. She'd given something away. Ridiculous cultural building? Then Bob knew where he was. He was on Hope Island. Of course. Halwell would have thought it deliciously ironic to kill him and Ruth at the site of one of her first killings, and where the discovery of human remains — Ruth's sister — had threatened to expose her.

How could this information help him? Bob didn't know, but Halwell had made one small mistake, and even though it was the faintest of hopes, she might make more.

229

She carried on speaking. "It seems the police are looking for you. You are on their wanted list. So we are going to invite them here to get you. But not before you gun them down, kill the lovely Ruth and then, of course, kill yourself. The brilliant journalist Bob Hinton will forever be known as a crazy cop killer who believed his own conspiracy theories."

The police wanted him? He didn't understand. But if the police were looking for him, that was a good thing. He said, his voice a little stronger, "Whatever you're planning, my daughter will make the truth known."

Halwell laughed. "Did you think I killed Juanita just to show you how tough I am? Remember Sebastian? Some powerful friends will make sure he's released pending a new trial in a few weeks. He'll want revenge for his sister's death. He'll come looking for your daughter. Then you'll both be gone. Journalists are hated almost as much as lawyers and politicians. Nobody will miss you. Or her." She jerked her head in Ruth's direction. "What's the old saying about Indians?"

She repeated the tired, bigoted old saying about dead Indians and laughed again. Bob had never hit a woman in his life. If his hand were free, he knew he'd make an exception, just this once.

Bob realized that Ruth had been silent for a while. She was slumped forward with her head on her chest. Bob hoped she'd fainted. This experience was terrifying, and Halwell hadn't finished yet.

The sound of static filled the room. One man walked behind Bob, and he heard words exchanged, although he couldn't make them out.

Halwell said nothing until the man walked back and whispered in her ear. She nodded.

"Cover their heads," she ordered.

Once again, Bob's head was covered. He heard footsteps leaving, but he daren't say anything to Ruth. He sat silently, his muscles numb, wondering if it was better or worse to know they were going to die, just twenty minutes away from everyone who loved them.

CHAPTER THIRTY

Andi held the copy of the article she'd written about Sebastian Romero, Elizabeth Halwell's bodyguard. He'd been convicted of two homicides and one attempted homicide. He'd refused to implicate Halwell, so was facing a considerable stretch in prison without the chance of parole. It was too much of a coincidence. Juanita Romero must be his sister.

Her father must have suspected something. The clues were there. Why would a young woman from Argentina look for work in Coffin Cove? Why else would she want to get close to Bob and Ruth? And then there was the overt hostility towards Ruth, the muttered insult after the so-called "accident" with the wine.

"You idiot," Andi said out loud to herself. She had allowed herself to be blinkered by the police investigation. Fowler had assumed there was a connection between Bob's disappearance and Professor Weber's murder, and Andi had just accepted their theory and run with it.

She'd sent Charlie to Quadra Island and the young woman had believed she was on a quest to find clues to Bob's disappearance, and she'd put herself in harm's way.

Not only that, but Andi had also wasted valuable time. She couldn't afford to waste any more.

If Juanita was still in town, she would need somewhere to stay, and there was only one place that could be. Andi picked up her phone and then changed her mind. She needed to look Juanita in the eye.

* * *

It was late, and the motel was in darkness except for a faint glow of light coming from the office.

Peggy Wilson opened the office door on the first knock. Her face was pale, devoid of the heavy make-up she'd been wearing of late. She had dark circles under her eyes, and instead of her usual colour-coordinated outfit, she was wearing a baggy sweatshirt and joggers.

"Are you all right?" Andi asked, startled by Peggy's appearance.

"Of course," Peggy snapped, but her tone lacked conviction.

Andi didn't have time for small talk.

"I'm sorry to bother you this late, Peggy. I'm looking for someone who might have been staying here recently. You remember the server at the Cove Bistro? Juanita?"

"The foreign one?"

"Yes." Andi resisted the urge to roll her eyes. "She's from Argentina."

"She's not staying here."

"Not now, but recently, maybe?"

Peggy sighed. Andi's questions clearly annoyed her. "Not ever."

"OK, then. Thanks anyway." Andi turned to walk away.

"Why are you looking for her?"

Peggy couldn't help herself, Andi knew.

"I think she might know something about my father's disappearance," Andi said.

"He's still missing?" Peggy asked. "I'm sorry about that." She sounded genuine.

Andi looked at Peggy closely. "Peggy, are you sure you are OK? You look . . . well, you don't seem your usual self."

"I'm fine," Peggy said sharply, and closed the door.

* * *

Back at the office, Andi called Harry. The call went straight to voicemail. She left a message and as soon as she ended the call, her phone buzzed.

"Andi?" Hephzibah's voice sounded anxious. "Andi, I think something has happened to Ruth. She hasn't come home."

* * *

"Hep called me half an hour ago. Ruth didn't come home. She told Hep she was working late, but by ten o'clock, Hep got worried. She called Ruth on the office number and her cell, but no answer. Then she called Chief George, and he said Ruth was getting ready to leave the office around seven. He's going to the office now, and he'll meet us at the café."

Harry had picked up Andi's second call.

"Have you called Matt?" he asked immediately.

"Not yet. I was waiting to see what the chief found. Ruth has been exhausted lately. Maybe she just fell asleep in her office and didn't hear the phone."

"I hope so. I'll meet you at the café in a few minutes."

The words in that note came back to Andi. *Please God, it can't have been an actual threat to Ruth's life.*

Light flooded out from the café as Andi met Harry on the boardwalk. She wondered briefly where he'd been, but there was no time for that now. As they walked, she told him about Juanita Romero and her suspicions.

"There's more you should know," Harry said grimly. "I'll tell you in a minute. Let's hear what the chief has to say first."

The chief's truck was parked by the marina, and he was waiting in the café with a white-faced Hephzibah.

"She's not there," the chief said as soon as they walked in. "But her car is. I checked in all the offices and then I looked all over the parking lot. I found these." He held up a bunch of keys.

"They're Ruth's," Hephzibah confirmed.

"I have to say—" the chief looked at Hephzibah with worry in his face — "I also found scuff marks and footprints around her car. Large prints."

"Oh God." Hephzibah's legs buckled, and the chief grabbed her arm. "Sit down, my dear."

"Is it possible she's with someone on the rez?" Harry asked. "What about the lawyers she's been working with? Maybe she went for a meeting and forgot the time?"

The chief shook his head. "No. They went back to Vancouver. I'm not sure who Ruth would stay with, but I'll make some calls."

"OK, thanks, chief. Hep, phone Matt Beaufort. Don't bother with 911, they dispatch from Nanaimo, it'll take an hour for someone to get here. Use Matt's home number," Harry said, urgency in his voice. "Plus, Matt knows about the note."

"Note?" The chief looked up from his phone.

Andi told him about the anonymous note Andi and Hephzibah received.

"I reported it this morning," Hephzibah said. "Matt said he would make it a priority."

"We think a server from the Cove Bistro wrote it," Andi said, and told him about Juanita and her disappearance.

"You think she took Ruth? Or attacked her?" The chief looked puzzled. "Why?"

Andi took a deep breath. "Chief George, we might be making connections where there aren't any, but we think Juanita Romero may be connected with Elizabeth Halwell."

Chief looked at her, and Andi could tell he was making connections in his mind. "Your father too?" he asked.

Andi nodded. "I think so. But I have no idea where Dad and Ruth might be. Halwell has all the money and power in the world. They could be . . ." She stopped as she heard a low moan from Hephzibah.

"Andi," Harry said, and there was an urgency in his voice.

"I think I know where Ruth is. I think your father is there too."

CHAPTER THIRTY-ONE

Beth Stanton sat in an interview room at Campbell River detachment with Inspector Fowler. They both had plastic cups of lukewarm coffee in front of them.

"What do you think?" Fowler asked. She'd lost her hostile attitude, Beth thought. Throughout the interview with Sylvie Hamm, Fowler had deferred to her several times. Now she was asking Beth's opinion.

"She was at Weber's cabin a few days before she reported the death. She admitted she knew he was dead, and she had no good reason why she delayed calling the police. She stole the wedding rings, but nothing else we know of. She is very . . . *strange*. If she had said she was in shock, or frightened, that might be a reason for her silence, I suppose. But she seemed . . . matter of fact about it all."

Fowler nodded. "She wasn't fazed about his death at all. But in her first interview, she was crying and seemed shaken. So, which is it?"

Beth said, "It's all circumstantial. Officer Vaughan is working on the financials. That might be a motive."

Fowler thought for a moment. "She might have been panicked that his son would discover money missing, so she went after him too?"

"It's possible. We're attempting to track her movements and see if there are any witnesses who saw her in Coffin Cove. She's certainly memorable. But the problem is there's little other evidence to tie her to either murder. And another thing."

Beth spread out the photographs from the file and her own pictures she'd printed off.

"I think the murder weapon was Randolph's own cane. See, in every recent picture, he has a cane. John Simpson, his handyman, said Randolph could hardly move without it. But his cane is missing."

Fowler nodded. "Right, a team will go through Sylvie Hamm's house. Make sure everyone knows what they're looking for. Good work, Sergeant."

Before Beth could acknowledge the rare compliment, Fowler's phone rang.

"Sergeant Beaufort?"

Fowler listened for a few minutes, her face serious. "Do it, Sergeant. How long will that take? Right. We're on our way."

* * *

It was nearly eleven o'clock and Harry was relieved the snow had only amounted to a few flakes and the blanket of cloud had lifted. Instead, the ocean reflected the pinpricks of light from a million stars and the silver shimmer from January's wolf moon lit the bay.

Sergeant Matt Beaufort had told him not to move from the office.

"Gunshots are a priority," he'd said. "We'll get patrol boats and see what's going on out there. Inspector Fowler's on her way."

Harry had been silent.

"It could just be a couple of overzealous security guards," Matt continued. "But leave it to us to check out."

When Harry still didn't answer, Matt sighed. "Just don't do anything stupid, Harry."

Harry had the same success in persuading Andi to stay with Hephzibah.

The *Pipe Dream* was too big and slow for Harry's plan. Ike kept a speedboat tied at the dock, and Harry knew where he kept the key.

"Go home," Harry had said to Hephzibah. "What if I'm wrong and Ruth arrives home? You need to be there. We'll be two hours, no more."

Two or three hours at the most was all they'd have, Harry knew.

"We're not going to the north side of the island," he told Andi and Chief George as he untied Ike's speedboat. "We'll go to Mercy Bay. It'll be tricky in the dark, but I should be able to navigate by the moon's light. There's an old dock, and it's about a ten-minute hike through the bush to where the contractors have been working. If it is Halwell's men I saw, and they've got Ruth and Bob, then that's the only place they can be."

Harry looked at Chief George. "Chief, are you up for this?"

"I am prepared." The chief had taken a quick detour to his truck and was now holding his hunting rifle. Harry nodded at the firearm. He'd been hunting with Chief George. They both knew how to use a gun and they didn't panic easily.

"That's a good idea. I'll get mine." Harry left the chief and Andi and jogged along the dock to the *Pipe Dream*. He took his gun from the safe, along with a box of ammunition. He did not know who or what they might face on Hope Island, but whoever it was on the island hadn't hesitated to open fire. Harry picked up two flashlights. What else? He thought for a moment and then grabbed his first aid kit and a couple of blankets. If Ruth and Bob were there, they might be hurt. He didn't want to think about the alternative.

In a few minutes, he was back on the speedboat. The chief untied the last line, and Harry held his breath as he turned the ignition. Ike didn't use the boat much. Harry

238

breathed again as the engine spluttered and then caught, and then he idled the speedboat away from the dock. Once they were clear of the breakwater, he pushed the throttle wide open, and the engine's growl split the night air.

Harry kept the boat moving as fast as possible, while keeping an eye for floating debris. Earlier, he'd taken the *Pipe Dream* to the north side of Hope Island. With its sloping beach and well-built dock, it was the best access onto the island. Mercy Bay was on the south side. The locals called it "No Mercy Bay" because there was a rock outcrop which formed a barrier across it. At low tide, it was impossible for any boat to cross through the narrow entrance. At high tide, it was still tricky, but someone experienced could get through.

Harry knew he had to focus, but his thoughts went back to the complicated history his family had with Hope Island. His mother had lived in a woman's commune with Hephzibah, after fleeing his violent father. Ed, his father, had witnessed the brutal murder of Essie George, Ruth's sister, and now it was probable that Ruth herself was captive on the island.

"Damn place is cursed," he muttered, slowing the boat as they neared the rocky entrance to Mercy Bay.

He knew Andi had heard him, and felt her body lean in to his. "It's not ghosts we're up against," she said.

"No. I wish you'd stay with the boat," he said, knowing what the response would be.

"Not a chance. If we're certain Dad and Ruth are here, I'll text Matt immediately. And if we catch sight of Halwell, I want evidence." Andi tapped her phone. "This takes decent pictures at night. If we see her, this time she's not getting away with it."

Harry nodded. "All right. But you do what I say. This is a reconnoitre mission, right? Nothing else."

He slowed the boat as much as he could, and the engine was just a low rumble as they glided past the rocks. Mercy Bay was a half-moon-shaped cove cut into the island. It was surrounded by dense bush, and as they moved past the rock outcrops, they were plunged into darkness.

Harry cut the engine and waited until his eyes adjusted to the darkness. The boat was drifting towards the shore. Luckily, they were only a few feet from the old wooden dock, jutting out from the cliff. Not wanting to start the motor again, in case they were heard, Harry grabbed wooden paddles from under the seats and handed one to the chief.

In a few strokes, Harry reached out and grabbed a wooden pylon. He put one hand over another, pulling the boat with his hands until he felt metal. The starry night was enough for Harry to see now, and he knew he'd found the metal steps attached to the dock.

The chief tied the boat to a pylon. Harry went first, hoping the steps would hold his weight, and knowing if they did, Andi and Chief George would be fine.

The dock creaked, and the rotting wood sunk a little under his feet, but the structure held. The chief handed up the flashlights and Harry's rifle, before helping Andi get her footing on the steps. When she was standing beside Harry, the chief climbed up.

"What now?" Andi said, and then dropped her voice to a whisper when Harry hushed her. The cleared site and cabins where Bob and Ruth were likely held were a ten- or fifteen-minute walk away, but Harry was concerned about men patrolling the island. They had been aware of Captain Ron almost as soon as his troller had arrived at the northern dock. When the police arrived, they'd dock in the same place. Hopefully, everyone's attention would be there.

But then, he reasoned, it would be easy to monitor Mercy Bay, just by setting up game cameras, which would be activated by movement. Their only hope was that Halwell and her men were unaware of this access. They were taking a chance. Again, Harry wished Andi had stayed behind.

The chief spoke into his ear. "I used to hunt deer here with my grandfather. In front of us is the main trail which leads to the old lighthouse site. That's where the contractors have been working. Before we get to the clearing, there is another trail which circles around the clearing. I will take that trail. It will get me near the cabins. I might locate our people."

Harry nodded. "What if you do?"

He felt the chief's breath and there was a long pause. "If these people are as ruthless as you say, I do not want to wait for the police. You will need to create a diversion, and I will attempt to free Ruth and Mr Hinton."

Briefly, Harry and Chief George made a plan. Then they got out their phones and made sure they were set to vibrate. Harry motioned for Andi to do the same.

"Chief, it's risky," Harry whispered.

In the dark, Harry saw the chief's bright smile. "Yes, it's risky. It's risky to wait. I think, if the opportunity is there, we must act. If I can free our friends, then I will guide them to Andi, who must lead them back to the boat. She must keep in contact with the police. Is Andi able to get them back to Coffin Cove alone — if it is necessary?"

Harry nodded. "I think so, if she's careful."

He leaned forward and relayed the plan to Andi, murmuring into her ear, as Chief George had done with him. Her eyes widened, but she nodded. "I can do it," she whispered back.

Harry calculated in his head. Two hours max before the tide turned, and even the speed boat wouldn't be able to get out of Mercy Bay. Then they'd be stuck until the following morning.

"Let's get going," he whispered.

Harry took the lead, with Andi following, and Chief George at the rear. Harry kept the flashlight on the lowest setting and pointed at the ground. He hoped the bush was dense enough to cover their presence.

The track was narrow and rutted. Even the pinpricks of starlight and the large moon were obscured by the fir trees which lined the trail. Two good things, Harry thought. They were walking on a bed of needles, which dampened any noise from their footsteps, and the trail was so overgrown it was obvious nobody had used it for a long time.

He heard Andi gasp twice as branches scraped their arms and faces, but their progress was uneventful.

Harry stopped suddenly and felt Andi press into his back. He turned around and whispered, "There's somebody near."

They were at the edge of a large clearing the size of two football fields. The moon was high, and Harry could see the outline of buildings at the farthest edge of the clearing. He couldn't see any movement, but he could smell somebody smoking a cigarette. He waited and watched, and there it was. In front of the dark buildings was the faintest red glow of light.

Harry had not seen the new cabins in daylight, but he knew they faced east, onto the beach. The plans which Ruth had described for the cultural centre had large windows facing the ocean. Harry hoped Chief George could get a good look at whatever — or whoever — was in those cabins.

The chief tapped him lightly on the shoulder and motioned that he was taking the trail to their right. He'd keep in the treeline, but the firs had given way to large maples and oaks. Harry hoped the recent rain would have dampened the undergrowth so the chief wouldn't be detected. The slightest noise travelled long distances in the night.

As if to confirm his thoughts, Harry heard the murmur of men's voices. He stood absolutely still, and he felt Andi stiffen against him. Chief George was also motionless as they saw a blue glow light up a doorway. There were two men standing on a porch, one of them holding a phone which was emitting the light. Before the light clicked off, Harry saw they were both armed. He knew guns, and he was certain one man was casually holding a semi-automatic rifle. Assault weapons like these were banned in Canada. Now he was certain Bob and Ruth were being held hostage in the guarded building.

The chief moved silently away from them.

The moon was slipping across the night sky. Harry moved himself and Andi further back into the trail. They needed to wait for Chief George to message Harry — either *Yes* or *No*. *Yes* meant Harry was to move away from the clearing towards the main dock and fire his gun to create a diversion. Then it was all up to Chief George. *No* meant they were to wait for the chief to join them, and they'd retreat down the trail to the boat, and let the police figure out what was going on.

Harry was relieved he couldn't hear Chief George move in the bush. He'd been with the chief once when they were tracking a herd of elk. The animals had been unaware of the chief's presence until he was near enough for them to pick up his scent. But this was different. The chief wouldn't be able to see where he was putting his feet. The sound of the smallest twig breaking would echo in the darkness and give away his presence.

Harry kept his eyes on the cabin. The tiny red lights went out, and then he saw an orange flare as they lit more cigarettes. He heard a low murmuring. Neither of the men seemed on high alert.

It felt like hours had passed, and Harry's muscles were stiff. Andi was crouched down, and he could hear her breathing. She was leaning in against his back, her arm around his waist.

Then she moved back, and Harry felt the vibration of his phone next to his chest.

He turned around with his back to the clearing so he could check the screen.

He looked at Andi and could make out her anxious face looking up at him.

"It's 'yes'," he whispered in her ear. "They're in the cabin."

CHAPTER THIRTY-TWO

Bob's head was uncovered now. This wasn't a good thing, he knew. If they didn't care what he saw, then it was obvious they planned to kill him.

It was quiet now. A while ago, the men and Elizabeth Halwell had been talking animatedly, and moving in and out of the cabin. In the distance, he'd heard a faint *pop-pop* and then Halwell had raised her voice in anger. Then there was the static of the radio again.

Bob couldn't make out much, but it was clear something had happened, and they were changing plans. Someone had pulled the cover from his head and given him a mouthful of water. Ruth's head was still slumped forward, and they hadn't bothered covering her again.

Juanita's body still lay in a dark pool of congealed blood. He wondered if they intended to leave her there. Halwell was right, he realized. When Juanita's brother was released, he'd go after Andi in revenge.

Bob felt the panic rise in his chest. He couldn't let that happen. Maybe he could offer an exchange. They could take him and torture and kill him in exchange for Ruth and Andi.

As he was frantically thinking of how to negotiate with a psychopath, he heard a sound.

Bob looked up to see Ruth with her head up, looking straight at him. She was grimacing and struggling in her chair.

"Ruth! Are you OK?" His voice was a hoarse whisper.

She nodded and pursed her lips together. She was frowning as if she were concentrating, and then, to Bob's amazement, pulled one of her arms from behind her back. There was a red welt on her wrist. She struggled a few seconds more and then her other arm was free.

She didn't say a word, just held up a small object. A copper bracelet.

She bent down and freed her legs. Bob could see her hands were shaking, but in moments she was standing, and then she moved across to his chair and knelt behind him. He could feel the pressure on his wrists as she worked at the thin nylon rope.

"Through the window?" Bob whispered.

"Yes."

He was sure the windows would be locked. Maybe they could smash the glass with the metal chairs.

"What the fuck?"

One of Halwell's thugs was standing in the door with his rifle pointing at them. In two strides, he was across the room and had grabbed Ruth by the throat, dragging her away from Bob's chair.

Her hands swung uselessly at his head, but he held her with his arms outstretched as if she were as light as a doll, and Bob could hear her gasp for air.

He pulled as hard as he could and got one hand free from the frayed rope.

"Leave her!" he shouted as he used his one free arm to drag him towards the man. He couldn't hear Ruth breathing now.

As Bob got near, he heard a loud cracking sound coming from outside.

Gunfire.

The thug heard it too, and for a split second loosened his grasp on Ruth's throat. Bob heard her take a shaky breath.

Bob fell forward, still partially tied to the chair, but as his free hand touched Ruth, he heard a loud explosion and shards of glass flying. Bob instinctively pulled his hand back to protect his face. His ears were ringing, and he looked up and around the room to see where the explosion had come from.

Halwell's thug stood with a stunned expression on his face. His arm went slack, and Ruth dropped to the floor on the carpet of broken glass. The big man fell backwards, and it was then that Bob saw the hole in his forehead.

In a second, Bob tried to pull himself to Ruth, but he felt a hand on his shoulder.

"Wait," a voice said, and Bob felt cold metal against his tied hand. Chief George Timms then sliced through the rope on his legs, and he was free.

Ruth was on her hands and knees, struggling to get up. The chief hauled her to her feet, and then with the butt of his rifle, he cleared a large, jagged pieces of glass from around the window he'd just fired through.

"Go," he commanded, and although Bob's muscles were burning and he felt warm trickles of blood on his face and neck, he obeyed. In an instant, he was in the cold night air.

CHAPTER THIRTY-THREE

Harry kept moving north, his flashlight pointed down, until he could hear the waves crashing on the shore. He was as far away from the cabins as he could be without leaving the safe cover of the trees. Hopefully, in a short while, patrol boats would be arriving.

He unstrapped his rifle, loaded it and fired once into the air. Then he waited and fired again. This time, he waited longer until he could hear men shouting.

He fired again for good measure and then moved back into the bush, off the trail. He thought he heard a shot in the distance and hoped Chief George was all right.

Harry crouched behind a fallen tree as he heard the crunching of fast footsteps coming nearer. He peered through the trees and in the moonlight he saw two men, both of them carrying weapons and wearing some kind of mask.

Fuck. Night vision goggles.

Their vision was as good as if it was daylight. He'd have to move carefully, otherwise they'd spot him in a moment. He needed to get back to Andi and get her to the boat.

Then he paused.

When the police arrived in patrol boats, they'd be sitting ducks. These men had military-style weapons and tactical gear, giving them a clear advantage over the local RCMP, if he didn't warn them.

Moving as slowly as possible, Harry put down his rifle on the ground and pulled out his phone. Hunching over the screen, Harry tapped out a quick text message to Matt Beaufort. He hoped that would be enough.

"The shots came from over here," a man shouted. He could hear bodies crashing through the bush. In a few minutes they'd find him, so Harry took a deep breath, stood up and started running.

Branches whipped his face and tore at his jacket. His eyes were adjusted enough for him to move quickly without crashing into trees, but he was stumbling over tree roots and brambles. Adrenaline was pumping through his body and his breath came loudly. He was sure he was making as much noise as a bull moose, and any second he'd feel a bullet go whizzing by or worse. Then his brain kicked into gear, overtaking his flight response. It was against all his instincts, but he forced his body to stop. He was leading his pursuers right to Andi. He stopped for a second to listen.

Nothing. Where were they?

Then he heard the roar of engines on the water. It was faint but getting louder. The patrol boats would be here at any second. If the men had stopped looking for him, and their attention was on their unwanted visitors, he had a chance to get back on the trail, where he could move faster.

Cautiously, he pushed through the bush until his feet found a smooth surface. The moon was visible again and cast enough light for him to see he was back on the trail and close to Andi. It was eerily quiet, no voices or footsteps. The sound of approaching boats had stopped.

Then, just as Harry was about to move again, light flooded through the trees and the clearing like floodlights in a stadium. It was as if daylight had arrived in a second.

A voice bellowed through loudspeakers, "Police! Show yourselves with your hands up!"

The words were still echoing when a burst of automatic gunfire ripped through the night air. Harry instinctively threw himself to the ground. The hail of bullets seemed to last for minutes. Then Harry could hear shouting, and gunfire started up again. The drama was unfolding behind him at the boat ramp. He needed to get to Andi. He hoped the chief had got Ruth and Bob, but either way he needed to get them all off the island.

Harry pulled himself to his feet and started running towards the trail head. It was only then he noticed he wasn't carrying his rifle, and he cursed to himself. He didn't know how many men Halwell had on the island, and it was unlikely they were all down at the boat ramp. Sweat was stinging his eyes, and he paused for a moment to wipe his face with the back of his sleeve.

Then he was aware of light above him. Harry heard the rhythmic *thwump-thwump-thwump* of a helicopter hovering above. A police helicopter? Harry couldn't be sure. Either way, he was standing where the canopy of tree branches had cleared, looking directly at the stars above him. He was an obvious target.

Harry ran as fast as he could along the trail. At least the lights from the helicopter illuminated his path, and he was moving quicker now he could see to avoid ruts and tree roots. He neared the trail head, and relief flooded through him as he saw Andi standing with other figures in the shadows. Thank God for Chief George.

The noise of the helicopter was deafening as it lowered onto the ground. The wind from the blades stung Harry's eyes as he finally reached Andi and the others. Bob Hinton and Ruth were slumped on the ground, and Chief George was leaning over them.

Harry shouted at them, but nobody heard him over the roar of the helicopter. Now Harry could see it wasn't a police helicopter.

As Harry watched, two figures emerged from the cabin. One was smaller, a woman, probably Halwell, and she was being helped along. Looking back in the direction of the boat landing, Harry saw three other men retreating towards the helicopter and then turning, crouching and firing. They were giving cover to the other two, who were about to board the helicopter.

Then, to Harry's horror, he watched as a small figure dashed from her hiding place and headed straight for the helicopter.

"Andi!" he screamed and then hurtled towards her. He saw Andi hold something up in the air, and then he was on her, pulling her to the ground as one of the armed men caught sight of her and swung his rifle in their direction. Harry felt the air move above his head as bullets narrowly missed them. He dare not look up or move, but then he heard the high whine as the helicopter prepared to lift off. He took the chance to grab Andi's hand, and crouching as low as possible, they both ran back to join the others.

All the armed men were gone. As the sound of the helicopter faded, Harry pulled Andi into an embrace and whispered fiercely, "I don't know whether to kiss you or kill you, you idiot."

She reached up and decided for him.

Bob and Ruth both seemed numb with shock, and Harry knew he needed to get them to a hospital.

Chief George knelt beside him as he checked them over for injuries, thankfully finding nothing serious except cuts and bruises.

"Harry—" the chief's voice was low and urgent — "I have killed a man. There is also a dead woman in that cabin."

Harry knew the police would find them any minute. He looked at the chief and said, "Get back to the boat. Take it back to Coffin Cove and ditch your rifle before you get there, OK? You were never here."

Harry looked into the chief's worried eyes and nodded reassurance. "Thank you. You saved lives tonight. It will be all right."

Wordlessly, Chief George nodded, stood up and started jogging down the trail back to the speedboat. Harry watched the round orb of his flashlight bounce until it disappeared into darkness.

Harry could hear voices and running footsteps getting nearer. He kissed Andi on her forehead and then stood up.

"We need help over here," he shouted and then stepped into the clearing with his hands up.

CHAPTER THIRTY-FOUR

January 10

Andi sat in the waiting room at the hospital. It was nearly four o'clock in the morning.

Hospital personnel in white coats and scrubs were swarming the corridors. Andi heard snippets of conversation and knew there was at least one officer in surgery with a serious gunshot wound.

"Miss Hinton?"

"Silvers," Andi replied automatically and looked up at a young doctor standing in front of her.

"You are Mr Hinton's daughter?"

She nodded. "How is he? And Ruth?"

Both Ruth and Bob had sustained minor injuries, the doctor explained. Ruth had a cracked cheekbone, they both had bruises and abrasions, and they were both in shock and dehydrated. Both of them would be discharged in a day or two with no lasting damage.

Except for the unseen injuries, Andi thought. She had experienced her own struggles with nightmares and anxiety after traumatic events. Both Ruth and Bob faced a long road.

She thanked the doctor. "The officer who was shot? How . . . ?" The doctor was already shaking his head. "Sorry, I can't say," and he left the room.

Andi pulled her phone out and was gazing at the screen when she heard someone cough.

Sergeant Matt Beaufort stood in the doorway. "How are they?"

Andi told him.

He sat beside her. "It's Fowler," he told her.

She had taken two bullets to the chest and one bullet had caught her in the neck on the right-hand side but had missed the carotid artery. She was still in surgery but was expected to recover, thanks to the bulletproof vest which had taken the brunt of the shots from Halwell's men.

He was silent for a moment and Andi had the feeling he wanted to talk. In the end, he said, "Coffee?"

She nodded, even though she didn't want anything.

"Walk with me."

She and Matt walked down the corridor and passed a small waiting room crammed full of police officers waiting for news of Diane Fowler's condition. The enclosed space smelled of stale coffee and sweat, even from the corridor.

Beth Stanton called after Andi and asked how Bob and Ruth were doing.

Andi told her and then said, "I'm sorry about Inspector Fowler." Beth nodded and went back to her seat.

Matt took Andi's arm.

He walked with her until they were out of earshot of the waiting room and standing in front of a vending machine.

He said, "We've been told not to talk."

"Sure, I understand, but—"

"No, you don't. We've been told not to talk — ever. Directive from way up."

It took a moment for Andi to fully comprehend what he was saying.

"This is going to be covered up again? Are you serious?" Andi glared at Matt. "Well, guess what? I don't work for

253

your bosses and Halwell will not get away with this again. She kidnapped my father and Ruth. She killed Juanita in *cold blood*. If your top brass think this can be just swept away, they will find out how wrong they are. There is *no way* my father and I will let this drop."

Matt's expression didn't change, but his tone hardened and his eyes went back to the waiting room.

"I'm just telling you what we've been told." And then he walked away, leaving Andi staring after him.

Harry was sitting in a chair when she got back to the waiting room, his legs stretched out and his head tilted back, his eyes closed.

Andi touched his arm lightly, and he struggled to sit up straight.

"I feel like I've been run over by a truck," he said. "You see the doctor? He told you they're going to be fine?"

Andi nodded. "Thank God. How did it go with the police?"

Harry shrugged. "Not sure they believe anything I said, but I stuck to the story. Ruth and Bob must have backed it up, because here I am."

"The chief?"

"I called him a few minutes ago. The speedboat is tied up, his rifle is at the bottom of the ocean and he had ten people who will swear he was tucked up in bed at nine o'clock and slept like a baby the whole night."

He looked at Andi and took her hand.

"Andi . . . ?"

"I know, I'm sorry. It was dumb, but . . ."

"Really dumb," Harry agreed. "What were you thinking, Andi?"

"I know," Andi said. "I just couldn't let Halwell get away with it again. So I didn't think, I just ran and took a picture. But it doesn't matter now. Wasted effort."

Harry listened as Andi told him about her conversation with Matt Beaufort.

He rubbed his face with his hand. "There are two dead bodies out there, and it was a firework display last night. How can they possibly cover it up?"

Andi shrugged. "Elizabeth Halwell got away with it before. I guess if you have enough money, power and influence over the right people, you can do anything."

Harry bent forward and kissed her. "The main thing right now is that we are all alive. Let's think about the rest of it tomorrow, right? Hephzibah is in with Ruth. She'll drive us home."

It was still dark when Hephzibah left Harry and Andi at Bob Hinton's house. Harry was too tired to argue about the impropriety of sleeping next to Andi in Bob's bed, and he was soon snoring.

Andi pushed her body next to his so she felt his warmth, and finally her mind closed down and she sunk into a dreamless sleep.

CHAPTER THIRTY-FIVE

Andi woke to the faint sound of her phone vibrating. She found her phone tangled in her clothes beside the bed and saw Charlie's number on the display. It was eight thirty. She'd only been asleep for about three hours, and her head was groggy.

"Charlie? Are you OK?"

"Andi, I'm at the office and there's someone here to see you." Andi listened for a minute more and told Charlie she'd be there soon.

As she got dressed, Harry stirred and turned on the bedside light.

"You going to work already?"

"Yep. A woman is waiting for me at the office. Charlie's there too. It's urgent, apparently."

Harry nodded and then leaned over the bed and grabbed Andi around the waist. He pulled her in close. "I nearly lost you again," he whispered in her ear. "Sometime soon, Andi, we need to talk."

Andi looked into his eyes but couldn't read him. She waited until the feeling of falling backwards into the abyss subsided enough for her to speak again.

Then she turned her head and kissed him. "I love you."

"I know, girl. I love you too."

But Andi had the feeling there were words left unsaid between them.

* * *

Rain soaked Andi's hair and jacket as she walked to town. She could barely see the waves hit the shore through the gloom.

Charlie was waiting for her when she got to the office.

"Hi there, Andi," she said in an overly bright tone, and widened her eyes as she gestured to a tall woman standing beside the story wall.

The woman was smartly dressed in a stylish black raincoat and leather gloves. She was carrying a small attaché case which she did not put down. She seemed fascinated by the pictures and documents pinned to the wall, and didn't turn to look at either of them as she said, "Charlene, get coffee for Ms Silvers from the café." Her tone was pleasant, but it wasn't a request. Charlie looked at Andi with an anxious expression before obeying the command.

"Can I help you?" Andi asked.

The woman ignored her but gestured at the wall with her free hand. "Very thorough work."

"Who are you?"

Andi kept her voice steady, but she felt a stab of fear.

The woman must have sensed it, because she smiled. "No need to worry, Andi. We just need to chat. Sit down."

Andi sat behind her desk and the woman moved a chair and seated herself opposite. Her hair was iron grey, pulled back into a bun, and she wore just a hint of lipstick. She could have been fifty or even sixty. Her eyes were dark and her features unremarkable.

"Who are you?" Andi tried again.

"We are all very glad that Ms Cloutier and Mr Hinton are recovering from their ordeal," the woman said, ignoring Andi's question.

"We?"

"You are a talented reporter, Andi," the woman said, still ignoring the question. "I've read your work. Impressive, really. But you will not be writing about last night's events on Hope Island, or anything or anyone at all."

"Oh, really? Says who?" Andi remembered the conversation she'd had with Matt Beaufort and wondered if this woman was an RCMP officer.

The woman smiled and said nothing. Just then Andi's phoned buzzed, and the screen lit up. The display said *number unknown*.

"Take the call, please," the woman said pleasantly.

"Andi?" It was Jim Peters. "Andi, I'm sitting in an office in the Canadian Embassy."

Andi listened as Jim talked and then ended the call without saying a word.

The woman watched her, and as Andi placed her phone on the desk, she said, "We found two bodies on the island last night. A young woman who you know as Juanita Romero and an as yet unidentified male. We also found a gun we believe belongs to Harry Brown. It has been fired several times."

She paused, leaving the unsaid implication hanging in the air.

"The RCMP, however, has closed the investigation. For now. Do nothing, Andi, which will change that decision. Listen to Mr Peters and concern yourself with local events."

Andi thought of the blurry picture she still had on her phone. She nodded at the woman, who smiled. "Andi, I wish I could take you at your word."

She produced a document from her attaché case. "Please sign this."

Andi read the document slowly. She had no choice, she knew. When she'd finished reading, she picked up a pen and signed the document. She pushed it across the desk.

The woman picked it up, placed it in her attaché case and stood up, just as Charlie arrived back.

"Ah, here's your coffee. Have a good day, ladies." And she was gone.

* * *

Ruth had woken to find a woman she didn't know standing beside her bed. It was dark, but a bedside lamp illuminated the woman's face. For a moment, the strange clicking sounds and smell of antiseptic disorientated Ruth. Her head felt heavy, and it was hard to form coherent thoughts. In fragments, flashes of the previous days came back, and in a panic, she tried to swing her legs out of bed.

In an instant, a nurse appeared beside the strange woman, put her hand out and pressed Ruth backwards onto her pillow. She said in a soothing voice, "It's all right, dear. You're safe." And then in a sharper tone to the woman, "You have two minutes."

It didn't take two minutes. Despite her grogginess, Ruth understood the message perfectly. She had struggled to a sitting position long enough to sign a legal document which closed the door on justice for her sister's death forever.

She didn't know what to think or feel, so she succumbed to the painkillers and her exhaustion and slipped into a dreamless sleep.

When Ruth woke, it was daylight. Nurses measured her blood pressure, checked her fluids and replaced her drip. They smiled and chatted about the weather and rearranged pillows. A doctor examined her cuts and checked her cheekbone.

"You may have a small dent," he said cheerfully, "but nothing that will show much."

Ruth refused more painkillers and food.

The nurse shrugged about the painkillers, but food was served anyway, and Ruth pushed unidentified grey mush around a plastic plate until she heard a discreet cough.

"May I come in?"

Ruth looked up to see her visitor and was immediately overwhelmed. She did not know where the waves of emotion came from, or why the kindly tone of Chief George's voice should prompt them, but tears ran down her face, soaking the bandage that covered her cheek and splashing into the unappetizing food. She couldn't stop them and couldn't speak.

The chief sat down in a chair beside Ruth's bed and waited.

When Ruth could compose herself, she told the chief about the woman visitor the night before, and her message. He listened without interrupting, his expression inscrutable.

"There will be no justice for Essie," she said, the tears threatening behind her eyes again.

The chief smiled at her. "Patience," he said, the one word an echo from distant years and Grandma Nora's kitchen table.

"I have news," he said after a minute, and produced a piece of folded paper from his jacket pocket.

Ruth read it.

"Approval for the hatchery grant," she said surprised. "I only submitted the application last week."

The chief nodded. "A handful of trade beads for silence."

Ruth understood. The woman who visited her in the early hours of the morning had made a simple statement. There would be no civil case against Elizabeth Halwell. The grant approval was a message to show their power. Whoever "they" may be.

"What is this?" the chief pointed to Ruth's copper bracelet.

She smiled, even though it made her face hurt. "A gift that saved my life," she said and explained how she'd used the bracelet to free herself.

The chief picked it up and studied it. "Hmm. The raven," he said, looking at the faint carving. "The trickster, but also a guardian spirit. It served you well."

He held the bracelet in his hands and then spoke again.

"The raven is the transformer, the trickster and the creator. The raven gave us the moon and the stars and the sunlight. A powerful spirit, don't you think?"

Ruth nodded. She knew the legend of how the raven stole the sun from a locked box and transformed the darkness into night and day.

"The power of a raven would be useful for a mayor," the chief continued, and Ruth saw the twinkle in his eye.

CHAPTER THIRTY-SIX

Charlie sat and listened as Andi told her about the events of the previous night. Andi chose the details carefully. The document she had signed bound her to the Security of Information Act.

Charlie, for once, was stunned into near silence, asking only whether Ruth and Bob would be OK.

"They'll be fine. Inspector Fowler was in surgery when I left, but she's expected to be OK too."

Charlie sat back in her chair and exhaled a long breath. "That's an amazing story."

"Yes, but one we will never tell." Andi explained her editorial decision was to not publish the story.

"Sometimes we have to make hard decisions. I've talked to Jim, and we decided legally we'd be too exposed on this one."

"Really?"

It sounded lame to Andi's ears, but she nodded. Elizabeth Halwell was forever off-limits. In return, her and Bob's safety was assured, and Harry would never be prosecuted.

Andi wondered how often shadowy powerful figures had cleaned up Elizabeth Halwell's mess and why, if "they" were so powerful, they continued to do so.

"Andi, I hope you are enjoying that coffee," Charlie said, breaking into Andi's thoughts.

"I am. You're a lifesaver."

"Good. Then hopefully you won't be too mad at me."

"And why would I be mad at you?"

Charlie's face fell. "I've written my article about Randolph Weber's death, and Sylvie Hamm. But I don't want to publish it. Not yet, anyway."

Andi remembered today was the deadline she'd given Charlie for her assignment about Randolph Weber's murder.

"Charlie, you've had a horrible ordeal. Don't worry about the article. In fact, take a few days off."

We all should, she thought, and suddenly felt exhausted.

Charlie pulled a face. "No, I want to work. Besides, Monica Drummond called me. She works at the ferry terminal on Quadra Island and she's the source for some of the background on Sylvie Hamm. The police are questioning her about Sylvie's movements on the day Professor Weber was killed, whether Sylvie left the island that day."

"They think Sylvie killed the professor? Makes sense."

"I know. But Monica didn't see Sylvie get on the ferry, and she says nobody else at the ferry terminal saw her either. I know she wasn't at the lecture, Andi. You've seen a picture of her. She stands out in a crowd."

Andi sighed. "You know, she fooled the police when she reported finding Weber Senior's body. And she kidnapped you. Isn't it possible she's just a great liar, Charlie?"

"Yes, but even when she was attacking me, I think she was just really frightened. And she was obsessed with her stuff. She kept saying over and over again, 'It's mine, it's mine.' She's nuts, but I don't think she's a killer."

"OK, what do you want to do?" Andi asked, eyeing Charlie and wondering if she'd found someone more obsessed with chasing a story than herself.

"I was supposed to talk to Maeve and Monica Drummond about Randolph Weber, but I . . ." Charlie shrugged and smiled. "I was Sylvie Hamm's guest instead. I want to find out more about Randolph Weber."

Andi smiled at her junior reporter. "OK, but there's one thing you have to do."

"What's that?"

"You have to take me with you. I'm not letting you out of my sight for a while."

Charlie hesitated.

Andi grinned. "Don't worry. The story is yours. Now, what are you waiting for? We'd better get to Quadra Island before the *Tribune* scoops the story."

* * *

"I should have told that police officer what I knew. But I was so upset, and they said it was a robbery gone wrong. It wasn't until Monica told me they'd arrested Sylvie Hamm, and then I found out about poor Gerald, that I thought I should tell someone."

Andi sat next to Charlie on a floral sofa and smiled reassuringly at Maeve Drummond. The elderly lady sat upright on a chair next to the fire with her hand in her lap, and they all waited until Monica, Maeve's daughter, arrived with a tray and poured them all a cup of tea.

Monica talked.

"I think we may have given you the wrong impression of Sylvie Hamm. That's the problem with living on the island; someone gossips, then it spreads, and then it all gets out of hand. People have been telling stories about Sylvie since we were in school."

"The police don't arrest people just on the strength of gossip." Andi smiled at Maeve. "There's evidence that Sylvie was at the cabin and knew about Randolph's death several days before she reported it. And she kidnapped Charlie."

Maeve Drummond looked sad. "It's terrible. I'm so glad you're all right. But as awful as that was, I just can't believe Sylvie would kill Randolph. She's looked after him for years. He was a very private man, and since Inga died, he hardly let anyone get close, but he let Sylvie visit. He never said anything bad about her."

She looked down at her hands. "Sylvie has never been violent before now. She was always just . . . odd. Even as a little girl."

"In what way?" Charlie asked. Andi watched her tap her phone and place it on a small coffee table between her and Maeve Drummond. They had already asked permission to record the interview.

"She was a shy child. She was always very quiet. Monica and Sylvie were never friends at school, even though they were the same age. She came to one of Monica's birthday parties once and instead of playing with the other children, she gathered up all the garbage and took it home."

She hesitated and looked at Monica. "She stole from me just last year. It wasn't anything valuable, but it was precious to me. Sylvie got fixated on an ornament which Monica had made for me. I loved it. One day, after a visit from Sylvie, it was gone. We couldn't prove it, of course."

Monica said, "There were rumours she'd taken other things from people's houses. But the Community Health office wouldn't do anything without proof, and Sylvie's son threatened to sue if they fired her."

Maeve sighed. "When Sylvie was very little, her parent's house burned down and everything in it was lost. Nobody was hurt, but they had nothing. It took years for the family to get back on their feet. I think that must have affected Sylvie."

"Mrs Drummond, we're really here to find out about Randolph Weber and his son. If Sylvie Hamm didn't kill them, then their murderer is still out there somewhere."

Andi didn't want to get distracted about Sylvie Hamm. She was obviously a troubled soul, but she sensed Maeve Drummond held the key to the real story they were pursuing.

Maeve nodded. "I know." She looked sad. "The last time I saw Randolph was just before his hundredth birthday. He gave a talk at the Historical Society about Ripple Rock. There were so many people there, and he was in his element. He was a kind of hero in our lives. If you had known how treacherous the Narrows was, before the blast . . ." she trailed off lost in thought for a moment.

"They came from all over," Monica said. "It was quite the event. The *Tribune* advertised it and ran an article about Randolph and Ripple Rock. Mom, do you still have a copy?"

"I do, I'll find it for you," Maeve said. "I wish I had made time for him," she continued. "But my husband died, and I was . . . anyway, I know he was struggling. Monica said he even had a pastor visit him. Randolph used to argue with my husband about religion. He was an atheist, so I know he must have been facing his mortality." She shook her head and dabbed at her eyes with a tissue.

"It's OK, Mom," Monica said gently. "You couldn't have known. Tell them about Inga."

Maeve started to talk.

"Inga was much older than me. I knew her when I was a young girl. The Webers were neighbours as long as I can remember. I always looked up to Inga. She was such an intelligent woman. She and Randolph were engineers. Randolph got all the credit. In those days, they did not recognize women for their achievements. She and Randolph had lost a child, a son called Theo. I think it was meningitis. Inga was devastated, and I think she enjoyed having me around."

She paused and then continued.

"Then, after Ripple Rock, they adopted Gerald."

Maeve shrugged. "We thought little about it. Everyone was glad for them. Gerald came from a troubled background. We knew that. His mother had worked at the miners' camp on Maud Island, and when the blast happened, she disappeared. Everyone thought she'd abandoned Gerald, and it seemed like God's gift to all of them. Gerald filled the hole that Theo had left, and he was a boy who never wanted for anything after that."

Maeve looked at Charlie and Andi, who were listening intently. "They really loved Gerald. It was only when Inga got sick that she talked about Ripple Rock and finding Gerald. I think she wanted someone to know the truth."

1958, BLAST DAY

Gerald grabbed Randolph's hand.

"Hurry," was the only word he spoke. The rain was blowing in from the ocean, coming sideways in gusts. The boy's shirt was stuck to his skin, and Randolph could see the jutting outline of his shoulder blades.

Randolph was wheezing. Too many months behind a desk and his heavy coat were hampering his pace.

"Wait up. Tell me what's going on. Who's trying to kill your mother?"

The boy glanced back but didn't answer, just tugged harder on Randolph's hand.

"All right, I'm coming, I'm coming."

Gerald slowed when they reached a house near the trail to Maud Island. Randolph realized he must have passed it every day for three years, but it was set back off the track and was obscured by high unkempt brambles and a dilapidated fence.

For all the haste the boy had made from the beach, he now seemed reluctant to open the gate. He looked at Randolph with large eyes sunk in his pale face. He was shivering, but Randolph couldn't tell if it was from the cold or because he was frightened.

"Come now. Let's see what's going on. It'll be all right, I'm sure." Randolph kept his voice calm and reassuring, but seeing the boy's obvious anxiety, he was getting worried.

Randolph pushed open the gate.

There was a well-trodden path through grass and weeds which were flattened by the rain. It led to an open door, and Randolph could see it was hanging off its hinges. It didn't bode well. There was no noise, just the rhythmic patter of rain on the roof of the two-storey house.

As they got nearer, Randolph could see that the door led directly into a kitchen. There were red flagstones on the floor. They appeared wet.

Randolph stood at the doorway with Gerald trembling behind him.

He rapped on the door. "Hello there, is anyone at home?"

He peered inside. The light was dim, but he felt some warmth. There was a large table in front of a wood stove. Nothing looked out of place, except a chair which was lying on its side.

"Hello?" Randolph said again in a louder voice. He stepped inside. His foot squelched in the dampness, and he looked down. It was only then that he saw the flagstones were not red. His shoe was covered in blood.

Just then, he heard a moaning sound.

"Ma?"

Gerald pushed past Randolph and before he could stop him, the boy was behind the kitchen table, and then he screamed.

Randolph moved quickly and found Gerald on his knees with his arms around a body lying prone on the tiles.

"Let me see." Randolph pulled the boy away.

A woman lay face down on the floor. Randolph could now see where the blood had come from. One side of her head had been caved in. A cast-iron pot lay on the floor beside her. Randolph drew back, trying not to touch anything and trying not to scream himself. The floor was a river of blood. Randolph had never seen such a horrific sight, but he couldn't look away. It was as if the dead woman mesmerized him.

A small whimper shook him out of it. He looked down at Gerald, but the boy was silently sobbing, tears running down his cheeks.

The whimper came again, and Randolph looked around. There was a narrow staircase in the corner of the room. In the gloom it looked like a heap of clothes was piled on the bottom step.

Then it moved.

The outline of a man's head emerged. Randolph moved towards him. "What happened here?" Randolph asked.

"That . . . fucking . . . bitch . . ."

The man coughed and spat.

"Dad!"

Randolph looked up. At the top of the staircase was another boy. He was taller than Gerald, but his voice was thin and reedy with fear.

"See what that bitch did to my dad!" he shouted. "Who the fuck are you?"

Before Randolph could reply, he heard a wail from behind him. It wasn't grief. It was a howl of rage, a shriek of anger.

"He killed my mother!" Gerald screamed.

Randolph moved to grab Gerald by his shoulders, but in a quick move, the boy ducked under Randolph's arm and stood over the coughing man slumped on the staircase.

In horror, Randolph saw Gerald was clasping the cast-iron pot with two hands. Shaking with rage or the weight of the pot, Randolph didn't know, the boy raised the pot above his head and brought it down on the man's head with all the force his thin body could muster, before either Randolph or the other boy could intervene.

Blood sprayed the wall. The man made a gurgling sound, then a loud rasping breath, and his body twitched before lying still.

"Dad!"

The other boy threw himself down the stairs. Moving quicker this time, Randolph pulled Gerald out of the way and used his own body as a shield.

"He killed my dad!" the boy tried to get around Randolph, but ended up flailing against his chest instead.

"I'm gonna kill him! I'm gonna kill him . . ."

Randolph didn't stop to think about his next words.

"No, you are not. There has been enough killing here. I'm taking Gerald and I'm going to the police right now."

"He's going to prison for murdering my dad!"

Randolph took hold of the boy's shoulders and shook him hard.

"I'm going to the police. I will tell them I found two dead bodies when I arrived. I work for the government, and I am a very important person. Who do you think they will believe? So, you better think about that because I will tell them you were the only person alive in the house when I got here. I think, when the police hear my story, they might suspect *you*. Do you hear me?"

"I didn't kill nobody," the boy said and sobbed. "I didn't kill nobody."

"Then you stick to what I say. There was a terrible fight. They both ended up dead. You hear me?" Randolph shook the boy again.

He nodded, still sobbing.

Randolph turned around. He took the cast-iron pot from Gerald and placed it beside the dead man.

"Come on, Gerald. We're leaving now."

CHAPTER THIRTY-SEVEN

Present day
January 10

The cabin looked grey and lifeless. The windows were dark, like mournful eyes. Bright yellow crime scene tape had been left attached to the front door and was fluttering in the breeze.

Monica Drummond unlocked the door and pushed it open.

"If you don't mind, I think I'll wait here," she said and moved to let Andi and Charlie step inside.

Andi had asked if they could see Randolph's cabin. Maeve Drummond got them a key. The police hadn't been back, she said. Nobody had said they couldn't go inside.

The living room had once been cosy. Andi could imagine Randolph sitting in the high-backed chair, reading and dozing by the warmth of the open fire.

Charlie shivered. "It's creepy," she said and then sniffed. "What's that smell?"

"Bleach? Or some kind of cleaning fluid," Andi said.

"What are we looking for?" Charlie asked.

"I have no idea, really," Andi said, looking around for a light switch. The power was still connected, but the light

271

bulb only emitted a faint glow. "Just some sense of who Randolph was, background for the Weber family, that kind of thing."

"This must be his wife, and Gerald Weber when he was young," Charlie said, looking at a black-and-white photograph in an ornate silver frame. "She was pretty. Do you think Randolph really covered up a murder so his wife could have a son again? Do you think they were both killed because of that?"

Andi said, "I don't know. Why wait until he was one hundred years old? Why not come looking before now? The trouble with small communities is that rumours and gossip somehow morph into the truth, if they're repeated often enough."

"I still don't think Sylvie Hamm killed him," Charlie said with conviction.

One wall of the living room was lined with books. Andi ran her eyes over the titles. They were mostly non-fiction — engineering textbooks, world history, geology and a few classics.

"Is this where he died?" Charlie asked. She had left the living room and was standing at the foot of a narrow staircase. There was a dark stain on the wood floors and the smell of bleach made Andi's eyes sting.

"Yes. Looks like the forensic team thinks whoever attacked him came through the back door and into the kitchen. Look at all the fingerprint dust."

Almost every surface in the small kitchen was covered in white powder, including around the door frames. The cabinets and countertops were yellowed and worn, and the stove and fridge were a mustard colour, apart from the white dust.

"It doesn't look like Randolph spent a lot of money," Charlie commented.

"You're right." Andi walked back into the living room and looked around. "There's nothing that suggests he was wealthy. Maeve said nothing seemed to be missing, so why attack a one-hundred-year-old man? Unless you've stolen something and he threatened to tell the police?"

Andi turned to look at Charlie, who was looking up the staircase. "Let's look up there. There might be a clue."

Andi smiled. The young woman wasn't going to be easily convinced.

Upstairs were two bedrooms. One was a narrow room with a small window looking out over the backyard. Andi imagined there was a peek-a-boo view of the ocean on a clear day. This had probably been Gerald's room. There was a single bed, a closet and a chest of drawers. There was only one picture on the wall.

"Look at that," Charlie said. "That's Ripple Rock."

Andi stepped to take a closer look. Someone had printed *April 5th, 1958*, in tiny letters in the corner of the picture. It depicted the epic moment of history at its most dramatic point. Thick grey plumes of smoke and rocks had been flung up through the ocean's surface, and the photographer had caught the moment just as the debris had reached its highest point and had just started the arc of descent back into the water.

"Didn't Maeve say Gerald's birth mother worked in the Ripple Rock camp? This could be significant."

"Or Gerald could be proud of his father's engineering achievements." Andi smiled. "Come on, we'll take a quick look in the other bedroom and then get out of here."

Randolph's room was just as sparsely furnished. A double bed with a wrought-iron frame stood against one wall. The floral wallpaper was stained in the corners and peeling. There was a chair in one corner and an oak dressing table with a large oval mirror facing the bed.

There was only one bedside table with a lamp. A pair of glasses and a magnifying glass sat beside a book. Andi stood looking at the table. Charlie reached out to touch the book.

"Don't," Andi said more sharply than she intended. It didn't feel right being in this bedroom. They were trespassing in the private moments of a man's life.

Charlie withdrew her hand. "Sorry," she said. "It's just that most old people I know have the Bible beside their bed. This is some book about math."

Andi looked at Charlie and laughed. "Not all old people have the Bible beside their bed. Some people read romance novels or . . ."

She stopped. A thought vibrated in the corner of her mind, not quite formed yet. She looked at the book and thought through all they'd been told about Randolph Weber.

"What?" Charlie asked.

Andi led the way down the stairs and out the front door. Monica was still waiting for them.

"Find anything useful?" Monica asked and stepped forward to lock the door.

"You said Randolph used to argue about religion with your dad, didn't you? Did he believe in God?" Andi asked.

"Randolph?" Monica laughed. "No, he thought religion was ridiculous. He thought God was a 'social construct to calm the masses'." She used air quotes to emphasize her point. "He could be quite offensive about it. I was glad he was too old to be invited to Dad's funeral, because he might have said something to upset Mom."

Andi nodded. "I thought so."

"Why? Is that important?" Charlie was looking at Andi with a puzzled expression.

"Could we talk to your mother again? I have a couple more questions."

* * *

"You said that lots of people came to Randolph's talk, including people who'd seen the *Tribune*'s article. Is that right?" Andi asked.

They were back in Maeve's living room.

"Yes, lots of people showed up. It was a nice crowd, all those people interested in Randolph's achievements. Why?" Maeve was puzzled.

"You said earlier that a pastor had visited Randolph, is that right?"

"Come to think of it, I don't know if the pastor ever visited. Monica just said that a pastor was asking after him." Maeve looked at her daughter questioningly.

Monica nodded her head. "I didn't see him myself. Christie, the café owner, said that a pastor was asking after Randolph. I don't know if she told him where he lived, or if he visited."

"You never actually saw him?"

Monica shook her head. "No. But there was a pastor who showed up at the talk. He seemed very interested in Ripple Rock and Randolph Weber. Mom, did you find the *Tribune*'s articles?"

"I did. This one is the first advertising the event, and this is the article with the pictures." Maeve handed them to Andi.

"Do you remember anything else about the pastor?" Andi asked.

"He spent a lot of time looking at the display of photographs. He asked about Gerald too, wanted me to point him out at the party. He seemed surprised when I said Gerald wasn't there, and then he asked a lot of questions about Gerald's life — you know, what he did for a living, where he lived, that sort of thing."

"He didn't really know Randolph, then?"

Monica shook her head. "I didn't think about it, but no, he hardly knew anything about Randolph or his family."

"I don't suppose you took any photos?" Andi asked.

Monica shook her head again. "No, there was the photographer from the *Tribune*, but that was it."

Then Andi remembered something. She pulled out her phone and found the picture she had taken at the Concerned Citizens meeting only five days ago. Then she held out her phone so Monica and then Maeve could see the screen.

Monica looked at Andi in amazement. "That's him. That's the pastor. Do you know him?"

CHAPTER THIRTY-EIGHT

January 11

"Sergeant Stanton and Sergeant Beaufort aren't taking my calls," Charlie said. "The only officer who will talk to me is a Sergeant Vaughan in Campbell River, and he was rude. He said someone will get back to me in a few days."

"I just got off the phone with Monica," Andi said. "She was talking to Sylvie Hamm's son who showed up yesterday, and he told her the police were tearing Sylvie's house apart. They've taken truckloads of boxes and garbage away to dig through. They won't tell him what they're looking for, but he thinks they're trying to find a murder weapon or some physical evidence to tie Sylvie to both the murders."

They both leaned on the edge of their desks, studying the story wall.

"The police say Randolph was murdered on or around New Year's Eve. They can't say exactly when. Sylvie Hamm reported finding the body on the fifth. Professor Weber arrived in Coffin Cove on the morning of the fifth and was murdered that night." Andi said. "So, if Pastor Michael Nelson had anything to do with these murders, he had to be on Quadra Island on the thirty-first. The Quadra Island ferry won't give us ticket information, and if he paid cash, we won't know anyway. Christie at the café didn't see him, but I'm going to the motel to get a photo of his truck to send to Monica. She wasn't working that day, but she can ask her colleagues if anyone saw the pastor arrive or leave on the ferry."

"He got to the New Year's Eve party at seven thirty," Charlie said. "And we know the last ferry from Quadra is at four o'clock, so that's just time enough to get to Coffin Cove from Campbell River."

"And we know he didn't take the time to dress up," Andi said, remembering how Pastor Michael's scruffy clothes stood out in the glamorous crowd.

She stood up and walked to the wall. She moved the pictures of Randolph Weber and Gerald Weber, so they were side by side. Above them, she taped the picture of Pastor Michael Nelson she'd taken at the Concerned Citizens Committee meeting.

Andi turned to face Charlie. "He had the opportunity to kill them both. But we don't know why. Professor Weber had been living and working in England for decades, and according to the Drummonds, Randolph Weber rarely left his house after Inga died. All we have is Maeve's story, which she heard from a very sick woman. We need more than that."

"I'm not sure," Charlie said. "The pastor is pretty old. Could he have dragged Professor Weber into the museum?"

Andi thought for a minute.

"He has a lot of energy," she said finally. "And if he had a strong enough motive, I think he's capable. We just have to find the connection and the motive."

Andi pointed to the three pictures. "You need to dig into every corner of these people's lives. Start with Maeve Drummond's story about Gerald's adoption. We need verification from several sources and documented proof if we can get it. Then let's see where Pastor Michael Nelson came from. Even if he had nothing to do with these murders, I'd like to know why he's here in Coffin Cove. I just don't trust him."

"Captain Ron knows something." Harry was standing behind them. "Ike and I are going to have a little chat with him later."

"That's great. Are those for us?" Harry was holding a cup of coffee in each hand.

"Yup. These too." He fished a paper bag from his pocket. "Muffins. I've just seen Hephzibah. Ruth and Bob are being discharged this afternoon. I'll pick them up. You want to come with me?"

Andi nodded. "Yes. I had better get going, then."

"Where are you going?" Charlie asked.

"To see a man of God."

"Andi . . ." Harry said, a note of warning in his voice. Andi understood. They'd talked when she'd got back the previous evening. Harry had been waiting for her.

"Andi, you can't keep taking risks — with your life, or with the *Gazette*. I know it's tough, but we need to let the Halwell story go and move on." His tone had been firm.

She had agreed, promised even, and didn't want to have secrets between them. But she knew she'd never tell Harry about the printed photograph of Elizabeth Halwell looking straight at the camera just before getting on the helicopter and evading arrest again.

Andi had deleted the picture from her phone, and in the next few days, the hard copy would rest in a safe deposit box until another day. There would be another day, she was certain.

Andi smiled at Harry.

"Don't worry. I'm just going to talk to him about the Concerned Citizens Committee and his fundraising. It's a legitimate issue for us to report on, and my guess is his ego is so large, he won't be able to resist an interview. I'll just let him talk and hopefully he'll drop some information we can follow up."

She checked her phone. "Let's meet back here at lunchtime and see what we've got."

* * *

The motel parking lot was empty, except for the last persistent piles of dirty snow, heaped up beside the office building. Andi hesitated, wondering where else she could find Pastor Michael Nelson. There was only one person who might know. Andi walked over to the office building. Maybe Peggy knew more about the good pastor and would be willing to talk.

Peggy answered at the first knock.

She looked expectant, as if she'd anticipated a visit, but her face registered disappointment when she saw Andi. She glanced over Andi's shoulder, as she thought Andi might not be alone. "It's you again. What do you want this time?"

"I need to talk to you, Peggy. Do you have a minute?"

Peggy was still wearing the baggy sweatpants and shirt. If anything, she looked worse, Andi thought. There was a caked orange line of make-up in the crease of Peggy's neck, as if she couldn't be bothered to clean it off, and Andi could smell stale sweat.

"I'm busy."

"Peggy, this is important. It's about Pastor Michael."

Andi expected another rude retort and a closed door. To her surprise, Peggy leaned against the door frame as if her legs were about to give way. She rubbed a hand over her wan face, and when she took it away, her cheeks were wet with tears.

"Does everyone know already? I don't know what to do," she said in a whisper, as if someone might be listening.

"About what? Peggy, what's going on?" Andi reached out and touched Peggy's arm. "Do you need a doctor?"

"No, no, nothing like that," Peggy said wearily. "You might as well come in."

Peggy stepped back to let Andi inside.

The room smelled of burnt coffee. The blinds were open, but the room was still dark. Papers were strewn across Peggy's desk, and the only light came from a computer screen.

Peggy sat in the chair behind her desk and Andi sat across from her.

"Peggy, what's going on?" Andi repeated, as Peggy wiped the tears from her face with both hands and sniffed.

"He's gone," she said dully. "He's gone, I don't know where, and he won't return my calls."

"You mean Pastor Michael?"

Peggy nodded, her eyes filling with tears again.

Andi took a breath. "Look, Peggy, I know you held the pastor in high regard, but . . ." Andi hesitated, not wanting to alert Peggy to their suspicions, and also not wanting to upset her further. "But I think he might not be who he says he is."

"I know." It came out as a whisper.

"You do?" Another surprise. "How do you know?"

"Because he took all the money . . ." Peggy's voice cracked, and this time she held her head in her hands and sobbed.

"You mean the donations he was collecting?" Andi was shocked. She hadn't been expecting this.

"Yes. The bank called me. We opened a joint account to collect donations. He . . . *Pastor Michael*—" Peggy nearly spat his name out — "he withdrew everything in cash this morning. At first, I thought he must have taken the money to pay some bills, but when I called the lawyer he said the committee still owes his invoice, and I got an invoice today about the fees for the Community Hall. I don't know why he would have taken the money, but he has."

The words came tumbling out, punctuated by sobs.

"How much did he take?" Andi kept her tone gentle but couldn't help but feel infuriated with Peggy. She was a businesswoman, a shrewd one. How had she allowed herself to be conned like this?

"Five thousand dollars," Peggy said, sniffing, and pulling a well-used tissue from her pocket. "But there's more."

"More cash?"

Peggy nodded. "The grant money I got last year. Twenty thousand."

"Holy shit, Peggy, why did you give him that?"

"He told me we would sue the city, and I'd get more than double, and I really needed more money, Andi. I lost so much money when I . . ." Peggy stopped.

Andi remembered the gossip she'd heard in the café, about Peggy spending the grant money on a holiday.

"Peggy, why did you close the motel last year?"

With a trembling hand, Peggy reached up and tugged on her hair. The wig slid off onto her lap.

"Oh Peggy," Andi said, and reached out to hold Peggy's hand.

CHAPTER THIRTY-NINE

Fred Harding rested his hand on the rusty chain that held up Sarah's swing. He pushed it gently, wanting to be transported back in time.

Abruptly, he turned away. He didn't have time for this now. He'd be with Sarah soon enough.

Fred's legs felt stronger, and his hands had stopped throbbing with arthritis. Last night he'd slept well.

God had made everything clear to him the day before. God had made sure he was in the hardware store at the exact time he needed to receive His message.

Fred had been waiting to pay for his propane tank and had overheard the harbour manager, Ike, talking to a fisherman.

"That damn pastor. I don't trust him," Ike was saying. "He's collecting money now. He's got all the old folk riled up and now he wants money."

"Sounds like a scam to me. My old aunt was caught like that once. Some con artist took her for thousands . . ."

A false prophet.

Fred had left the store without his propane. He'd prayed and then he'd slept like a baby.

Now he knew why God had kept him alive.

Fred climbed into his truck and set his loaded shotgun carefully on the passenger seat. He turned the key in the ignition. For once the truck started first time, and Fred smiled. It was a sign from God.

CHAPTER FORTY

"He's done this before. Look."

Charlie's hair was plastered to her head, and she left a damp trail on the café floor. The rain was torrential, and the wind was whipping spray off the ocean. Charlie gave Andi her phone to read an email displayed on the screen.

"Church of the Guiding Light of the Lord, Church of Redemption and Light, Church of the Spirit Bear . . ." Andi looked up. "Really? This checks out?"

Charlie nodded. "Yeah, he doesn't care. He uses a different name every time. I guess nobody checks because everyone trusts a pastor, right?"

There were pictures attached to the email. Andi clicked on each of them. It was Pastor Michael Nelson, sometimes with a moustache, sometimes with shorter hair, but the same thick glasses and arrogant sneer in every photograph.

"He dupes vulnerable people, down on their luck. What a piece of shit." Andi handed back the phone. "I've tried calling the number that Peggy gave me, but no answer."

Charlie sat down and pulled a notebook from her bag. She shoved a strand of hair behind her ears and wiped the raindrops off her glasses.

Hephzibah brought Andi another mug of coffee and mint tea for Charlie. She sat down with them as Charlie read from her notes.

"The *Campbell River Tribune* reported the horrific double murder of Doris Duffy and John Jennings on the fifth of April 1958. It was the same day as the Ripple Rock explosion, so they buried the report a few pages in."

Charlie looked up. "By the way, I had to pay by the page to get access to the online archives. The *Tribune* must make a fortune. We should definitely do that."

Andi gestured with her hand to get Charlie back to her notes.

"Right, so the bodies were found by her young son Gerald, who ran for help. Randolph Weber, the renowned young engineer who'd been part of the famous Ripple Rock project, alerted police. Neighbours say that Doris Duffy's common-law husband, John Jennings, had a violent temper, and Doris often appeared with black eyes. Jennings had a record of petty crime. He had a son, William Jennings, who was found by police at the scene. The boy was in shock and unable to tell police what happened, except there was a brutal fight which resulted in both Doris and John succumbing to their wounds."

"That ties in with Maeve's story. Anything else?"

"Not about the murders. I searched under Gerald Duffy and Gerald Weber and found an article about Gerald Weber's acceptance to the brand-new University of Calgary in 1966. I then went back and checked and found that Gerald Duffy was legally adopted and changed his name to Weber in 1960. So the story all checks out. Gerald Duffy is definitely Gerald Weber, and his biological mother was murdered."

"Anything more about William Jennings?"

"He dropped off the radar in 1958. I found court records about a William Jennings in 1970. He was charged with breaking and entering, and did a short stint in prison. Then . . . nothing. I'll try in Alberta. He might have left the province after coming out of prison."

Andi nodded. "Good work. Keep going. See if we can link Jennings to Pastor Nelson, or whatever his name is."

"Has Peggy reported the pastor?" Hephzibah asked.

"Yes. It took a while to persuade her. He humiliated her. But I told her there was no way she could get the money back unless she reported Pastor Michael, or whoever he is, to the police."

"Is there much chance of that?" Hephzibah asked.

"Who knows? He's probably long gone by now." Andi took a sip of her coffee. "Harry and Ike are leaning on Captain Ron for information. Ike is certain he knows something."

"What do you mean by *leaning*?" Hephzibah said with alarm in her voice.

"I don't think he'll be in any trouble." Andi smiled. "And by leaning, I mean bribery. If Captain Ron tells us what he knows, then Ike will waive the moorage fees and put in a good word with the Coast Guard about the illegal dumping."

Andi smiled at Hephzibah. "Harry is getting to be a very effective investigator."

* * *

Captain Ron was a weaselly little man, Harry decided. When Ike and Harry stepped onto Ron's boat, at first he was belligerent, even shaking his fist at them. When it was clear that Harry and Ike were not leaving, he backed off, promising to pay the moorage and be out of there as soon as the tide turned.

Ike was happy enough with that arrangement, but Harry needed more.

"Tell me about Pastor Michael," Harry had asked conversationally. "A friend of yours?"

"Never heard of him," Captain Ron had said quickly, but the fearful expression on his face gave him away.

"You know," Harry said, lying, "those guys shooting at you the other night? I know them. They're pretty pissed with you . . ."

"I didn't do anything!" Captain Ron blurted. "I just tossed some garbage bags on the barge, I thought nobody would care!"

"Just tell me what I want to know, and I'm sure I can smooth things over for you," Harry said reassuringly. "So, Pastor Michael Nelson, what do you know about him?"

Twenty minutes later, Harry left a frightened Captain Ron with Ike. Harry pulled out his cell phone. Andi wouldn't like it, but he had to call Matt Beaufort first. He'd definitely want to talk to Captain Ron, and Ike wouldn't let him leave until Captain Ron told the police everything he knew.

Matt was out on a call, so Harry left a message and then hurried up the dock. He'd just go to Andi's office and tell her everything in person. It was quite the tale, and he wanted to get it straight.

It started to rain, and dark clouds descended below the cliffs. Harry kept his shoulders hunched against the cold. When he reached the boardwalk, he looked up for a moment and caught sight of a man hurrying towards him.

Harry squinted in the gloom. "Hey!" he shouted when he realized who it was.

The man had seen him and had already changed direction, running across the road towards the town.

"Watch out!" Harry bellowed, as a truck skidded to a stop, missing the man by inches.

In amazement, Harry watched as Fred Harding got out of the truck and pointed a shotgun at Pastor Michael Nelson.

CHAPTER FORTY-ONE

"We should wait for Matt." Harry didn't look at Andi as he spoke.

He was driving his truck — at Andi's insistence — and kept his eyes on the track ahead. She could tell he was shaken. From the moment he'd turned up at her office. White-faced, he told her what he'd witnessed out on the street. Fred Harding, Pastor Michael . . . and the shotgun. Without thinking, she'd ushered him straight out the door and into the driver's seat of his truck.

The melting snow had carved streams into the gravel since Andi had been to the Valley and Harry couldn't help bouncing over the ruts. It was raining hard, and the wind was whipping the branches in front of them. Andi was glad Harry was driving. She steadied herself by holding on to the side of her seat, and Harry swung the steering wheel to avoid a waterlogged pothole.

He tried again. "Fred had a shotgun. He's crazy. We should wait for the police."

"You're the one who came to me with this," she said, not intending to sound so irritable. "We can't always wait for the police to get their shit together."

Harry said nothing.

"Sorry. I know you're right. But as you said, Fred is nuts. We need to get the pastor out of there, even if he is a piece of shit."

Harry glanced sideways at her. "You know, this sounds a lot like a saviour complex to me," he said, straight-faced.

"You're a funny man," Andi said. "We'll be careful. We'll just go there and see if Fred will listen to us. I want Pastor Michael in prison, not dead." She looked sideways at Harry. "Why don't you tell me exactly what Captain Ron said?"

"Pastor Michael is definitely not a pastor. His name's not Michael either. He's been operating this con for years, apparently."

"What's his real name? Jennings?"

Harry stared at her for a second. "How did you know?"

"William Jennings left Quadra Island in 1958 after his father was killed. I wonder if the Webers had a bigger part to play in it than they let on."

"Holy shit."

They drove in silence for a moment, but Andi's mind was working overtime. "How does Captain Ron fit in to all of this?"

"William Jennings met Ron in a children's home or juvenile detention, I think. He was a talented thief and took Ron under his wing. Jennings passed on all his skills and they worked together for a while until Ron got caught breaking and entering. When Ron got out of prison, Jennings had moved on. Ron came out to BC. He kept his nose clean for a while, and then thought of the salvage con all by himself."

"When did Jennings get back in touch with him?" Andi asked.

"Just after Ron started making money. Jennings found out and wanted a cut. He was already running cons on little old ladies with money and had morphed into a pastor."

"Charlie found out about that. So, Captain Ron didn't know Pastor Michael — I mean Jennings — was in Coffin Cove?"

"No. But get this. When he was in Campbell River, he got a call from Jennings, who wanted a ride to Quadra Island, but wouldn't say why."

That made Andi snap her head around. "He took Jennings to Quadra? When?"

Harry nodded. "New Year's Eve. After that, he left Jennings in Campbell River and then came down to Coffin Cove. The contractors who left all that crap by the Fish Plant hired him to get rid of it."

"Dump it in the ocean?"

"I'm sure they'll claim they didn't know what Captain Ron would do with the garbage, but yes, he intended to dump it. Then he found out about the barge at Hope Island. He bumped into Pastor Michael, and apparently the pastor threatened to tell on him unless Captain Ron did him a few more favours."

"Such as?"

"Keeping his mouth shut for one, and dumping a bag of garbage for him." Harry said grimly. "He took the bag along with his other garbage out to Hope Island and that's when he got shot at. It freaked him out. He's just laid low ever since."

"What was in the pastor's garbage bag?" Andi asked.

"I don't know. That's all he would tell me. Then you called, so I left the captain with Ike. He isn't going anywhere."

Harry slowed the truck. Andi could see the lopsided outline of Fred Harding's wooden church loom up through the rain. As they got nearer, she could see the dim glow of a light around the old oak door.

"I guess we're in time for tonight's service," Harry said as he parked in front of the door. They both got out of the truck, and he looked at Andi. "What now?"

"Time to pray," Andi said as she pushed open the church door.

It took a moment for Andi's eyes to adjust to the dim light. She could smell wet timber and heard faint splashing sounds, just audible above the creak of trees bending in the wind. She looked up and could see clouds racing across the sky through gaps in the roof.

"If, however, you do not obey me and keep all these commandments, if you reject my statutes and abhor my regulations so that you do not keep all my commandments and you break my covenant, I for my part will do this to you: I will inflict horror on you, consumption and fever, which diminish eyesight and drain away the vitality of life . . ."

Fred Harding was standing behind a pulpit. His face was lit up by a candle, which was struggling to stay alight and casting flickering shadows on the old man's face.

His voice was powerful, and Andi thought he was standing straighter as he emphasized the words of his sermon by periodically thumping his fist on the lectern in front of him. His eyes rested on Andi briefly, but he carried on his sermon.

"You will be struck down before your enemies; those who hate you will rule over you, and you will flee when there is no one pursuing you. If, in spite of all these things, you do not obey me, I will discipline you seven times more on account of your sins. I will break your strong pride and make your sky like iron and your land like bronze."

"Where's Jennings?" Harry whispered. He had followed Andi inside but was standing well back in the shadows.

"Over there."

At the end of a pew, a figure was slumped forward.

"Doesn't look like he's praying," Harry whispered. "See what Fred has on the pulpit?"

"Oh shit," Andi murmured. Fred raised his hands, and she saw the barrel of a shotgun glinting in the candlelight.

"He hasn't seen me," Harry said. "I'll try to get behind him and grab that gun."

"No, that's insane . . ." But it was too late. Harry ducked to the floor and moved on all fours, away from Andi.

"Sinner! Get on your knees and repent!"

Fred was looking directly at Andi now.

"Mr Harding . . ." she started, but Fred grabbed his gun and pointed it straight at her.

"*Repent!*"

Andi made a quick decision. "I will, I will repent," she called, and she slid into the pew beside Jennings, her heart thumping.

Her movements seemed to satisfy Fred Harding, because he continued to preach. She breathed a sigh of relief.

"If you walk in hostility against me and are not willing to obey me, I will increase your affliction seven times according to your sins. I will send the wild animals against you, and they will bereave you of your children, annihilate your cattle, and diminish your population so that your roads will become deserted . . ."

Jennings's eyes were glassy behind his thick lenses, and his breathing was laboured. Andi bent her head as if in prayer and whispered, "Are you OK?"

Jennings grunted and shifted slightly. Andi could see a dark stain on his shoulder.

"That crazy fucker kidnapped me and then shot me when I tried to get away," he rasped. "Get me out of here."

"The police are on their way, Mr Jennings," Andi whispered back. "Did you kill Randolph and Gerald Weber? Do you have Peggy Wilson's money?"

"Fuck you," he whispered back.

"If in spite of these things you do not allow yourselves to be disciplined and you walk in hostility against me, then I myself will also walk in hostility against you and strike you seven times on account of your sins. I will bring on you an avenging sword, a covenant vengeance . . ."

"I know," Andi whispered back, "why don't I ask Fred Harding what vengeance is appropriate for a sinner who pretends to be a man of God, who murders and steals? What do you think he would suggest?"

She made a movement, as if to stand.

"You're fucking crazy," Jennings whispered urgently and turned his head to look at her. "You can't prove anything."

Andi raised her head and saw a movement in the shadows behind Fred Harding.

"If in spite of this you do not obey me but walk in hostility against me, I will walk in hostile rage against you, and I myself will also discipline you seven times on account of your sins. You will eat the flesh of your sons and the flesh of your daughters . . ."

The old man's voice rose in animation and he raised his arms high and turned his head up to the sky.

Andi stood up and shouted, "This man is a sinner! He has murdered and stolen. He has pretended to be a man of God." She took a breath. "He is Satan and has walked among us in sheep's clothing . . ."

She saw Harry lunge forward to grab the gun, but the old man was fast and got a hand to it. Harry grabbed his arm. The shotgun swung up and there was an explosion, followed by a flash.

Andi ducked behind the pew.

"I will destroy your high places and cut down your incense altars, and I will stack your dead bodies on top of the lifeless bodies of your idols. I will abhor you!" Fred Harding screamed.

As if in answer, Andi heard a loud crack. She looked up and saw branches hurtling down towards her. She shouted at Jennings, "*Run!*"

As Andi scrambled from behind the pew, she felt the air rush around her, and she hit the floor again. The tips of the falling undergrowth whipped her face and arms as she crawled. She held her arms over her head as rotting timber cascaded down around her. She felt a heavy thump on her foot and couldn't pull it away.

"Harry?" She opened her mouth to scream, but the wind carried her words away, and all she could hear was sirens in the distance.

* * *

"It's a revolving door for your family in this hospital," the doctor commented as he bandaged Andi's ankle. It was the same doctor who had spoken to Andi two nights before.

"That should do it," he said. "Just a bad sprain and a few cuts. You were lucky." He smiled at her as he left the treatment room.

Harry stood in the doorway. "Must have been divine intervention," he said dryly.

"How is Fred?" Andi asked.

"Oh, he'll be fine. He's a tough old guy. But he won't be living in the Valley anymore. That tree clipped the church but destroyed his house. He'll have to move to town with all the sinners."

"But he shot Pastor Michael — I mean, William Jennings." Andi stood up and winced.

"Fred says he was trying to rid Coffin Cove of evil, doing God's work. And it was only a flesh wound. Jennings is in all kinds of trouble, so who knows how it will all unfold? Fred apprehended a murderer."

Harry slipped an arm around Andi and helped her limp out of the hospital.

He stopped and looked at her. "Satan in sheep's clothing?"

Andi shrugged. "It was the best I could come up with in the moment."

EPILOGUE

Two months later

"What's on your schedule for today?" Harry asked as he handed Andi her second cup of coffee.

She didn't answer for a moment, as she took a sip and then placed the mug on the deck beside her.

"Nothing exciting." She smiled at Harry as she pulled a wool blanket closer around her shoulder. It was a windless morning so far. The sky was clear and the palest of powder blue. Watery sunlight danced on the surface of the ocean. It would be one of those bright, chilly winter days that were an occasional February gift.

In the distance, Andi could see the peaks of snow-capped mountains on the mainland. It reminded her of her father's departure. By now he'd be boarding a plane at Vancouver airport to take him back east. She would miss him.

"I'll be back for visits," he'd said. "And you can visit me too."

"Will you have time for a lowly reporter working for a local rag? Now you're a famous talking head?" she'd asked her father, trying not to sound too serious. An old friend in the industry had recommended him for a new job working for a national TV station headquartered in Toronto.

"I'll always have time for my daughter," her father had answered seriously, and he hugged her tight.

Andi came back to the present and Harry's question. She held up her hand and counted her planned tasks off her fingers. "I have to edit Charlie's article—"

Harry interrupted her. "She gets the byline for this one?"

"Absolutely. For the entire series of articles. She's taken Sylvie Hamm's story as a start and worked it into an in-depth examination of mental health. She's matured as a writer."

"What happened to Sylvie?"

"She was convicted of fraud. She forged Randolph Weber's signature on a government benefit application. When the cheques arrived, she paid them into her bank account. She always used an ATM, so nobody picked up that the checks weren't in her name. She knew it was all over when she found Randolph's body, but she needed one more cheque to arrive before she reported his death."

"Sounds pretty cold-hearted to me," Harry said.

"You should read Charlie's article. Hoarding is a mental illness. All Sylvie cared about was her stuff. She couldn't stop buying and storing it, but the more she got, the more stressed and crazier she became. If you want an example of cold-hearted and callous, then William Jennings is your man."

She fell silent for a moment. William Jennings had been charged with the murder of Randolph Weber and his son Gerald. He'd made wild accusations against Gerald Weber for the murder of his father in 1958, but they were dismissed as there was no evidence to back them up and nobody left to prosecute if there were.

William Jennings had seen the article in the *Tribune* and had intended to blackmail Randolph Weber, or so he told police. He'd wanted revenge, and it had seemed like a gift when he found out Professor Gerald Weber, the same boy who'd killed his father, was giving a lecture in town. He'd dumped the body in the museum to make a point, he said.

Following a statement made by Captain Ron, police recovered the murder weapon used in both killings from the garbage barge moored at Hope Island. It was the cane owned by Randolph Weber.

"Police are still making appeals for victims of Jennings' fraud schemes," Andi said. "But Peggy Wilson has retracted her statement and dropped the charges."

"What? Why would she do that?"

Andi shrugged. "She got her money back, and she doesn't want the public humiliation. But she confessed to one thing. Don't be mad, Harry," she warned.

"What did she confess?" Harry was suspicious.

"She was the one who wrote the notes to Hephzibah and Ruth."

Harry exploded. "That evil old witch! Damn her!"

"Calm down. She's written to both of them to apologize. Hephzibah let me read her note. It seems genuine."

"They should both press charges," Harry said, still fuming.

"Hephzibah said they just want to move on. Look to the future," Andi said softly. "Not a bad idea."

Harry looked at her. "About the future," he said. "I have something to show you. Are you done with your coffee?"

Ten minutes later, Andi walked up the dock with Harry. They both waved at Ike, and then Harry pointed left towards the Fish Plant. "This way."

Katie Dagg arrived at the main door in time to hold it open for Andi and Harry.

"How are you doing, Katie?" Andi asked, pleased to see Katie looking better than she had for a while.

"Oh, I'm doing fine. I'm focusing on my next exhibit, the history Seymour Narrows and Ripple Rock. A kind of tribute to Randolph and Gerald Weber."

"That sounds fascinating," Harry said, and patted Katie on the shoulder.

"Why are we here?" Andi asked, when Katie had disappeared into the museum.

"This way," was all that Harry would say as he climbed the stairs to the second floor. When they got to the top, he pulled a set of keys from his pocket and unlocked the door in front of them.

"I thought you'd like to see one of the finished apartments," he said, as he held the door open for Andi.

"They're finally finished?"

"Just this one. But Lee Dagg says it's just a matter of fitting the new appliances in the others and then the city will put them up for sale."

Andi stood and looked around. A small entrance hall led to an open-plan kitchen, dining and living room, with vaulted ceilings, polished wooden floors and glass sliding doors which led onto a balcony.

She pushed open a door to the right and found a large room with a closet and the same sliding doors.

"Wow, this is swanky," she said when she saw the large ensuite bathroom. "I bet the city will want a stack of cash for these places."

"Their plan is to offer local people a deal first, before they open sales up to non-residents. I think Mayor Thompson is expecting a strong candidate to run against her this year, so she's doing all she can to appeal to the 'concerned citizens' of Coffin Cove." He grinned.

"How do you know all this?" Andi asked.

"You're not the only one who can do a little investigating," Harry said. "Anyway, what do you think?"

"This is a wonderful space," Andi said. "It feels so inviting, and so much light. I'm impressed at the finish too. Are those real granite countertops?"

"They are. They're not standard in every apartment, I asked for granite especially. It's been a while since I've cooked in a half-decent kitchen. And look over here . . ."

Harry opened another door to the left. "This could be a guest bedroom, but maybe an office? It hasn't got as much light as the master, but it's still a nice size, don't you think?"

"What is going on here?" Andi demanded. "What are you talking about?"

"Andi. It's not just you who feels the cold on the boat. As much as I love being on the water, it was never my plan to live on the *Pipe Dream* forever. And I'm tired of renovating old properties. I made an offer to the city for this apartment, and the deal closed yesterday. We can move in whenever you want. If that's what you want?"

Harry's voice was calm, and Andi was shocked into silence.

"You kept all this secret?" she demanded when she could get the words out.

"Some secrets are good." Harry smiled, and for a second, Andi remembered her safe deposit box. She pushed that to the back of her mind.

She squeezed Harry's hand. "We can move in today? But it's an apartment. Are you sure you want to live in an apartment?"

"It's ten times the space we have on the *Pipe Dream*." Harry smiled, the relief showing on his face. "And besides, look at this."

He walked over to the sliding doors and pulled them open. "Come out on the balcony."

Andi did. She stood beside Harry and held his hand.

"We can have coffee out here every morning and watch the sunrise, same as on the deck. Doesn't Coffin Cove look beautiful from up here?"

The ocean had taken on the pale blue of the cloudless sky, and Andi could hear the gentle break of waves on the steel pylons of the pier beneath them.

She could see Hephzibah and Ruth setting tables outside the café to make the most of the rare winter sun, and she could hear the hum of traffic as the residents of Coffin Cove went about their daily business.

"Yes," Andi said, squeezing Harry's hand. "It looks beautiful."

THE END

THE JOFFE BOOKS STORY

We began in 2014 when Jasper agreed to publish his mum's much-rejected romance novel and it became a bestseller.

Since then we've grown into the largest independent publisher in the UK. We're extremely proud to publish some of the very best writers in the world, including Joy Ellis, Faith Martin, Caro Ramsay, Helen Forrester, Simon Brett and Robert Goddard. Everyone at Joffe Books loves reading and we never forget that it all begins with the magic of an author telling a story.

We are proud to publish talented first-time authors, as well as established writers whose books we love introducing to a new generation of readers.

We have been shortlisted for Independent Publisher of the Year at the British Book Awards three times, in 2020, 2021 and 2022, and for the Diversity and Inclusivity Award at the Independent Publishing Awards in 2022.

We built this company with your help, and we love to hear from you, so please email us about absolutely anything bookish at feedback@joffebooks.com

If you want to receive free books every Friday and hear about all our new releases, join our mailing list: www.joffebooks.com/contacts

And when you tell your friends about us, just remember: it's pronounced Joffe as in coffee or toffee!

ALSO BY JACKIE ELLIOTT

COFFIN COVE MYSTERIES
Book 1: COFFIN COVE
Book 2: HELL'S HALF ACRE
Book 3: HOPE ISLAND
Book 4: THE VILE NARROWS